PAY DIRT ROAD

Samantha Jayne Allen

MINOTAUR BOOKS
NEW YORK

First published in the United States by Minotaur Books, an imprint of St. Martin's Publishing Group

PAY DIRT ROAD. Copyright © 2022 by Samantha Jayne Allen. All rights reserved. Printed in the United States of America. For information, address St. Martin's Publishing Group, 120 Broadway, New York, NY 10271.

www.minotaurbooks.com

Library of Congress Cataloging-in-Publication Data

Names: Allen, Samantha Jayne, author.
Title: Pay dirt road / Samantha Jayne Allen.
Description: First edition. | New York : Minotaur Books, 2022.
Identifiers: LCCN 2021051058 | ISBN 9781250804273 (hardcover) | ISBN 9781250804280 (ebook)
Subjects: LCGFT: Detective and mystery fiction. | Novels.
Classification: LCC PS3601.L4355 P39 2022 | DDC 813/.6—dc23
LC record available at https://lccn.loc.gov/2021051058

Our books may be purchased in bulk for promotional, educational, or business use. Please contact your local bookseller or the Macmillan Corporate and Premium Sales Department at 1-800-221-7945, extension 5442, or by email at MacmillanSpecialMarkets@macmillan.com.

First Edition: 2022

10 9 8 7 6 5 4 3 2 1

For Dane

Part I

Chapter 1

At night we rode up to the old railroad tracks on the west side of town, turned the headlights off, and waited for the dead to appear. My cousin Nikki and I had seen the phantom lights of the old passenger trains maybe, just once when we were kids and sneaking out, but it was—and I believed this even at twelve—likely a trick of the light, our eyes bleary and tired. And still, whenever we went cruising, this was the place we ended up. Staring into the dark, wishing to be scared.

"Annie, why do we come out here?" Nikki said, her blond curls making a funny halo around her wide, sharp-boned face.

"Something besides doing donuts in the Walmart parking lot?" I squinted my eyes, but the only speck of light was from a cell tower past the interstate, miles ahead and outside of town. "You see anything?" I ran my fingers lightly up her arm like a spider and she swatted me.

"God, we're so lame," she said, and tugged on the tight-fitting halter top she'd decided to wear. Without checking the mirror, I knew I'd already smudged my new liquid eyeliner.

"We're so lame? This was your idea," I said, and turned the

ignition. "We're all dressed, might as well get a drink some-where."

"Where?"

"Mixer's." Headlights on, a cloud of dust swirled in the beams. A tremor of fear—was something circling our car in the dark?—but branches swayed in the trees and I realized it was just the wind picking up. We bounced in our seats as I drove over the rickety tracks.

"And just you and me sit on barstools with all the sad folk? Come on, you know you can't go in there before midnight. Be-sides, I'm starving. Let's go by the café for a bit. That'll give my sources time. Got to be something happening. It's Thursday. Practically the weekend," Nikki said, and checked her phone again, sent a few texts, and I drove down the empty farm-to-market road, elbow out the open window. The night air was just cool enough to tickle my skin. The wind was all it was. Just coming a storm.

"I like Mixer's. They have a band," I said. I knew it was lame, but old dives like those had no pretenses of being anything but dives. I was burned on college bars and frat boys. "Sure, the band is usually the Donaldson kid, who may or may not be out on parole—hey, you sure you want to eat at the café? There's usually snacks at the bar."

"It's nine. Everywhere else is closed. And no, I don't want to eat stale popcorn everyone's dug their dirty paws in."

"Fair enough," I said, and turned right toward town.

Victoria yawned and pulled a pencil from her apron pocket. After a moment she started tapping it on the linoleum counter. "Y'all look nice."

"Thanks," I said, shifting uncomfortably. My thighs stuck to the leather stool, and it felt weird, her waiting on me. "You're on again in the morning, aren't you? I'm on at six."

"Shit, am I?" She looked behind her to the swinging door that led to the kitchen. "You know I don't check the schedule till I'm leaving. Which is soon. I do know that much."

"Chicken fingers," Nikki finally said, looking up from her phone. "Please."

"You eating, Annie?"

I shook my head and Victoria went to the kitchen. Nikki sat her phone on the counter and looked at me. "What's your deal?"

"That I basically live here," I said, and checked the wall clock, my new force of habit since going full-time. Waiting tables wasn't exactly how I'd envisioned using my degree. I'd say moving back to Garnett wasn't the plan either, but that would indicate I had one. College graduation four months in the rearview—a private school I'd gone on scholarship to, at that—you'd think the future would feel wide open with infinite choices, but I was circling, waiting for what else I wasn't sure.

"Those LSAT books under your bed might be lonely. No pressure."

"Trying to start a fight with me isn't unlike you, but damn."

"Oh, come on. I can't have you move again. You'd leave me high and dry," she said, and looked around the empty café, taking a plastic flask from my purse and dribbling the last of our whiskey into her Dr Pepper. She loved knowing where my goat was tied.

Victoria came through the swinging doors hip first with the plate. "Fernando just took these out of the fryer, so careful. Said to tell you go home already, Annie."

Nikki's phone vibrated on the countertop. "Hey, Momma," she answered, resting the phone between her shoulder and ear. With her other hand she shook a glass ketchup bottle, but

5

instead of her plate, the ketchup shot onto her baby blue top. Victoria and I both reached for napkins, but Nikki took off toward the bathroom, cussing, then apologizing to my aunt.

I leaned my head back and stared up at the high pressed-tin ceiling. A rotating fan was mounted in the corner, but it barely made a dent in the cloud of cooking grease and batter smell that hung in the air. Victoria propped her elbows on the counter and stuck her tongue out at me. The last part of this shift was always either really busy or really quiet, depending on if there was a home game. I wasn't sure which I preferred. At least when it was busy the time went by and before you knew it Dot, the overnight waitress, was at the door tying her apron on. Victoria looked tired—pretty, but tired. Her black-brown eyes were glassy, shadowed underneath, but it somehow softened her face, made her doe-eyed instead of drawn. She was my age, twenty-two.

"Vic, want to hear a ghost story?"

"No."

"Fine." I laughed. "Hey, what did—or what do you want to be when you grow up?"

"Annie always with the questions."

"Come on." I smiled.

"Sounds stupid, but I always thought I'd be an actress. Like, even into high school. Now I don't even know. Something that pays decent. And one day I'd like to have horses. . . ." She paused like she'd say more but rolled her shoulders and ducked into the back, returning with a slab of cobbler and two forks. "Here. On the house."

I narrowed my eyes.

"Swear to God they didn't touch it!" She had a loud laugh that caught you off guard, but before you knew it you were laughing too. "I literally just took it to this couple when they had to leave. You need something on your stomach," she said, and sat in Nikki's place.

"Trusting your judgment," I said, and took a bite. The owner, Marlene, made all the desserts from scratch. She was known for her pecan pie, but in late summer the special usually involved freestone peaches from the hill country. The cobbler was sweet and a little tart and cinnamon dusted the golden lattice top. I savored the taste, knowing it was probably the last of the season.

Victoria leaned forward with both hands cupping her chin, emphasizing the heart shape of her face. "Slow night. Even my favorite regular stood me up."

"Playing favorites now?"

"This one's cute. I think he's a professor or something. Bet you'd try and steal him from me."

"Doubt it," I said. She was the flirt who got good tips, not me. "You still haven't shown me your ways out in the wild. What're you up to later?"

She grinned and set her fork down. "There's this place I've been meaning to tell you about. You'd get a kick out of the music—"

"All right," Nikki said, coming up behind me. "Let's get out of here."

"Everything okay?" I spun around on the stool to face her. The ketchup stain looked worse—half her shirt was wet and the cheap fabric pilled where she'd been rubbing it.

"Oh, yeah, Momma was just nagging me about Sunday. But I found us a party. Bonfire west of town. We need to run home so I can change," Nikki said, bouncing on her heels. She looked down at Victoria in her seat, and then to her plate. "Hey, uh, can I get a doggy bag?"

The tops of Victoria's cheekbones flushed as she stood and walked back behind the register.

"This will be fun," Nikki said, and reached for her wallet. "Everyone's going."

Finally, a destination. Someplace to arrow toward with all our pent-upness. "Vic," I said, and pointed up at the clock. "Want to come with? It's nearly time."

"No, no," she said, and busied herself with a Styrofoam container. "And I'll be waiting here until either Dot shows or a handsome stranger comes to steal me away, whichever happens first."

"Hey, you never know," I said, already inching toward the door. "Wait, what's the place you were talking about? With music?"

"Maybe some other time," Victoria said, and handed Nikki her change. "You two be safe driving around at night."

Yellow light bled onto the pavement as we shoved through the door. There was always that exhilaration when I left the café, working or not, and I wondered if that was a kind of sign. Main Street was empty. Dark but for the water tower's blue glow, still but for the flags flown above the courthouse snapping in the wind. Back then, nights were never-ending—expansive or oppressive, depending on my mood—but always had a certain quiet to them. Foolishly, I thought nothing ever really changed. I followed fast behind Nikki, car keys pressed in my palm, but stole one last look behind me. Victoria stood at the café window with her arms crossed over her chest. I waved good-bye to her, forgetting that from inside you can't see past the glass. That at night, only the darkness peered back.

Chapter 2

"Is that Annie McIntyre?"

Thirty or so people stood around a tall, raging bonfire ringed by pickup trucks in the Schneiders' south pasture, but it was Justin's face that found mine. He squinted in my direction and tipped his beer, his face distorted through the wavering heat coming off the fire.

"Hey, Justin," I said, making a beeline toward an old card table that seemed to buckle under the weight of a keg, open bottles, and stacks of red plastic cups. We were friendly, if not friends, and I'd seen him around since coming home. It shouldn't have been weird to be at his party, but I felt unsettled and unsure. I took my beer and stepped back from the light where it was cooler, opposite him and a handful of boys I'd gone to high school with, hoping the shadow would disguise the girl I felt like just then. To my right, the popular girls—women now, but in Garnett homecoming queen was a lifetime appointment— held court on a tailgate, swinging their tanned legs, using their freshly polished toes to point at different people, then whispering loudly about them. Ashley Alvarez was still pretty. Sweet, too, so you couldn't properly hate her. Sabrina and Macy Wiggins, on the other hand, while both pretty, were not so sweet. And unfortunately had a minor history of violence with my cousin.

"That girl better not say anything about me," Nikki hissed in my ear. "I swear, Annie, she does and I'll pour this beer on her."

"Don't make me drag you out of here," I said, and watched a couple I didn't know walk hand in hand toward a parked car. "There high school kids here?" I did a double take on some guys wearing our school's purple and gold jersey.

"Don't think so, but you should probably check ID before making any moves," Nikki said.

Cade Johnson sauntered over, every few seconds checking for Macy, who'd hopped off the tailgate, hands on her hips and staring down Nikki. "Ladies," he drawled, and gave Nikki a sideways hug. "What're you two carrying on about? Planning some kind of trouble?"

"Not talking about you, so don't you flatter yourself," I said, and punched his arm. I'd known Cade since preschool.

"Y'all remember that party out at Canyon? I came over and you two were having a whole conversation with hand gestures and weird noises? Like little kid twin-speak."

I didn't doubt Cade. Nikki and I were always finding our own corner in the middle of a crowd, no matter how large. Had been since we were born. Our mothers are sisters and we grew up in houses about a mile apart. Nikki's a year older than me, and while you can tell we're related, we have noticeably different features—her blond to my brunette—yet people often ask if we're twins. I think it has to do with our mannerisms and our vocal tics, the tint of red in both our hair. And I loved her like no one else. That was always visible to the world in the way certain things are more felt than seen.

"I remember something else about that night," Nikki said, and squeezed Cade's hand. Macy saw and started toward us.

"Come on," I said, and pulled Nikki with me. She laughed, winked at Cade, and I found a couple of empty camping chairs closer to the fire and sat down with my beer. Nikki plopped down in the chair next to mine, dabbed a Kleenex in her beer, and reached toward my eye with it.

"What the hell, Nik?"

"You look like a raccoon; hold still."

I let out my breath after she finished fixing my ill-fated eyeliner. "How drunk are you? You know Macy and Cade are back together."

"She says I'm some kind of slut? They broke up! Plus, he always liked me better." She stared at Macy, her head cocked to the side and her lips pursed—a face I'd seen her make the last time she got in a fight, at a bar on spring break after a woman cut her in the bathroom line—and I wished we'd stayed home.

"Here we go," I said under my breath, and looked for an escape plan.

"Don't worry, Annie; I'm not going to *start* anything." She poked me in the ribs. "Now tell me why did you turn three shades of red when Justin said hey?"

"He asked me out once."

"How come you never told me?" Nikki's eyes widened and she tipped back her head to take a swig of beer.

"You were up in Austin." I flicked her cup. "Hey, slow it down. Anyone else—single, I should add—you got your eye on?"

"Don't change the subject. Did you?"

"What?"

"Go out with him, you goose."

"It was very brief and is very much over," I said. Nikki laughed and I forced a smile. Truth was I had a bad night and, after it, he never called me. Why I felt queasy again remembering that night I wasn't sure, other than the time warp it felt like I'd been trapped in.

"Justin does have those big blue eyes. I know lots of girls, maybe even me, who'd be jealous he asked you out. You know it's about time you started dating again, now that you can't use school as an excuse—"

A group of guys whooped and hollered from a jacked-up truck. The driver jumped from the cab—literally jumped because the truck was so high off the ground—wearing a racing T-shirt and grease-stained work boots. Him and his friends looked middle-aged to me, even in the dim light, and I figured them for roughnecks, probably new to town and looking for trouble. There had been an uptick in drilling in our county. Oil and gas leases were nothing new, but this level of interest was. To the counties west of us it was worse—workers came in droves, skyrocketed the rent, trashed the roads—and talk around town was there'd be a pipeline built through Garnett.

"Babe, you know where a guy can get a beer?" the driver said to me, and I shrugged, tried to ignore them so they wouldn't sit next to Nikki and me. Even five feet away I could smell the whiskey they were sweating out.

"Hey, man, keg's over here," said Troy, Justin's older brother. "Girls." He tipped his head with his carefully tousled blond hair, smiled with his white-strip-bright teeth. Though he was only four years ahead in school, he'd always seemed more removed from our orbit. Probably because he'd been a championship-winning quarterback and the Schneiders were wealthy by Garnett standards. He was a landman now and it clicked these guys might be people he'd met through work.

Nikki turned to me. "I told you this whole town would turn up."

"You make it sound like a good thing."

One of the guys threw a green branch into the fire, making it hiss and smoke. The air burned my throat and the heat made my eyes water, but there was something mesmerizing about the flames licking the blue-black sky. It was dangerous, given the wind that night and the long, dry days. And it wasn't near cold enough for a fire, but it was early September and we were tired. Couldn't will it to feel like fall, but we could pretend.

Walking back from the keg a second time, Nikki stopped and tapped me on the shoulder. "Isn't that the girl you work with?"

I turned to see Victoria stumble out of the dark pasture. It took me a second to recognize her without her hair in a bun or dressed in the dorky aprons we wore. She'd changed into cut-offs and a tight red blouse knotted at her navel, and her long, inky hair swung over one shoulder.

"Long time no see," I said, and tapped her on the arm. "Changed your mind, huh?"

"Um, okay." Victoria seemed to struggle like her tongue was numb, her eyes trained on me but vacant. "You, you always are like a sweet girl, good girl Annie. I need a man," she mumbled, and leaned sideways, waved to one of the roughnecks. He looked her up and down and licked his lips, nudged the guy next to him.

"Someone's having fun," Nikki loudly whispered, mocked tipping a glass back, and slurred her own words a little, though unintentionally, I thought. The only thing keeping me from keeping up was the fact that I drove, but Victoria leaned into me and I smelled something sickly sweet and astringent, like Hawaiian Punch and cheap, vanilla-flavored vodka, and didn't regret tonight's sobriety. Her tongue through slack lips was a bright artificial red. She turned her cup and a red stream trickled into the dirt by her boots.

"Where'd you get that punch?"

"I looove, I love, sangria wine," Victoria sang, and tried handing her cup to Nikki.

"Girl, that smells . . . potent. Let your friend Annie get you some water while I make the rounds." I grabbed Nikki's arm, then looked at Victoria, who seemed to have regained her composure, if only to sniff out more punch. "I'll be right back," Nikki said, and walked toward a group of guys on the other side of the fire, the foam of her beer sloshing over the lip of the cup. Victoria closed her eyes, bobbed her head to the heavy bass line emanating from one of the pickups' speakers.

"Want me to see if they'll put on Hank for you? Maybe some Cash?" Victoria loved traditional country uncritically and without irony, which our coworkers delighted in teasing her about, but the truth was, I loved it too. We'd take a fifteen to sit in her battered green Honda with the windows down, bitch about the customers, and listen to the old songs. Marvel how clear and crisp the sound came through those new speakers she had installed. Highlight of my afternoon, most days. "Vic?" I nudged her, but she didn't react. Her arms hung loosely at her sides and her neck bent so she looked like a rag doll.

"Will have another, I think," she said, and twisted around, looking for someone who wasn't me.

We were work friends. We didn't grow up together like half the people here. What I knew about her personal life—her exes, her dates—I didn't know well, but I sensed her desperation in the brassy smell of sweat and citrusy perfume, her body so tense it hummed. "Who do you know here?" I asked. And, sorry I sounded snotty, added, "What I meant was you shouldn't drive yourself."

"Ain't going home unless it's with him." Victoria looked across the fire, smiling a little, her lips spreading uneasily over her teeth, trying to be coy and tossing her hair over her shoulder.

"Who?"

Hand to hip she swayed, sang, "Why don't you mind your own business and—"

"Hey, now there's the girl I know!"

Then I heard a sound like a bird of prey or maybe a car alarm: Nikki's drunk laugh. I turned to see her lean on Cade's shoulder, then slap her knee.

"And there she goes," I sighed, and started toward the car for the water bottle I had in the cup holder. "I think she meant I ought to get *her* the water."

I came back toward the fire and saw Justin doing that search beam stare people do when they hope someone, anyone, will rescue them from standing alone at a party. We locked eyes and he waved. I blushed—maybe I still had feelings for him, it occurred to me—and I couldn't think of a way to avoid him this time, or anything to say but, "Nice night."

Justin put his arm around my shoulder for a hug and I felt the blush spread all over my body. "Both of us back home, we're living the dream," he said.

"Some dream," I said, not sure if he was kidding. The Schneider ranch was huge and I always figured Justin would stake his claim, if not now, eventually. My granddad owned land nearby, but it was unused and about a tenth of the size. If growing up in a town like this made you a dreamer, coming back made you aware of wanting too much. Maybe I did—but isn't that why I'd worked so hard to leave? There was all this momentum getting to college that once I was there, I felt like I'd *made* it. Maybe that's why I didn't think so much about next steps. Maybe that's why I only had vague dreams about smart-looking blazers and owning a briefcase.

Justin had sandy hair just long enough to move behind his ears. "Troy wants to go to the game tomorrow. I don't know if I will. Feels different this year," he said.

"It does feel weird, school starting back," I said. The whole town was decked in purple and gold. Whenever I caught myself staring at the banners and the window paint, knot forming in my throat, I wasn't sure if it was because I felt left out or because it reminded me that time was, in fact, passing. That in November I'd need to start paying back my loans. I heard the crunch of dry grass underfoot and turned to see Wyatt Reed approach Justin.

"Hey, man, thanks for the invite," Wyatt said, shoving his hand out to shake. "Wasn't sure if you remembered me the other day."

"Dude, come on. I'm glad you made it," Justin said, and patted him on the back. "Annie, this guy's going for more school, if you can believe that. I couldn't walk across that stage fast enough. You two know each other, right?"

I nodded, thinking five years had been a long time. He seemed taller. Good-looking, eyes a hazel color with long lashes you would call pretty on a woman. Wyatt Reed had been my first boyfriend. A year older, shy, I don't think he'd ever spoken to me before that home game. He'd played basketball, lanky and learning his height, and I had loved him first. I wasn't angry—it hadn't been that kind of ending—but I pushed him away. Took him out of my head and out of my heart, so when I thought of him I thought nothing. And yet he was no stranger to me after all this time.

"A bit," Wyatt said, and smiled warmly, a smile that lit up his whole face.

I smiled back. "How's your mom?"

Oh, and his mother had been my English teacher.

"Just fine. Will be happy to know I saw you," Wyatt said.

"Wait a minute," Justin said, moved slightly between us. "I forgot y'all were a thing. Hope this isn't, uh, uncomfortable."

"No." I flapped my hand awkwardly.

"Well," Wyatt said, crossing his arms in mock discomfort. Not fully getting it, I realized. He had already gone off to college when Justin and I hooked up, would have had no idea.

"Well indeed," I said. "Good to see you both. Quite the reunion tonight."

Justin tapped his cup against ours. "Go Steers."

I looked at Wyatt. "You're starting grad school?"

"Yeah, at State."

A loud crash set our heads spinning in the direction of the keg, knocked over on its side and rolled into some guy's pickup. Macy Wiggins was crying. Cade lay on the ground clutching his shoulder yelling a string of cusswords. Justin ran to help his brother pick up the keg as Nikki came up beside me. "We have to go," she said. "Now."

"What in the—"

"I poured my beer on Macy, and when Cade started laughing, she pushed him into the keg. Come on," she said, and grabbed my arm, both for emphasis and to steady herself. She must have finished a beer, then gotten a new one just to pour on Macy— evidence of premeditation.

The wind changed course and smoke gusted in my face. "It's not a Garnett party if people don't burn shit and have a fight or two."

"At least no one's bleeding," Wyatt said. "You two need a ride?"

"I've only had one beer." Still had the keys and the water

bottle in my hand—I'd forgotten. "Real quick let's find Victoria," I said.

"Who?" Nikki squinted at me.

"The girl I work with. She was gone when I came back."

"She had her legs hooked around some guy. Giving him, like, a lap dance."

"Lord, never mind." I looked at Wyatt and shrugged. "Sorry."

"We have to go. Now," Nikki said, and pulled me toward the car.

Away from the fire I smelled rain. We needed it. The river was low, the ground so dry it cracked. Rain hitting dust was the best smell in the world—I was thinking about how Victoria and I had run out to the café parking lot yesterday when the sky clouded up, to breathe it in, when a coyote ran out into the road. I braked hard and its flash of green eye gave me a caged, anxious feeling. Like being seen when you thought you were alone. I turned off the dirt road, onto the asphalt and closer to town and the little pink house Nikki and I shared off Main Street. The road smoothed out and I picked up speed.

"Annie?"

"Yeah?"

"You think you're leaving again?"

"Can't. Someone's got to mind you."

"But really."

"I don't know."

Nikki's head lolled to the side as she fell asleep. Her temper would someday get her in more trouble than this, but not tonight. I knew every inch of that highway, could make out the pale blue water tower and the red-light railroad crossing, and so I wondered why my heart beat faster. I wished for a sign, believing destiny was like a wisp of cloud moving across the moon, visible if you looked closely. I didn't know to stay or to go, only that what I had in Garnett—my family and my friends, our favorite haunts, and all the stars in the vast night sky—was real, realer than the coasts and private schools and jobs in big cities.

"We're almost home," I said, and tucked a stray curl behind her ear. "Safe."

Chapter 3

The overnight waitress told me to hurry and get out to the floor. She wanted to go home and soak her feet. Tying my apron on, I surveyed the room: our regulars, farmers and ranchers up before dawn, ready for a third cup of coffee and their plates of steak and eggs hot and popping with grease to appear before them.

"Spooky Sheila's in a bad mood." Dot motioned toward the elderly woman wearing a purple caftan.

"Premonitions?" I asked, referring to the older woman's shaky relationship with reality, or, as some believed, her psychic abilities. I pulled my hair into a ponytail and the smell of woodsmoke, as I lifted it off my neck, turned my stomach. The storm had broken overnight, all that lingered a still heat. Moisture fogged the picture window, and outside, tiny curls of steam rose from the damp patches of grass.

"Feels like the other side is telling her someone is up to no good," Dot said, and rolled her eyes, but I knew that she'd actually taken Sheila seriously. Once I saw Dot coming out of the tarot shop Sheila had set up off the highway.

"Lady's been listening to the police scanners again," a husky voice said from beside me at the counter. "Like me."

Mary-Pat Zimmerman and my family went far back, having both been the law in Garnett for many years. Before he was the county sheriff and before he was voted out almost as fast, my granddad, Leroy, had been partners with Mary-Pat, and now they ran a private investigation firm together. Well, she ran it. My granddad was all but retired. Not long after starting the firm, they'd solved a cold case widely covered by the media, so they maintained a level of notoriety not just in Garnett, but also across Texas. The publicity got them a steady stream of clients, and the closing of that terrible case—a home invasion gone wrong that left a young couple dead—procured in the community a sense of goodwill that for a time absolved my grandfather of his other notorieties: drinking and general recklessness chief among them. That had been over a decade ago. Still, whenever Mary-Pat spoke, the table next to hers quieted, straining to hear any juicy tidbit she'd let slip.

"There was a bad accident out off the highway last night. One of those trucks taking brackish water from a drill site, driver hadn't slept."

The men at the table groaned.

"That's awful," I said, and poured her a cup.

"It is," Mary-Pat said. She made me a little nervous—had dirt on my family, for one—and with her ice blue eyes, it felt like she saw right through me. Nearly six feet tall, she was strong and severe looking. She wore her silver hair in a long braid she twisted tighter and tighter around her finger. "I'd better eat. How about steak and eggs."

"You bet." I smiled, wondering how in the world all these people could stomach steak so early. Not like the chorizo and

21

egg I'd gotten from the taco stand behind Texaco and wolfed on my way in was much lighter.

"Marlene makes a strong cup," she said, and ripped open three sugar packets at once. "Good thing, I'm about to get on the road. Got a job out to Gonzales."

"Cheating spouse?"

"That'd be easy money." She chuckled. "By the way, Annie, Leroy told me you might be looking for extra work."

"He did?"

"Yep."

"You mean at the firm?"

Mary-Pat nodded and took a sip of coffee. *What on earth— they wanted my help? They wanted me to help them with a case?* She put down her cup, met my eye, and I felt a strange sensation in my chest: like a drop of ink in water, something dark and unexpected bloomed.

"You can type well, can't you? Might could use someone to transcribe my notes, do some filing in the office."

"Oh, of course," I said, color rising in my cheeks.

Sheila wailed at the top of her lungs. Every chair in the café turned to watch her as she closed her eyes and waved her arms in the air. "Don't think this will be the last of the bad news. I can feel it."

Startled, a man seated a few stools down knocked his water over. "Miss! Missy! Get some napkins," he said, snapping his fingers.

Avoiding the temptation to snap right back, I dropped Mary-Pat's ticket at the kitchen window and grabbed a rag from behind the counter. "Yes, sir."

"We can talk later!" Mary-Pat called after me. "Seems you got your hands full."

Garnett's police chief, Melvin Baker, and a young male officer came in and sat in the usual place, the cop booth as we called it, the only large table where no one had to sit with their back to the door. It wasn't my section, but I brought waters anyway, overheard them talking in low tones to Mary-Pat about the highway accident. I bussed the table behind theirs, and from what I could gather, a man had been going home from the Te-jano club out off Highway 125, thinking he was being safe by walking instead of getting behind the wheel. The driver of the water truck accidentally drifted into the other lane, and a sec-ond vehicle, a pickup truck, swerved onto the shoulder, hit the man, and sped away. I felt a chill down my arms—how could a person just drive off?—and hoped Sheila was wrong about more bad news. I hoped the man would live.

Up and down the rows of the narrow, high-ceilinged room, sick to my stomach now, I gathered more dishes and wiped down the faded blue-checked tablecloths as people came and went. It was busy, and would stay busy all day. Tonight was the home opener. In addition to everyone in Garnett, we'd get out-of-towners coming to see the Steers play. I checked the clock on the wall behind the counter: thirty minutes past the start of our shift and Victoria hadn't shown, hadn't even called in. Dot me-andered her big behind between the tables and ignored a woman trying to flag her down for more coffee. Put her hands on her hips and waited for me to pick up a bottle of ketchup someone asked for despite her being closer. Not normally a go-getter, but she made her point about having to stay late.

"I can't cover. Cannot do it again. I have to sleep for at least a couple hours before my grandbaby's sitter goes home," Dot said, not bothering to lower her voice when customers' heads turned.

Marlene removed her glasses and pinched the bridge of her nose. Her swoop of feathered bangs had fallen and stuck to her forehead, despite what I knew to be a generous spritz of Aqua Net.

"It's not that bad," I said, walking with them into the kitchen. "I'll handle it alone." I changed the coffee filter to put on a fresh pot. Working with Dot in a mood was worse than the extra hustle.

Marlene shook her head, donned an apron. "I needed to run errands and go to the bank before the weekend. That girl does this at the worst possible times."

"Maybe she's got a good reason," I said, remembering her swaying, her slurred speech last night at the bonfire, stopping short of saying she was likely sleeping off a hangover.

"No call, no show, anywhere else that would get you canned!" Fernando called from the freezer, carrying out a bag of pork chops and hefting it into a basin of water to thaw. "This is her what—third or fourth time missing? If it were me, I'd can her ass." He was a year younger than me, a football player who blew out his knee the first game at the junior college nearby. He was still going to school, but part-time since he had lost his scholarship. He hated the café. And most people, I thought.

"I don't remember making you manager." Marlene squinted in his direction, her normally sunny face tired and drawn.

He shuffled back to the griddle with his head down. "Just saying."

"Maybe I should call her," Marlene sighed. "Don't want to let someone go without a warning."

Marlene wouldn't fire Victoria. She wasn't that kind of manager—meaning she didn't like to think of herself as a manager, more like an older sister, the fact of which was usually good but often resulted in situations like this—and besides, Victoria had problems at home. She had been taking care of her grandmother up until she'd passed a few weeks before. Victoria had a kid, a little girl, and no one wanted to put a single mom out.

"Don't bother," said Dot, halfway out the back door, holding her purse and her tennis shoes by the laces while sliding her red, swollen feet into a pair of flip-flops. "That chick blew in here and will leave just as quick. I've seen it a hundred times. People come and go. Just the way it is."

Chapter 4

I came around the bend in the road, imagined the house before I saw it: white limestone and tin roof, low-slung single story like most places in Garnett. Imagined the front porch as it always had been: crowded with two humming brown fridges next to a plastic-covered recliner, echoing wind chimes, and Mamaw's orange trumpet vine tangled on a chipped white lattice. Couple of stray cats with patchy fur and chewed-up ears mewing around an old basting pan full of kibble.

Loose gravel popped under the tires as I pulled under the carport and parked next to the blue Ford with the busted camper shell. Weeds choked the cracks in the walkway and a fine layer of dust coated the porch. Leroy's left arm was in a sling and I startled when I saw his face—redder than normal, and puffy, his cheek slick with ointment and scabbing around three small stitches—I'd almost forgotten he'd hit his head when he'd fallen a few weeks back, forgotten he got sent to the VA up in Big Spring, and my stomach wrenched all over again imagining my strong, fierce grandfather suddenly helpless, lying in his own blood on the floor. He'd always been such a powerful presence, had seemed immortal to me. His hair—full and mostly dark even into his eighties—was wild and long. He had sharp brown eyes, nearly black, and a tall, straight back and wide shoulders.

"Hello, little darlin'."

I bent to hug him, moved toward the chair he had set out, but it was piled with boxes of river rocks he'd collected. The swing was covered in braided rugs and already occupied by a tabby cat with a runny eye. Leroy leaned back in the recliner, feet up and looking like a king in court. So I brushed off the top porch step and sat down.

He drank his beer and set the can on the armrest. "You come by to bring me more refreshments?"

I laughed and went to the fridge to get him a cold one. "You told Mary-Pat I need work?"

"Don't you?"

"It would help."

"All right, done. That it?"

"What're you kicking me out? My parents told me I'm supposed to invite you to Aunt Jewel's birthday party this Sunday."

He shook his head, took a swig of beer.

"They'd love for you to come. I can even drive you." I bit my tongue remembering what Momma had really said: "Just make sure the old man's alive. Tell him he's invited, not like he'll make it." Leroy was my father's father, but he and Dad didn't get along. Dad's mother, my mamaw, had been the last tether—a funny, sweet-natured woman—and after she passed we'd seen less and less of Leroy. But really, the relationship between the two men felt frayed for as long as I could remember. They couldn't go much longer than a single meal before they started picking, picking turned to fighting, and fighting turned to each not speaking to the other for months. Dad was a cop, once. When I was a baby, he was badly injured in a car accident while on duty.

Leroy, sheriff at the time, had been the driver of the vehicle. Dad took disability and Leroy retired not long after. Dad was never the same, according to all who knew him, and neither was Leroy. I knew no difference, but one picks up on things, overhears hushed late-night discussions while sneaking out of bed to read by the light in the hallway.

No one ever said it outright. No one spoke the word "fault," and yet a sliver of something ugly shone under a door I'd long been too afraid to open.

"Oh, now, I don't know about a party. Ask me Sunday," he said.

"What else have you got to do?"

He finished the first beer and cracked open the other. "Been thinking about going across the river. You know I'd like to take you out to the place. How 'bout it?"

"I'll be in sad trouble if I miss that party. If you want a ride out there today, just ask."

"Hell, right now I've got nothing better to do than have you drive us around. How's your silver bullet?"

"Just fine." I smiled. I drove a 2007 Pontiac Grand Prix I'd dubbed the "silver bullet," for its color and in some ways, too, for protection, for luck and for speed. It was a steal—fifty thousand miles on it and cost me four grand—and buying it on my own had been a proud moment. It was sturdy and wide, a muscle car with get-up-and-go. I jingled the keys, motioning him to follow.

Leroy always said this part of Texas is God's country. I don't know if Garnett is God's country, but as we headed west and out of town, as the houses disappeared from the road, it opened up something inside of me—a melancholy, perhaps—all because the sky seemed so big yet the world so small.

We drove toward the river where the land seemed to break and rise upward. There is a fault line in the middle of our county and beyond it the land is hillier. The Salt Fork River—to the southeast it becomes the Little Angel, runs through town and is spring fed, clear and cold, and to the southwest continues the twisty, ever-widening Geronimo River—is about a mile from the start of my family's land, what we called "the place." I drove over the bridge and Leroy sat up straight, his eyes alert. He had helped build the bridge sixty years ago, long before he became a lawman. Mamaw told me that while he had the road construction job they moved every six weeks or less, often into motels and boardinghouses. She'd just have spent hours cleaning a tar-papered apartment when Leroy would come in and announce they were moving in the morning.

But before then, when Leroy was a boy, he broke horses. We came close to the neighbor's quarter-horse ranch and Leroy leaned forward in the car seat at the sight of the horses running full speed the length of the fence, as far as the eye could see.

"Pull over; let's watch the ponies first. Right here is fine," he said as I eased the bullet to the shoulder. The Shaver property was wide and flat, the grass yellowy from the drought but still good grazing. We watched as two mustangs played with each other, jumping and racing, muscles rippling under the sheen of their black coats. A rust-and-white-colored mare came closer as we hung our arms over the metal rail.

"That paint looks like a smaller version of this mean old pony we had when I was a boy out on the place. We called him Riot."

"Did you ride him?"

"Took me long enough, but I got him muzzle broke. Could

lead him around a pen, even rode him to school," he said, his laugh coming in short, tumbling bursts like a snare drum. "Shit, but not before I got thrown twenty, thirty times."

"Bet that hurt."

"I can still see my father's and my uncles' faces, the young kids sitting on the wooden fence posts near the troughs. A cold norther blowing in," he said, and whistled to call the paint closer. "When that mean pony threw me it was like time stopped, though it was only a second—the pulse of the animal under my thighs, a jolt, and I'm upside down, turning over. Landed and hit so hard on my back it knocked the breath from my lungs. All I seen was black. That next gulp of air was like being born again."

Leroy's childhood felt impossibly long ago, but standing beside him, I, too, felt a pang of desire for those days. This feeling of being caught between the present and the past. The sharp smell of the animal and the scrub cedar on the breeze and the high, thin clouds—the sky, too, was like a memory that we breathed but couldn't touch.

I looped my arm through Leroy's good arm as we walked. "Isn't that how your granny lost the tip of her finger? Breaking horses?"

"No, she'd rode out to rope cows. Noise scared her horse. The calf she had went one way and the horse bucked. The rope wound so tight around her finger it cut off the circulation and popped it right off at the top joint," he said. "Granny was tougher than any of these drugstore cowboys you see strutting around nowadays."

I'd heard the gruesome details many times but knew he enjoyed telling them. The paint drew just close enough to us that I could hear her heavy breath, see her nostrils flare and the soft plane of her neck as she shook out her mane and flicked her ears. But when I reached through the fence to pet her, she bolted.

"Let's go," Leroy said, and motioned west.

After I'd driven onto the place about a half a mile on nothing more than a deer trail, I pulled under the shade of a live oak and parked. Leroy got out and started walking uphill.

"You ought to be taking it easy," I said, jogging to catch up to him. For someone his age, he climbed quickly and nimbly. "I thought you wanted to check the fence line." The Schneiders' ranch bordered the place to the north, the Shavers' to the east. Leroy didn't get out here as much anymore, and usually when we did come out it was to check on what needed maintenance.

"Naw, not today," he said.

"And it's the middle of the hottest part of the day."

Leroy kept walking uphill. "I'm not hot." He wore long shirtsleeves, cowboy boots, and stacked Wranglers every day, even during the summer. I kept pace with him as we moved through the tall grass, wishing I'd worn boots instead of my work sneakers.

Just when I felt like I couldn't stand the burning in my calves and the sun beating down on me any longer, we crested the hill and beyond us the land seemed to flatten and open wide like a palm. In a circle of trees at the top of the escarpment was where the old house had once stood, all that remained a foundation and a stone cistern. The house had burned in a fire caused by lightning twenty years before, when my great-uncle still lived there. He had died in the fire and the land became Leroy's. Their intention had always been to rebuild out on the place and move, but for a variety of reasons—the cost, Mamaw's preference toward town—they never did.

"It's been too long," Leroy said, and leaned against the

cistern. I leaned my arms back next to his, the cool, shadow-dappled stone giving my skin goose bumps.

"I've always loved it here too."

"One day this will be yours—well, your father's and eventually yours. You have to take care of it," he said. I felt a knot forming in my throat. I knew he meant to be kind, this was his way of telling me he loved me, but I hated foretelling future sadness.

"Maybe the business," he added. I thought about his and Mary-Pat's office above the town square. Up a narrow staircase and through a pebbled-glass door, just like in the old movies. My dad had made it clear he'd rather sell the space than "get involved" in any type of law enforcement again.

Leroy walked toward the center of the circle of the trees, a house without walls made of light and branches. "Sometimes when I'm up here I think I smell my granny's pipe. She kept a little tobacco purse on her lap and smoked and rocked, that pipe in the corner of her mouth. I always thought she was the bravest person I ever knew, braver than most men. Sarah Anne. She lived out here all by herself, never scared. Lonely sometimes, sure, but never scared." He smiled and tipped his head back to breathe in the air more deeply. He frowned.

"Feeling okay?"

"I get tired more easy; lately I've been forgetting where I am, feel dizzy of a sudden when I stand," he said quietly.

I reached for his good arm. "You ought to go back to the doctor. I can take you Monday."

"Don't worry about me," he said, and waved me off, then spun around for effect. "It's called getting tooted."

I laughed with him, despite my actual concern. He'd gone to the hospital, and considering how much he hated doctors it had to have been somewhat serious. He really shouldn't be drinking so much, but there was little use going down that road with Leroy.

"You going to tell me what's going on? Seemed nervous when you pulled up."

"I'm worried about you," I said.

"Don't be, darlin'. What else?"

"Just a weird, sad day. Coworkers arguing at the café made it kind of tense, and there was a hit-and-run in the county last night; cops were talking about it all morning. A pedestrian was involved—he's in critical condition, I think."

"Terrible shame."

I nodded, hesitating. "And I guess I'm all in my head too much. Thinking about what Mary-Pat offered." I watched two brown doves dance across a tree limb, unable to articulate why I'd felt stung. I wasn't a cop and didn't have any experience—what did I expect? And did I really want to follow people for hours at a time? I didn't know much about what the two of them did all day, but I did know it wasn't always glamorous. "You know I first thought she meant help her with investigating, and I wonder if—"

"You don't have a license."

"I know. I thought she meant, like, apprenticing."

"Well, now, it is in your blood. My grandfather, father, me, William. But I don't know."

"If I were a boy would you have suggested it for me?"

"Mary-Pat's a female."

I rolled my eyes.

"Your daddy wouldn't like it. He never really did want to be a lawman himself," Leroy said. "I'll see what old Pat allows. Work in San Antone keeps her busy. Thought she was fixing to retire. Maybe you could help—but things are different nowadays, so I don't know."

"How so?"

"Drugs mostly. But people are out of work, desperate in many ways. It's not the same round here as it used to be."

Sounds silly, but it never occurred to me that Leroy would be scared of anything. The nights Leroy spent working cases and the years spent searching for the missing and the dead had always seemed off-limits for discussion, among a million other things, feelings chief among them. On the occasion I used the words "I love you," he often replied, "Thank you," but here we were together, talking, me loving him and feeling for the first time in a while like I belonged anywhere.

"What made you want to be a lawman? It must have been hard, frightening a lot of the time. You could've been a rancher, or all kinds of other things."

He was quiet for a moment. "I don't always know. Felt called to. I think it was about knowing right from wrong, one's duty to help people. It's also about yourself and your vanities as much as one wouldn't like to admit." He walked over the foundation toward the downward slope of the hill. "Reckon it's about time for us to go, little darlin'. Don't want to miss my programs and you drive too slow."

Chapter 5

County Line was pretty traditional looking as far as icehouses go, half outside with picnic tables lined up under an overhanging corrugated metal roof like an old carport, the wooden building mottled brown and gray from years of weather. I could smell malt and smoke from the crushed beer cans and cigarettes in the dirt as we walked through the wide, unpaved parking lot rutted with tire marks.

"I need that fifty bucks. Watch her try to wriggle out of it again."

"Kelsey Kramer needs all the help she can get, you ask me." I laughed and pulled open the creaking wooden door. The smell of smoke was stronger inside and bad radio country, the kind that sounds more like pop music with banjos, blasted my eardrums.

Nikki raised her voice. "She doesn't is the worst part. The kind of tips she pulls in on a good night? You know, you ought to try serving tequila shots instead of Diet Cokes, but like I was saying, Kelsey just likes thinking she's smarter than everyone. Her hair does look good, though; I'm glad I lightened it." She motioned with her chin to the young, female bartender with a fresh trim and highlights, blended so they looked almost natural, not like the stripes you often saw painted on women's heads around here. Nikki only finished her cosmetology program and got a chair at her mother Sherrilyn's salon six months ago, but already she had a solid reputation around town and a full appointment book.

"The problem is that a lot of the girls we came up with got spoiled to you doing their hair at sleepovers for free," I said. Kelsey and I made eye contact; then her gaze shifted to Nikki. She dropped her paring knife and lime and rushed through a side door.

Nikki grinned. "Come on. She can't hide back there long." She pushed and the gaggle of men at the bar parted so she could order beers. While I could wait forever for service at a crowded bar, Nikki was always taken care of promptly. She commanded attention that way. It was mostly dark inside save for the blinking neon, and the blue color on her light hair and skin made her look kind of otherworldly.

I took a long pull of the beer she handed me and scanned the room. County Line wasn't a place we frequented, was a little far out, but every time I'd come before the pool tables had been full. Tonight, the crowd was thinner, likely due to the home game. A crowd of misfits like our neighbor Glass Eye Rick, who'd nearly lost his life shooting guns in the air over Fourth of July weekend, and Mr. Fritz, our former gym teacher who'd gotten fired over suggestive texts sent to Macy Wiggins, were scattered to the corners.

Nikki moved toward one of the long picnic tables under the overhang. "Let's sit. When she comes back out, I can see her from here."

"Speaking of money being due, sorry about the cable bill.

Wasn't expecting to take the bullet to the shop last week," I said. Nikki didn't charge me rent, just asked that I take care of half the bills and shared groceries. Our place had once been her paternal grandmother's. A small old house painted pink with a slice of unkempt yard, paid off long ago. Another reason I'd come back to Garnett: I could afford it, mostly, without being back in my childhood bedroom. I felt a flutter of nerves in my stomach. "I might be getting a second job soon, so that'll help."

"Hush." Nikki nudged me. "We're gonna have to do something about that junk bucket vehicle of yours, though." She took a sip of beer. "You talk to your old roommate much? The one I met? I liked her."

"Her parents sent her to Europe for a few months as a graduation present, so she's been out of touch," I said, tamping down the desire to look at my phone. The amount of time I spent scrolling through her posts despite the jealousy they inspired felt like getting sick after binge eating.

Nikki laughed. "Well, shit. Sorry I just got you a card. Maybe her parents can send you and me as chaperones next time."

With my roommate, as with most of my friends from college, I'd known pretty early on we'd be out of touch in more ways than one after it ended. Nikki laughed with less mirth than I—oh, I'd nursed those feelings whenever things got hard at school. But times like these, in some dimly lit bar, I hated how the same songs played. Everyone was familiar, yet not a friend. Limbs twitchy and my chest tight, I'd think, *You don't belong here.* Beer fizzed on my tongue, blandly sour. Maybe I was too much in my head. All I knew was that if I didn't get over myself quick, I'd topple under the weight of this chip on my shoulder.

A group seated inside howled at the television mounted on the wall. The game had gone off and one of those never-ending infomercials started up: a woman selling "fine" jewels and build-able charm bracelets. "Put it on the game," one of the guys hollered. The bartender ignored him and after a few moments the man just shrugged his shoulders and kept watching.

"He looks familiar," Nikki said. "Do we know him?"

"Him watching a muted TV commercial?"

"No." Nikki pointed with the neck of her beer bottle to a group at the periphery of the gravel lot beside the bar. Four guys with identical red polo shirts and stiff, industrial uniform jeans and boots were smoking and cutting up.

"I think they were at the bonfire last night," I said. One of the men turned and I saw the label on his shirt pocket: Artemis, the oil and gas company.

Nikki squinted. "The blond one's kind of cute."

"The one with a plug in his lip? That would be fun to kiss."

"No, the other one," she said, and waved. He was cuter than the others—a healthy tan and strong looking—and smiled at her. "He's coming over here." She giggled.

"Hi. I'm Randy," the man said, then motioned toward his friends behind him. "We were just saying you girls might be thirsty—if we get a pitcher you gonna have some?"

Nursing the first beer, I shook my head, but Nikki nodded yes. Up close Randy looked older—lines around his eyes and mouth, his deep tan made his skin seem stretched over his bones—and underneath his drugstore cologne smelled chemical, sulfurous like the air around the drill sites themselves. The rest of the Artemis guys approached, though they didn't sit. One stayed back a distance and stared at us while spitting into a gas station drink cup. The two who were closer blew smoke that hung thickly in the air and jabbed each other in the ribs, debating who would buy the first pitcher. Randy shook his head and grinned. "Be right back, girls."

Nikki whispered, "I don't know about them. Think we might've fed some strays."

"We?"

"And I realized why this Randy looked familiar—your co-worker, the drunk one? She was sitting on his lap."

"Hey there." One of the men looked down at me. The gauges in his ears only emphasized how far they stuck out. I met his gaze and his face reddened. "You play pool?" he asked.

"Not well," I said. He shifted and looked unsure of what to do with his hands now that he'd stubbed out his cigarette in the gravel under the picnic table and, like the others, looked vaguely familiar. Maybe he was kin to someone in Garnett. I didn't think we'd gone to school together. Feeling momentarily sorry for being unfriendly, I said, "As I drink I'm either better at pool or stop caring that I'm no good. I'm Annie and this is my cousin Nikki."

We shook. His hand was dry, calloused. "Steve. We saw you last night at Schneider's. Talked with some of your friends, just didn't get a chance to come over."

"Shame," I said, not hiding my sarcasm well enough. "Sounds like you met Victoria."

"Hey, who am I?" The other guy swayed and flopped his arms and let his tongue hang out. He laughed hard and held his side.

The hair on the back of my neck stood up. Nikki crossed her arms over her chest. The one with the spit cup still stood back, watching, but laughed with the other two and he started doing the thing with his arms again—like a zombie—and sang, or rather, slurred, "Why don't you mind your own business."

They were making fun of Victoria.

"Randy, dude," Steve said as he approached with a frothy pitcher and a stack of plastic cups. "You got a picture of that drunk bitch hanging—"

"Shut up, stupid," Randy said, sensing our unease. He turned to Nikki. "He's just joking."

"And I just thought he was having a conniption," Nikki said. "Y'all are rude."

They kept laughing, harder now, and suddenly it felt like someone was standing on my chest, like the world was too loud and too hot.

Randy shrugged and poured out a beer for each of us. As he handed Nikki a cup, she looked down at his ring finger and the dented gold band. "Shit, and you're married? Get outta here, man."

He pulled back his hand, clenched his jaw, and looked back and forth between us. "That's nothing you need to worry about."

"Fair enough. Now she and I are gonna have us a private conversation. Y'all have a good night," Nikki said.

Randy stood. Mumbled something under his breath before turning on his heels. The others followed him over to an empty pool table.

"Losers," Nikki said.

I felt a headache coming on, a throb intensifying behind my eyes. "I knew she was drunk last night, but I didn't realize Victoria was *that* drunk; did you?"

"Happens to the best of us."

I started to say something—to explain the sameness I felt seeing them mock her. The feeling of being pulled down a dark tunnel, a memory.

But I couldn't.

Nikki touched my arm. "You okay? You look a little green."

"Fine," I said, and took a drink of the beer they'd left, a mouthful of foam and almost tasteless.

Kelsey reemerged from the back. She shuffled out from behind the bar and stood in front of our table. Her denim shorts were tight and damp looking, and I thought she was picking a wedgie when she reached into her back pocket. "Here." She pushed a wad of cash into Nikki's hand. "I told you I got paid tonight. That's all I was waiting for."

Nikki relaxed her shoulders. Smiled and put the cash in the zipper pocket of her purse. "Bless your heart, that's why I came by—to make it easier on you!"

"Yeah, okay."

"Put it on the game!" a man at one of the barstools called out. The infomercial woman leaned over a velvety maroon box showcasing a necklace that was supposed to look like the one from *Titanic*.

"I can't find the remote and I can't reach up there without a ladder!" Kelsey yelled without turning around.

"Whatever. I was leavin' anyway."

"Fine," she said, and mocked putting a pistol to her head. "Y'all want anything else?"

Nikki looked at me, indicated it was my call. She'd gotten what she wanted.

"Nope," I said, the pain behind my eyes dulling. Kelsey sashayed back behind the bar. The place was getting busier and there would be more people to talk to. We could get a cold round. But home, to be home and under the covers, was what I really wanted.

Nikki watched the television, her chin resting in both hands, her eyes glazed over. "You think those are real gemstones she's selling?"

Letting out the breath I hadn't realized I'd been holding, I fished in my purse for the keys.

Chapter 6

Without thinking I'd run to the railroad tracks. The sky was wide, oppressively so, the ground flat and yellow to the horizon. The tracks themselves, blackened with age, ended in the middle of the field in an upward twist of crooked steel. There was nothing out here but the wind and a scatter of broken bricks, and yet there was this presence of another, a hum, a feeling like a ghost. If lonely had a texture, if the past was a whisper-like sound in the air around your head, that would be it, this ghost.

I hadn't gone for a run in months. My legs felt like lead. Not only out of shape, I hadn't slept. Angry over how those men had made fun of Victoria, but more so irritated with myself, I'd gotten up, downed a glass of water, then opened my laptop and ended up reading, again, the last email from my advisor, Dr. Berman. The email in which she had encouraged me to stay and enroll in the LSAT prep course on campus, that she'd help me find a cheap apartment, maybe land me a job babysitting for a colleague in the department.

She said we would figure something out.

While I loved being in school, going out of state was hard on me—I'd never even been to an overnight summer camp—and there were more than a few nights I lulled myself to sleep by cataloging sensations I worried I might forget: the sound of cicadas at night and crickets bouncing off my window screen, the wind at dusk carrying the sweet smell of dry grass, and the kind of dark it gets only out in the country, away from all the lights. Let those thoughts pull my heart into my throat with such an intense longing I thought I'd die of it. When the sun rose, I closed the laptop. Shook my head and got dressed. Pulled my running shoes out of the back of the closet. I was here, and the only way to truly be here was to be outside.

Rivulets of sweat ran down my arms. Panting, I seemed to have forgotten the simple logic that the farther out I ran the farther I'd have to go on the way home. I had a lot to do that day: errands to run and then back to the café for the night shift. I groaned, walked to catch my breath before turning back and picking up speed. Pumping my arms, lungs aching, muscles stinging—

But eventually the pain blurred. My body felt almost weightless. Like I was floating, my breath so loud it sounded like someone else's, and I thought, *Maybe the ghost is me.*

By the time I got to the H-E-B in Colburn it was packed. People drove in from all across the county to do their shopping for the week on Saturdays. Motorized scooters trailed behind women with one eye on a coupon book and the other on whatever sugar cereal their kid tried sneaking into the basket. State students ransacked the frozen foods. Out-of-towners stockpiled beer and Doritos for their final float down the river till spring. I pushed my buggy through the bakery, angling to get one of the last packs of fresh tortillas when someone nicked my ankle with theirs. I winced and turned around to see Justin Schneider inches from me.

"Hey, lady. Don't mind me," he said, and reached for the last bag. "Oh, did you want this?"

"You're kind of a bully, aren't you?"

Justin wore an old football T-shirt that didn't quite fit him anymore; his shoulders were broader now, his biceps more defined. He dipped his chin, smiled. "Come on. You know I'm going to let you take it."

"That's okay."

"All yours," he said, and touched my hand. *Lord, really?* I wanted to say. He was the kind of person who could make a conversation over a pack of tortillas seem like innuendo. But I looked up at him, at his handsome face, and just said "Thank you."

He let his hand linger on mine for a moment. "So, what're you up to this weekend?"

"Getting groceries for my great-aunt's birthday party. I lead a pretty wild life."

"You and me both."

"I didn't get a chance to ask you, how's your family? I saw Troy."

He frowned. "Yeah, kind of weird, us both back in the house. He and Megan aren't engaged anymore, so he's staying at home till he decides where he wants to go."

"God, they've been together forever," I said, trying to sound surprised. Nikki already told me—the Beauty Shoppe was a hotbed of gossip—plus I'd noticed Megan captioning a lot of her posts with sad song lyrics. All the pictures she'd posted of her ring deleted. "How's he doing?"

"I honestly don't see Troy that much. He's working a lot, for Artemis, and I'm working for Dad. My major was construction management, so Dad's getting me in touch with some developers around here, but so many projects are delayed, canceled. Wasn't the most recession-proof major."

"Tell me about it. Your dad doing well, though?"

"Ever since they finalized the divorce, he's had this new lease on life. Dating, weekend vacations with his old fraternity buddies." Justin laughed. "He's got a busier social life than me and my brother. Mom's remarried to this guy from Amarillo. Haven't been up in a while," he said, pushing out his lower lip. In high school the talk was that Mrs. Schneider, Sunday school teacher at the Garnett Church of Christ, was messing around on her husband—out late at night, someone else's car in the driveway, that kind of thing—a scandal big enough that all our classmates and teachers knew, causing people to look sideways when either of the boys came close. When the rumor reached its peak, people cruelly teasing them, Troy said one day on the school bus that his dad could do better than someone who behaved like a whore. The whole bus—our loud, spitball-throwing bus—fell completely silent. His words seemed unfair, even then, but also had further embarrassed us for both boys; I had never heard someone speak about his or her mother that way. Seated behind him, when Justin turned his face to the window, I remember seeing two fat tears roll down his cheek.

"Thanks for having us out the other night. It was good to catch up," I said.

"Your girl Nikki's crazy as ever." He chuckled. "She's always liked a party. Then again, I think you do too."

My face flushed. For one, I might poke fun at my family, but someone else, that's different. Two, was he referring to that night? I knew that was why he didn't call me. Heat pricked my neck, my chest. "You know me, always had a talent for embarrassing myself," I said.

"Hey, wait a minute. I didn't mean to, like, offend you. I meant it would be fun to hang again soon. Just you and me."

My heart pounded. An invisible, taut wire strung between us, and for that moment I wanted nothing more than to be seventeen again and out on the water. To forget all that came after. "Sure." I nodded, queasy with my own desire and a sense that everyone was staring at me.

And they were. I was blocking the aisle.

"Excuse me, sorry." I pulled my buggy to the side. "Justin, I'll see you later then."

It was September of my senior year, and Justin, flirty and passing notes in homeroom, invited me. I had extracurricular activities—cross-country team, newspaper, academic decathlon—was busy and had friends through those, but no one close, not since Nikki moved, not since Wyatt and I had broken up. More than a boy I was crushing on, Justin surprised me at a time when I felt everything exciting was elsewhere. He'd come back from summer vacation muscled from working on the family ranch, his hair sun streaked and face lightly freckled. He appeared like a wildflower-scented balm to soothe the loneliness I felt.

The stock tank was set far back off the road. Big as a lake and full of perch, bass, and enormous catfish with a camper and a floating dock at its edge. Kids went to party, naturally, but my parents really thought we were fishing—that's the kind of girl I was, no trouble—Dad even picking me up a bucket of minnows I had to dump in the creek after he dropped me off at the top of the dirt road before the others saw.

I was slaphappy on punch and cheap booze, but still self-conscious in the bikini I wore—a hand-me-down from Nikki I was pretty sure she'd shoplifted from the Victoria's Secret outlet—and nervous wading through the cloudy water. Worried over cottonmouths and rusted cans hiding below the surface. But then Justin came up behind me and grabbed me round the waist. I smiled and rocked back into his hips. The other boys jackknifed into the tank, and against the sky specks of mica free-floating in the airborne wave shimmered like glitter. Out of the water our skin was brown and shimmery, and we kept drinking. Darkness came on fast and was disorienting—I passed out in the camper's bunk and woke to a loud thud on the dock: everyone by the water, Justin dragging a small rowboat to the edge.

There was only room for two, and he begged me to go with him, tapping my butt with the oar when I turned back. I didn't really want to go, to be on the water in the dark, but he twined his fingers through mine and I followed.

The night was half-clear, only pinpricks in the sky from a few small stars. Once we were far out in the middle of the tank, Justin stood up and swayed. The boat dipped and tilted as he began to dance to the music blasting on the dock.

"You tip this thing over and I will kill you," I said.

He laughed and rocked the boat hard enough to slosh water over the side. Picking up the oar again, he slammed it into the water, where it stopped and stuck upright with a squish. "Chill out, girl. You could stand out here it's so shallow. What're you so scared of?"

"It's dark and I can't see."

"You can swim."

"My granddad and I nearly drowned out at Canyon once."

"No shit?"

"He'd taken his belt off, tied it around his waist and around mine since we didn't have a life jacket for me, but tethered to him like that, I went under when he did. I couldn't see or feel the bottom. I think he'd slipped into deeper water and sliced his foot on something, 'cause there was blood, and he kept pulling me under—"

"I'm not gonna let it tip," he said, and rocked the boat again. Dared me to scream. Dared me to not act cool. I felt so foolish having told him the story.

"I just like to see the bottom," I said, stopping short of the part about Leroy being drunk, about the horrible fight with my dad afterward at the hospital, about throwing away my favorite swimsuit, bloodstained. I looked up at the sky and counted breaths through my nose to slow my heartbeat.

Justin sat down across from me and leaned forward so I could make out the contours of his face in the dark. He moved his thumb on the knobby bone above my sunburned foot and pushed it like a button, all my nerves blinking and signaling. He pulled me closer, his hand inching up my thigh. There was beer on his breath, but what I remember most was that his mouth tasted like the ground smelled after a rain. Like he had swallowed gulps of that gold-flecked water. I kissed him back, hard, and I think now that kiss, a kiss I saw as a promise, was what led me to the awful thing a few nights later. But on that night, we would go back to his truck to be alone, then watch the stars from the bed of it.

Chapter 7

Fernando came out from the kitchen as I tied my apron on. "What're you doing here?"

"Nice to see you too. Victoria and I traded shifts. I've got family stuff tomorrow."

He blew a puff of air through his nostrils. "You better make sure she's actually covering you—you know she still hasn't called Marlene?"

"Yeah, usually she at least tells us. But she wouldn't miss now—again—if she didn't know I would be here in her place."

"Who knows." He shrugged and walked back to the kitchen. I reached for my phone where it was hidden in the small space between the register and counter under a napkin holder. Marlene didn't allow us to have them out while on shift. Fernando really couldn't have his out since he cooked, but Victoria usually hid hers under the menu box. I texted her: *Remember we switched? I'm here now, so you're still taking my 10–4 tomorrow?*

I waited a beat for her to text back, hoping for a quick *yeah* or *duh* like usual, realizing my mother might actually kill me if I missed Aunt Jewel's party. I thought back to the bonfire and winced. Victoria was in bad shape—worse than I'd realized, as evidenced by those men—but I was sure she wouldn't miss a second shift. She'd feel it if her paycheck was short. And she'd done worse than come to work hungover, even came in tipsy once, black rinds of old makeup under her eyes, smelling like booze and a stranger's cologne and winking when asked how her night was.

"Excuse me, can we get some service? Hello?"

"Sorry," I said, nearly dropping my phone as I scrambled to put it in its hiding place. It was early for supper and I hadn't noticed them come in: a young woman seated across from a man with a shaggy haircut, the one guys in alt-rock bands wore—not quite a mullet, but close. She was pale and petite, with a thin sliver of gold hooped through her nose. She had tattooed whimsical thin-lined drawings of sparrows and basic shapes on her arms that managed to make her look hip and oddly refined for someone with half sleeves. I figured them for State students driven over from Colburn, or maybe on their way up to Austin and had decided to pull off the interstate, looking for an abandoned building to take pictures in front of or something. I took out my pad and waited, prickly for having been scolded.

She touched her chin and tapped her lips, as if this were a major decision. "Dr Pepper with crushed ice. You have crushed ice here?"

"Sure, and we have some specials if y'all are eating. Meatloaf and mashed potatoes, chicken-fried steak—"

"Wait a minute. I know you," she said. She poked the guy, who was studying the menu like he'd find something we didn't have if he looked hard enough. "Babe, she went to my high school!"

"Uh-huh."

I looked closer at her face. "Cecily?"

"Yep." She giggled and adjusted the straw boater hat she wore. "You look exactly the same, Annie! Wow! We were on our way to *ACL* and when I saw the exit I told him we had to stop in Garnett real quick."

"Great," I said. Her sister and I had been friends, briefly, until she all but stopped speaking to me. It still stung and I tried keeping my voice even. "How is Elise?"

"Elise is really good. She moved to New York after graduation. Shoebox apartment and two roommates in Brooklyn, but she's happy."

"We lost touch," I said, feeling uncomfortably warm. "Nice to hear she's—"

"I'll just have a burger," the guy said, looking up from the menu.

"Got it." I nodded.

The supper crowd was trickling in, and it was getting busy enough that I didn't have to dwell on that particular blast from the past, but I wished Victoria were working with me. You need a certain level of camaraderie to get through any customer service job. I knew Victoria would have overheard our conversation, made eye contact with me, mouthed, *Put a bird on it,* her favorite line from *Portlandia.* Marlene came out from the kitchen and helped me when all the tables got to be full, but I was back in my groove by then. There was something serene in the work, I realized, an order to the present that kept you focused. When the last table settled up, I looked around, eager for something else to busy my hands with, but it was quiet, mostly clean.

"I'm fixing to call it," Marlene said, her hand on my shoulder. She lived above the café in a two-bedroom apartment she had shared with her son before he deployed. Something was off about Travis—people said he was touched, but he just had his head in the clouds—and while Marlene was proud of him joining the army, she worried. Stayed down in the café pretty late, and even when she didn't you could hear her moving around upstairs most of the night. Marlene's protectiveness is how the café came to be open 24/7: Travis was fifteen and sneaking out at night, so Marlene kept the lights on until he came in. In many ways, she kept the lights on for all of us. In a town where more businesses were shutting their doors than opening them, the café was a comfort, a sign of life.

"Okay, night." I hovered by the register.

"And, Annie?"

"Ma'am?" I turned to face her.

"Put your phone away."

The kind of people who came into the café late at night were the wayward types you'd expect—long-haul truckers come off the highway, shift workers, stoned teenagers—and some surprises too. Like the couple with the baby who won't sleep, or Mrs. Parrish, who does her grocery shopping after ten because she fears crowds.

I'd finished sweeping the scuffed-smooth hardwood floors and was rolling silverware when a handsome man came through the door. It was Wyatt Reed, his presence coincidental, or rather uncanny since I'd been thinking of him. About him and Justin and Elise. About timing. About how he was the type of person who would come in that night, a night I felt alone and somehow completely seen by all the people I'd ever known. It reminded me of a story Leroy once told: He was once on a road trip in New Mexico working a case, feeling lonely and anonymous, separate from all he'd left behind. He stopped at a gas station. The car at the second pump was left sitting with the doors wide open, but no one inside, and Leroy thought to himself, *That's just like my cousin Del.* Del, who always left doors open or his seat slung back from the table. And lo and behold, it was his cousin Del at that very Allsup's outside Clovis driving a rented car.

I wondered if I'd somehow summoned Wyatt.

"Oh, Annie." He smiled, his face crinkling around his warm hazel eyes. "It's usually Victoria—she have the night off? I was hoping to talk to her about something."

"Uh, yeah. Sorry to disappoint," I said, realizing how lame that sounded. God, was Wyatt the favorite regular Victoria talked about? Not a professor, but probably a TA since starting grad school. I pictured him teasing her, Victoria all happy to see him with her big, toothy smile and way of looking at you while you talked as if you were the only person who ever mattered. Standing with my shoulders a little straighter, I asked, "You usually spend Saturday night at the café?"

"Well . . ." He paused. "Tonight, I'm suffering a bout of sleeplessness."

That was one thing I couldn't decide if I liked or loathed about Wyatt: he talked in a lilting way, choosing phrases like "I'm suffering a bout of sleeplessness" instead of "I can't sleep." We traded in sarcasm, but this, his opaqueness, had often frustrated me.

"What'll you have? Marlene's made chocolate pie."

"I don't have much of a sweet tooth." He shook his head. "And I'm actually not hungry. I'd like some water. Well, I'd really like a fresh cup of coffee. Victoria usually puts on a new pot for me."

Oh, does she? "That'll help you sleep," I said.

"Maybe I like being up this time of night."

"You seem kind of cranky. Need to get your nap out."

"Or maybe I figure if I'm going to be awake I ought to be productive," and he pointed to a book and binder he had on the seat next to him.

Walking to the kitchen, I couldn't help but smile at Wyatt. He might bemoan homework, but I knew he really liked studying. And I remembered how he looked playing basketball: You wouldn't think someone so lanky could be as fast or as graceful as he was. Most of all I recalled the joy on his face, even when our team wasn't winning, which they often weren't. I wasn't much of a photographer, often caught up in the game so by the time I thought to click the camera the big moment had passed. I was better at accumulating, sifting through my notes and coming up with a story, but I wondered if I had captured any of the joy with which he played. I brought him a hot cup of coffee—we always had a fresh pot, per Marlene's rules, though I wouldn't spoil the illusion for him—with cream and a couple sugars. "Do you still play basketball?" I asked.

"Just pickup with my brother. Hey, why don't you sit down with me?"

I looked around. No one else was there beside Fernando and me. Marlene was upstairs—"just a holler away," she always said, "or throw something at the ceiling"—and it was quiet, not even the sound of her television wafting downstairs. "Just for a minute," I said, and slid into the booth. It felt deliciously good to get off my feet. "The other night, I didn't get a chance to ask what program you're starting at State."

"Master's in geography," he said and slumped his shoulders. "Already worrying about midterms."

"You'll be fine. I'm proud of you, by the way."

"Thanks," he said, his cheeks coloring slightly. "What about you? You just graduated, right?"

"Yeah. I don't know," I sighed. "I wonder if maybe I don't really know what to do when no one's telling me. In which case, what if I truly am the kind of person who drinks too much, or just wants to get high, then eat whole frozen pizzas with their cousin? I'm afraid—"

"Are you high right now?"

"Shut up!"

He laughed. "You're not the only one. Why do you think I'm going to grad school? Guess I always thought you would be this hotshot headed out of Garnett. Never looking back, that kind of way."

"It's not all for lack of effort. Seems like everything entry-level is actually an internship. I interviewed for what I thought was a copywriting job, found out it was for summer and only paid a three-hundred-dollar stipend," I said.

"You know my mom used to make me read your assignments?"

"I always wondered if the teachers could resist poking fun at us."

"She wanted to show me how good they were, always saying you were smart." He grinned, nudged my foot with his under the table. "I disagreed with her, of course."

"I still wonder where she went wrong with you."

"But really, Annie, whatever you do, you'll be good at it," he said, his tone a little softer, eyes meeting mine.

"Thanks, Wyatt," I said, surprised by the shake in my voice, the urge to hug his neck.

"I hope I'm not overstepping, but can I ask you something?"

Before I could respond Fernando swung through the kitchen door. "Look alive. Po-po's coming."

I scrambled out of the booth. "They'll want to eat," I said to Wyatt just as the bell on the door jingled. He nodded and opened his textbook, sticking his nose in it with mock serious-ness. I went to the counter to fill some water glasses and Fernando sidled up beside me.

"Wyatt the Weird distracting you?"

I'd forgotten that's what some kids called him back in middle school. Being a teacher's kid, therefore narc, with an unhealthy obsession with anime got him that one. I gathered up menus and the glasses, not daring to look back at Wyatt.

"Whoever did this is one cold sonofabitch," the deputy said as they sat down in the cop booth. "A real piece of shit."

"Hey, little miss." Police Chief Melvin Baker waved me over, then turned to his partner. "Now J.J., watch your fucking language in front of the lady."

I was pretty sure he'd made that joke at least three times before, but I laughed politely and took their orders. They would eat a full breakfast, fuel for the long night and morning ahead of them. When I first started, I wondered if the cops who frequented the café were at all wary of a McIntyre—Baker was my father's age and Leroy had been his superior—but if they were, they didn't let on. They talked to me like they would to any young waitress. They talked *around* me, as if I were barely sentient. Only once did I hear mention of Leroy, once when they were riffing on Sheriff Garcia, saying he might have a stick up his ass, but at least he was straight edge. "McIntyre," they snickered, mocked tipping back a flask.

When I came back with their food J.J. was fiddling with his phone, half listening to Baker, and I overheard they still hadn't arrested anyone for the accident out on the highway. And worse, the man, Chavez, had died. It was a homicide investigation now. I shuddered to think of those terrifying moments before the vehicle hit, if he even saw it coming. Saying a silent prayer for his family, I poured steaming coffee into two mugs and the remainder into Baker's open thermos.

"Whoever did this would have tried to get as far away as possible," Baker said.

J.J. nodded. "They're running."

They're running. A small, strangled sound came out of my mouth.

Baker looked up. "You say something, hon?"

"Nope," I said, and hurried behind the counter to hide and look busy so I could get my thoughts together.

Victoria could have hit the man.

That could be the reason for her being gone without explanation. She'd been hammered Thursday night—what if she'd driven home? Got into an accident? But even impaired, could she be so hard, so cruel? Or so stupid? I didn't think so, but—

Terrible things can happen. Mistakes can quickly spiral out of control.

"You're all spaced out and your hands are shaking," Fernando said, standing beside me. "Eggs are up. I rang the bell."

"Sorry."

"What's up with you?"

"Just thinking about this whole thing with Victoria. What if she had to get out of town in a hurry?" I said, and nodded in the direction of the cops.

"The hit-and-run? Jesus Christ." He mopped his forehead with the edge of his apron. "She didn't do that, wouldn't do that," he said.

"You're right. That would be a horrible thing to do and she's not like that."

He looked at me like I'd spit in his face.

"Forget I said it, okay?"

"Here," he said, setting the plates down loudly. I wondered why the suggestion made him so angry. They didn't have much of a connection that I witnessed, other than some light flirting when she first started, mostly from him. Maybe he had more of a crush than he let on. I balanced the tray on my arm. Fernando was right. I was being crazy, tactless. It's just that for however irresponsible Victoria could seem, she wouldn't completely flake without a reason. She still hadn't even responded to my text—I'd checked and re-sent it—so something wasn't right, but then again, how well did I really know her?

Hector Chavez. I'd been racking my brain trying to remember where I knew the name. He'd worked in the elementary school cafeteria. Tears over spilled milk my first week of kindergarten: I remembered my carton flying onto the floor and he'd come over, wiped it up, and given me a new one. Showed me how to open it correctly and tucked my straw inside. He'd been kind to me, to all the kids—tying our shoelaces, propping our feet on his bent knee to show us how the bunny went around the tree. Maybe that shred of closeness I felt toward Hector Chavez explained the need to insert myself, but lately I think something else. There are people who see a thing dark or ugly and look away, and then there are people who want to turn over the ugly thing. There are those of us who want to look closer.

After the cops had their meal and their check, I went to give Wyatt a refill, but he wasn't there. Must have slipped out without me noticing. A five and an empty mug were left on the table. I peered out the window onto the dark street and saw nothing but taillights.

Chapter 8

"Can I get ten on pump three and a Quick Pick, please?"

The cashier nodded, handed me the lotto ticket and my change. "Feeling lucky or feeling desperate?"

"Maybe both," I said. "Gerald, you know how much it's for this week?"

"To gamble is a sin," he mumbled, not fully paying attention to me, but to the men kicking the door, the bell sounding louder and weirder than normal as they charged through it. Clearly from out of town, just passing through—two of them made a beeline for the restroom; the other two loaded up on jerky and Mountain Dew and phone minute cards. As I felt their eyes on me, my palms began to sweat and I wiped them on my jeans. One caught my stare and winked. It was just after midnight and there was no one there but Gerald, who had to have been pushing eighty, so I tucked my head down and walked fast out the door.

It was dark and quiet save for the road sounds from the highway overpass. A single streetlamp flickered, throwing a dim, sickly green glow around the pole but not much farther.

I turned on my phone's flashlight, not willing to wait and let my eyes adjust. A gust of hot wind amplified the smell of gas, burnt rubber, and garbage, and an old chip bag brushed against my leg. If I hadn't been riding on fumes all day I would have gone straight home from the café, probably could have made it, but not back to the station again. The convenience store door opened. The men snickered as they came closer and I started pumping my gas, determined not to turn around, not to be so irrational. Determined to ignore the hair standing up on the back of my neck, because this was Garnett. It was fine.

"Girl, you paint them jeans on?"

The man who'd winked came close enough for me to smell the clove cigarette he puffed through his nostrils. He handed me a receipt with a number scrawled on the back. He was big shouldered and bald, a pair of white sunglasses atop his shiny head despite the dark.

"Party at our place tonight."

My body stiffened. "No thanks."

"Come on, we'll go right up the road," he said, and motioned west with his chin. "Gonna get us a room at the La Quinta. There's a pool."

Instead of making up an excuse or a boyfriend and shrugging him off politely as I could—as I'd normally do to not hurt anyone's feelings, to not start something—I yelled at him to get the hell away from me.

Shocked, he stumbled backward and spit. Muttered something about women in this town was bitches as far as he could tell and walked backward toward a sputtering beige Impala with Oklahoma plates. Hands shaking, I got inside the bullet and locked the door. I felt like someone else. And, Lord, how I hated that. How I hated that feeling of being looked at and suddenly frightened to be in my own skin. Like I was seventeen and seeing myself in those grainy pictures—

A fist banged on the window and my heart leapt into my throat.

"You okay?" Gerald stood with his legs squared, a pistol tucked into the front waistband of his slouchy jeans. I rolled down my window. Gerald kept turning his head back to stare meanly at the men in the car, but instead of tough he seemed somehow frailer; his bony arms shook and his skin hung loosely around his quivering neck.

With a squeal of tires, the car sped off. Back up the feeder road to the highway, only the stench of exhaust left hanging in the air.

"I'm fine," I said, gripping the wheel.

"I only didn't like the looks of them, and this ain't the last. Boom time, I reckon. Filling up the motels with trash," Gerald said, his eyes trained on the black night into which the car had disappeared. "Top off the tank and go on now, girl."

It happened at a fraternity party at State. I was supposed to meet Justin—it was his brother's frat house, and only seventeen, I had no business being at a college party—but Justin never made it. I was blackout drunk when someone took a picture of me with my clothes off. I have no idea what happened that night. No idea what happened in the time between arriving at the party and waking up hours later in my friend Elise's bedroom. The thought of it fills me simultaneously with rage and deep shame. For reasons I can't explain—self-preservation, most likely—I pushed it out of mind almost immediately afterward. Not to say the fact of it didn't linger like a bad taste, a humiliating reminder of my limitations. I didn't drink again until my twenty-first birthday. Certain relationships burned out: Justin never called and Elise grew increasingly distant. But I didn't dwell on it. I finished high school and got into college. It didn't ruin my life.

And yet the night came often to me in snippets, mostly in dreams.

Back at the little pink house after the shake-up at the truck stop and finding Nikki gone, I sat on the couch, and before I could even consider getting up to wash my face and change clothes I fell asleep. The kind of exhaustion you feel pulsing through your temples and neck, your body still waging war against the fatigue. It was sudden, the feeling like I was in between spaces, not awake but not asleep, and I had this vision of Victoria's eyes, blank and dilated, unfocused, but there was a trail of brown dried blood and bright red vomit down her shirtfront. When I went to her, I tried to scream and no sound came out. I couldn't speak or walk, my tongue a dry gag in my mouth. In a deep pool of water, I saw a reflection of myself, ragged, out of control of my own flopping movements.

I was searching for her and she had disappeared.

The television in the corner of the room came on suddenly— Nikki must have had it paused—and I woke in a panic. I'd only been sleeping twenty minutes or so, but I felt disoriented and scared. Like I had missed something important. I jumped off the couch, and though it was past one in the morning I dialed Victoria, the idea of her calling to me from a dream as disembodied from reality as the sound of her phone ringing endlessly with no answer.

Chapter 9

In our county, things are more spread out than most places. You couldn't really make it somewhere like here without a car, unless you were a State student and could ride the shuttle, but even then, beyond the campus in Colburn it only took you so far as the Walmart out on the highway and the Greyhound bus station. To get around the county takes time, but I don't mind driving—helps me think, lets me clear my head—and there is no traffic here, only distance. So, it took me a good thirty minutes to cross the river and head out to Cedar Springs where Victoria lived.

After waking up and seeing she hadn't responded to me, I had called the café. She wasn't in early for the "family" breakfast Marlene did on Sundays. Marlene had an unfamiliar sharpness to her voice: "You're on the schedule, Annie, you're responsible. One of you better be here before church lets out," she said. Angry with Victoria and concerned for both our jobs, I'd gotten in the bullet. But what would I do if she was home? Scold her? Somehow force her to cover for me? Tell her it wasn't fair? I hadn't quite worked it out, but I was already this far down the broken asphalt road crumbling to gravel, petering out to dirt.

A spindly metal mailbox that looked like it had been run over, then straightened out again, marked the beginning of a narrow drive, a double-wide up on cinder blocks at the end of it. The wood and rusted wire fence had no gate, only a weathered orange and black sign that said BEWARE OF DOG, though there was no animal, no sign of life really at all. I drove slowly up toward the slate-colored trailer and parked behind Victoria's green Civic. So, she was probably home, phone battery dead or on silent, sleeping something off. Maybe she had been sick.

There was a small deck with a couple of plastic lawn chairs and a charcoal grill that looked like they hadn't been used in quite some time. As I climbed the stairs, I noticed a kid's tricycle and some plastic play buckets tucked underneath the deck. She had a daughter, I remembered—I nearly turned around when it hit me how little I knew about Victoria's personal life.

"I'm just here for my grandmother," she'd said one day at work, her first day, the two of us outside, feeling each other out. I was taking my time emptying the trash, she taking her break and going on about how boring Garnett was. She was about my age—twenty-three in October she'd said—and so I wondered why she hadn't seemed familiar.

"I went to Parr City High and lived with my dad back then. Moved to Garnett after 'cause my ex and I were still together, and then my granny's emphysema got real bad and she needed someone to help out. I just moved in with her."

"That's nice of you," I said.

"She's the only family that's ever done anything for me." She shrugged. "She has some land out in the country. It's quiet."

Not two weeks later her grandmother had passed away.

"Victoria? You home?" I rapped on the screen door. I heard a rustle inside and a scratching noise against the siding. "Hello? You okay in there?" I said, my voice cracking as it rose. I pulled the screen door open to knock harder on the front door, and when I did it opened.

An open door is not always an invitation, a fact I tend to ignore.

I leaned into the dark front room. It smelled stale, a hint of something sweetly rotten, like the trash hadn't been taken out in a couple of days. "Victoria? Anyone home?" I stepped inside and immediately felt something furry tickle my leg. I jumped about a mile into the air and when I screamed the cat at my heels hissed and growled.

Well, there definitely wasn't anyone home; otherwise they'd have heard me just make a fool of myself.

Still, my shoulders tensed. There was no way I was getting out of work. Aunt Jewel would be mad, my mother too. The cat mewed and pawed at my arm. I looked around for his bowl and found it empty. "No wonder you're upset," I said, and rubbed behind his ears. He was black except for a patch of white under the chin, and I realized I'd seen him before: his picture was the lock screen on Victoria's phone, Oreo his name. How long had she been gone that Oreo was completely out of food? I found Fancy Feast in the pantry, surrounded by not much more—some rice, dried beans, an open bag of cheese puffs—and opened the can. The little beast was so grateful I could still hear him purring as I moved around the trailer.

Victoria met me at the road the couple of times I'd given her a ride to work. Hadn't invited me in when I dropped her back home. It was mostly messy inside, not dirty—there is a difference—piles of mail and unfolded laundry in the small living room and only a coffee cup, a wineglass, and some silverware unwashed in the sink. I knew I needed to get going, but I poked around, curious and intent on ignoring the sinking feeling in my stomach.

There was a child's pink and purple backpack hooked on the back of a chair and crayon drawings of butterflies taped to the faux wood paneling that said: *to Mommy love Kylee*. I wasn't surprised she had a kid old enough to be in school—around here if you don't have a kid before you're twenty-five you're more the exception to the rule. I could imagine the sex ed program at Parr City had been much like ours in Garnett: a woman from the Crisis Pregnancy Center telling us girls that abstinence was best, our virginity our virtue, that her biggest sin had been having an abortion and her unborn baby, Grace, was an angel in heaven now. The boys' lecture had been Coach Ryan coughing on a cookie, and then passing it around saying, "You wouldn't want to eat that now, would you?" It was more surprising that Victoria barely mentioned the girl in the months we'd been working together. Never a casual, *Oh, Kylee said the funniest thing*, or, *Kylee's obsessed with* Frozen *now*. Victoria mostly kept that part of her life private.

There were the effects of Victoria's grandmother: a stack of heavy blankets, a worn pair of terry-cloth house shoes in front of a recliner, pill containers, and a portable oxygen tank next to some cardboard boxes half packed with clothes and knick-knacks wrapped in newspaper. It didn't seem to me Victoria was moving, just quietly, slowly packing away the woman's belongings. I imagined her holding the porcelain Precious Moments

figurines in her hands. Pictured her with the sad-eyed angels in that empty, quiet trailer and felt a jab deep in the center of my chest.

I walked toward the back bedroom and saw a letter taped to the bureau mirror. I gently peeled it off to read when I heard a popping noise like gravel under tires. The hair on the back of my neck stood up. I waited one beat, two, but didn't hear it again. *I'm just jumpy,* I thought, *and of course I'm jumpy; I'm being a creep.* I refolded her letter. "And trespassing," I said aloud to Oreo, who'd since followed me into the bedroom. Out here, trespassing is likely to get you shot, no questions asked. Leroy used to tell me, only half joking, that if I ever needed to shoot a man to make sure I did it on my property or to drag him onto it if need be.

I placed the letter back on top of the bureau and walked toward the front room, looking out the window and down the driveway. Saw no person, no cars besides hers and mine. *This is wrong,* I thought. Victoria wasn't home and I needed to leave. And I wasn't so much mad at her anymore as I was unsettled and uncomfortable and, remembering the dream I'd had, felt my scalp tingle and my face grow hot. *Go on, get,* I repeated, shaking the traces of it from my head like you'd beat dust from a rug.

"Vic? The hell's going on in there?" a man's voice called from the back door.

I scanned the coffee table beside me for something I could use as a weapon and instead laced my car keys between my fingers, the metal slipping against my damp skin. Every muscle in my body tensed as I slowly turned around, bracing myself at the thought of staring down the barrel of a gun.

The man, barely a man he looked so young, wasn't armed and looked about as scared as I was.

"Who are you?"

"Who are you?" I shot back, and squared my shoulders. I learned from Leroy long ago that to gain the upper hand act like you've done nothing wrong. "I'm here to see Victoria," I said.

He had a strong, square jaw, but his body was as thin as mine and no taller than my five feet, five inches. His eyes narrowed and he crossed his arms over his chest. "Well, where is she then? And why's she not answering her goddamn phone? You nearly gave me a heart attack."

"I don't know. She and I work together. The door was open." I looked out the back and saw a mud-caked bicycle leaning against an old swing set. He must've ridden in on the ATV trails that sometimes cut through these properties. That he'd ridden a Huffy over made him seem even more like a petulant middle schooler.

"I'm Brandon Barnes," he said, and when I didn't react he added, "I come to see why she hasn't picked up Kylee."

"So, you're the father?"

He let out a long sigh. "It's not like I mind taking her. But Mom was going out of town for the weekend and my girlfriend and I made plans."

"Does Kylee's grandmother usually take care of her?"

"Yeah, but Vic was supposed to pick her up Thursday after work. We planned this, like, two weeks ago. She tell you to cover for her? Don't fucking lie to me."

"Whoa, calm down. She didn't say anything about all that." I took a deep breath and angled myself closer to the open door. "She missed her shift. Friday. Just thought I'd check on her while I was on my way in."

"I've texted and called her, like, a hundred times since Thursday. If Vic wants custody, she's gonna have to do better than this."

For as little as I knew about their arrangement, I didn't think Victoria would ignore calls about her daughter. Then again, if he was being truthful she had decided to leave the girl and instead go to a party on Thursday night. I debated telling Brandon about the last time I'd seen her, the way she was acting at the bonfire, and for whatever reason, maybe his tone, I decided not to say anything. The way his voice strained over certain words—"lie," "custody"—made me sure I shouldn't. Anger, I knew, was actually fear, and his anger made me feel as though there was a sharper edge to this situation. I wasn't so naïve to think Victoria had no fault in whatever drama had played out between her Brandon, but I couldn't shake that meanness in his voice. I didn't want to make it worse.

"You should call the cops," I said. "Something's clearly not right."

"The cops? No, no." He paced across to the kitchen, touched the rim of the wineglass in the sink. "She's just blowing off steam in some bar. I know you know she's been through hell with her granny. Don't blame her or nothing. But she ought to be straight with me, tell me she can't pick up Kylee. Mom's pissed, and damn it, I was supposed to go to the lake."

It hit me that he—the father of her child, her husband, a man she'd likely loved at some point—was more inconvenienced by her absence than he was remotely concerned, filling me with dread, and the nagging feeling that I, too, should have been more worried. "If you don't call the police now, then I will."

"Damn, why don't *you* calm down. I'll call, okay?" He opened his phone to wave in my face, 9–1–1 on the badly cracked screen, and I grabbed it from his hand. "Hey, give me—"

"I want to be in touch," I said, and dialed my number so I'd have his. "Save that number. Text me as soon as you hear anything, if you haven't heard from me first."

"Fine," he said, and reached for his phone. "You should know, though, that she's done this before."

"Whatever. I need to go," I said, and hurried out the door, bounding down the steps before he could stop me.

"What's your name?" he called to me from the deck.

"Annie," I said without turning around. "I'm just a friend."

Chapter 10

I looked around the room and wondered how exactly I could be related to these people. My cousin Candice sang off-key at a decibel normally only dogs could hear, and Nikki's dad, my uncle Curtis, had brought out homemade deer jerky that stunk to high heaven. And then there was the birthday queen herself, our great-aunt Jewel: she sat on the couch in a cotton candy pink sweat suit that belied her mean streak, while her teacup poodle—skittish from her spanking him so often—ran in circles around my ankles and bit me when I tried petting him, to which she seemed pleased. I had a headache. Marlene, either feeling generous or irritated with my presence, had let me leave early to get to the party. Despite my surliness, I'd had a table that tipped well, and my paycheck would be bigger than normal, with my having taken the extra night, but the whole shift that cold, empty trailer was all I could think about. I called and texted Brandon when I left but had gotten no response.

"Sweet pea!" my mother called, and I hurried into the warm kitchen. Instantly comforting was the smell of cake and fresh-cut lemons for tea, our family photos hanging on the bright yellow walls. I looked around for a pan to pull out of the oven or napkins to fold, but she just put her arms around me. "Wanted to give you a squeeze is all." She smiled. Between my odd hours, Dad's back hurting him, and Momma taking extra shifts at the bank where she was a teller, I hadn't been to the house in a few weeks.

"Missed you," I said, and kissed her cheek. She looked put together as always. My mother was my aunt Sherrilyn's guinea pig when it came to new hairstyles, colors, and makeup combos, and that day she had a new short cut: chunky blond layers framed her lightly freckled face and brown eyes. Her perfume was the same, though: sweet ambrosia oil, its scent calling to my mind soft pink clouds. Had I let myself relax I would've let her hold me forever, such was the combination of tired and sad I felt. Relieved to be home.

"Sorry I'm late." I turned my face from hers and looked for something to do. "Can I take anything to the table?"

"You can fill up that pitcher and give everyone water at their place. The beer's already been flowing; we need everyone to not get sick in my bathroom."

I laughed and went to the sink. "Granddad isn't even here yet. I called and he said Mary-Pat would give him a ride."

"Speak of the devil." She motioned out the window. Mary-Pat's vintage Silverado kicked up a dust cloud as it barreled down the long gravel driveway.

Dad poked his head in through the screen door. "Need a new plate for the done ones. Hey, sweetie." He nodded, unsmiling. Grilling was serious business around here.

"How're you feeling?" I handed him a serving platter from the cabinet.

"Much better." His dark brown eyes darted down. "I've got to flip these," he said, and slipped out.

Momma placed her hand on my shoulder. "He's embarrassed he hasn't been himself lately."

"It's just me. Why would I judge him?" I walked over to the table and poured water into the amber-colored Tiara glass Momma got out for birthday dinners and holidays, admiring the way the afternoon sun lighted them. My aunt Sherrilyn used to sell sets and this one had been my parents' wedding gift.

"He has a lot of pride," Momma said just as Aunt Sherrilyn came in with a plastic shopping bag in one hand, car keys still in the other.

"You and your cousin are in some sad trouble," she said, and jammed a carton of ice cream in the over-packed freezer, and Mom looked relieved, taking a moment to reapply her lipstick and then busying herself with the platters of burger fixings to go out on the table. She didn't want to talk about Dad's back or Dad's pride. I think *her* pride was often at stake when it came to his health. He'd been out of work for a long stretch this time.

I grinned at my aunt. "What'd we do now?"

"You two killed those plants I potted for you. I come to pick up Nikki and what do I see but a bunch of dried twigs—"

"Anne Louise," Jewel hollered from the living room. She used my full name whenever she had a bone to pick, which was often.

I scooted around Sherrilyn and out of the kitchen to find Jewel still perched on the sofa—the green, itchy one that reminded me of a hairy avocado. I approached tentatively. "Yes, ma'am?"

"Sit by me." She patted the sun-faded cushion. She had the television on, was halfway watching *Deal or No Deal* and letting the dog eat off her plate. I leaned my head on her shoulder. Her eyes flicked to the screen and she tsked at the contestants.

"Having a good birthday?"

Samantha Jayne Allen

"Hate birthdays, hate getting old. This party was your mother's idea. I'm missing water aerobics at the rec."

"Maybe you can convince Dad to fill up the hot tub with the garden hose. Splash around in there a bit." We had an old, busted hot tub that came with the house when my parents bought it in the early nineties, along with a water bed. The intriguing thing about the hot tub, according to the house's previous owner, was that the cover used to be George Strait's—but just the cover, not the tub.

"You need to start wearing clothes that fit you better if you're looking to attract a man. The shorts you've got on are all loose in the seat! You've got a cute seat. How're you going to get any attention if you don't show off some curves?"

"It's a mystery."

"I always wished I could lose weight like you and Candice but gain it in the right places with the ease of Nikki."

"Good genes," I said, thinking it a talent unique to Aunt Jewel to so artfully jab both her grandnieces at once.

Nikki bounded into the room and took me by the wrist.

"I wasn't done talking to you," Aunt Jewel said, and dug her brittle nails into my other arm. "Go on sit down with us, Nik."

"We'll be right back," I said, and followed Nikki out.

"You're welcome." Nikki smiled. "But for real, there's a code red William versus Leroy."

"Where's the Teddy Roosevelt?" I joked, but all the same looked up to where the commemorative rifle hung safely above the mantle. We walked to the backyard and found the two of them staring each other down, smoke curling from under the lid of the grill between them. "Hey there," I said, noticing they'd stopped talking a little too quickly. Nikki slid her feet into some flip-flops and walked off into the yard. She'd caught sight of her youngest brother throwing dirt clods at the bird feeders and seemed to take scolding him as an easy exit.

"Little darlin'." Leroy tipped his cowboy hat, making me laugh.

Dad rolled his eyes. The backyard seemed to hum with pent-up anxiety—shrill cicada sound, hot wind scratching the dry, untamable Johnsongrass—and it was my unspoken duty to bridge the gap between Leroy and my father. Momma was never impartial enough. I loved both men dearly, if differently. My dad regarded me with an intense protectiveness that some-times frightened me. And he was serious—it was life-or-death with Dad—and being in his orbit often felt like treading water in the deep end of a pool, the sway and pull of dark water sur-rounding you. Leroy, too, was of a melancholic persuasion, but he had his humor. At the end of the day, though, it could feel as if his love were shallow, not quite strong enough to carry those around him.

A car door slammed and Mary-Pat came around the corner of the house. "Sorry, had to make a call. Hello, Annie; hello, William. Your dad said it was okay if I stayed, and, well, those burgers smell right tasty," she said, and tucked her cell phone into the belt clip she wore. Her long legs were slightly bowed, and she kind of loped when she walked, leaning so you could see the black leather holster on her other hip.

"Grab a beer, make yourself at home," Dad said to her with a tight-lipped smile. Leroy and Mary-Pat went in through the back door and I heard them making their way to Aunt Jewel singing "Happy Birthday."

Leroy was pretty adept at acting like nothing was the matter with him and Dad.

Once they were inside, Dad put the barbeque tongs down and

sipped his Dr Pepper. Let his shoulders relax. "Hungry, sweet-heart?"

"Starving," I said, and hugged his side. "What are you guys arguing about now?"

He was normally clean-shaven, and when he rubbed his chin I noticed how much more gray than black his stubble was now. "Old man can't take care of himself or the house, much less the place," he said. "You know I had to hear from Lillie Anderson in the grocery store that the VA doctor wanted him to see a specialist. He refused and just went home! He's going to kill his idiot self."

A waft of charcoal smoke stung my eyes and nose. "You can't control anyone, much less Granddad," I said, deciding not to add my thought that his worrying over Leroy was only aging himself.

"What's this I hear about you going to work for him?"

"Isn't that something?" Leroy laughed, beer in hand, letting the screen door slap behind him. "She's getting into the family tradition!"

"Why didn't you say anything?" Dad said to me, his voice lowered. He came around the side of the grill and gripped my shoulder. "I don't think that's such a good idea."

"We only were just talking about it. Really more about doing secretarial work for Mary-Pat," I stammered. "But maybe I—"

"I think it's a fine idea. Mighty fine," Leroy said, and adjusted his arm sling so his shoulders were less slouched. "She could be just like her what, two-or-three-times-great-grandmother? She could be like Sarah Anne."

The Sarah Anne stories were more legend than fact, even I knew that, but another part of me beamed with pride. In addition to being good on a horse, she had been one of the few female Pinkerton detectives and, later, deputized as sheriff when her husband disappeared for two months. Her husband had been the law in Garnett County and they met during a train robbery investigation that brought her into town. That much is true—there are newspaper records in the county courthouse—but the other stories about shootouts and undercover missions had a volatile half-life, likely to grow or change shape depending on the teller. It's also true that she died out on the place, broke and alone. Sarah Anne was our origin story. Fitting that the tales be riddled with dead ends and false statements, yet seamed with veins of gold.

"This is not the Wild West, old man," Dad said, and tightened his grip on my shoulder. "This girl of mine didn't get a scholarship and go to her fancy school to end up a city cop. Or to follow around so-and-so's cheating husband. Hell, no."

"Hey, now." I took a deep breath and stood straighter, shaking off Dad. "I'm an adult."

"She'd like to try it, son," Leroy said, grinning.

How he'd changed his tune since our conversation at the place. I smiled, not even bothered that he'd blindsided me. Leroy had that effect on people—a way of anointing you with his attention—and I basked in the warmth of it, like the sun burst through the clouds to shine only on me. I knew he was going after Dad, that I was a pawn in their game.

But I also have an aversion to the word "no."

"It's a stepping-stone," I said, realizing the kernel of truth in that. "I can apply to law school later. This is another form of seeking justice, isn't it? Of searching for the truth? If I've learned anything from this family it's those values."

Leroy whistled though his teeth. "That's a right smart way of putting it, little darlin'. You're hired!"

Dad shook his head, and when he looked up, looked at me, then at Leroy, I could tell something had shifted. He thought

I'd taken Leroy's side against his, further confirming my hunch that this argument wasn't about a job.

"Whatever," he said, opening the lid of the grill. "Burgers are done. Y'all go and wash up."

"Daddy, come on," I said. "Lighten up."

He frowned. "We'll talk later."

Aunt Jewel had requested pineapple upside-down with those gummy-looking maraschino cherries that no one liked, so Momma made it personal sized. For the rest of us there was chocolate sheet cake and Blue Bell. The candles were lit and instead of singing I found myself staring out at the faces around me made soft by the flickering light. I wished I could press pause—I loved them, I thought—and *we're going to be okay* I sent up along with whatever Jewel wished as she blew the candles out. Smoke swirled around her and the smell of wax and icing filled the room. Sherrilyn passed out plates and nearly dropped Uncle Curtis's in his lap when Mary-Pat's phone went off with an earsplitting ring.

"Shit on a shingle." She scooted her chair out, nearly hitting Sherrilyn. "I have to take this. Be right back."

Sherrilyn rolled her eyes and continued her way around the table. "Mr. McIntyre, will your friend want cake?"

"Leave a piece at her place; she'll be back. She is my ride home after all."

The nature of Leroy and Mary-Pat's relationship had puzzled folks. I felt weirdly territorial of Leroy and my mamaw and so was wary of Mary-Pat for a long time. When I was growing up Garnett was still the type of place where being queer, if not frowned upon, went unsaid even if it was obvious. It wasn't until

I was older and a bit less naïve that I figured she wasn't inclined toward Leroy, not romantically.

"Nikki, you sure you want cream on that cake?" Aunt Jewel watched us with visible disdain, as if we were supposed to do something with food besides eat it.

"Jesus, lady, mind your own goddamn plate," Nikki said, then took a second scoop.

"I ought to wash your mouth out with soap," Aunt Jewel said, pointing with her fork. "Taking the Lord's name in vain is—"

The screen door rattled on its hinges and Mary-Pat came into the room with her car keys in hand. Her tall, imposing figure cast a shadow over the table. "That was the sheriff," she said, her face pale.

Slumped in his chair with a forkful of cake halfway to his mouth, Leroy searched Mary-Pat's eyes, concern slowly registering in his. "What's happened?"

"A body was found on your property," she said. "Garcia couldn't get ahold of you at home, Leroy. We've got to go out there to talk to them." She took Leroy by the elbow of his good arm and lifted him out of the chair with ease. Her face was stiff, her only tell of emotion a twitch, a quick tug at the corner of her mouth.

Aunt Jewel clutched her chest and Sherrilyn cursed. Momma's chair made a painful screech as she shoved it aside and Dad went to the door with Mary-Pat. Nikki was the only one who, like me, didn't or couldn't speak. The light in the room suddenly seemed brighter, taking on an eerie quality of stillness. Like the way the clouds turn yellow and the wind quiets just as it comes a terrible storm.

Part II

Chapter 11

The interview room at the Garnett police station was roughly the size of a supply closet and might've been an actual supply closet at one point. Windowless, sterile, over-air-conditioned, the room had no two-way glass, only the blinking red light from a video camera on a tripod to remind you this was an interview and you were being watched.

Police Chief Melvin Baker sat opposite me at a flimsy card table they'd set up with metal folding chairs. Garnett is small enough to not have dedicated homicide detectives—they're all supposed to be cross-trained and call in assistance as needed—and Sheriff Garcia and one of his deputies stood shoulder to shoulder in the corner. A Texas Ranger up from San Antonio had been in the room earlier but left. Baker had lines in his face that seemed to have deepened since I'd seen him last at the café.

He cleared his throat. "Remind me. How long had you known Victoria Merritt?"

"About four months," I said.

This was the second time I'd spoken with law enforcement. They'd come to the café a few days before and questioned all of us: Marlene, Dot, and Fernando, even the part-timers. And I knew they'd spoken to Nikki, confirming my alibi. *My alibi*—never thought I'd use those words—the thought made me both scared and slightly embarrassed for some reason. Like I'd gotten in trouble and needed to be reprimanded.

The medical examiner had since finished the autopsy. Confirmed Victoria had been dead for three days before the law found her and that's why they were so keen on finding people from the party to talk to, again—I'd seen Ashley, Macy, Cade, and Wyatt all leaving when I was coming in that day. Victoria died sometime between midnight and early Friday, before dawn, before the storm. Her clothes were disheveled and unzipped, a button on her shirt missing, and while no physical evidence of sexual assault was collected, it was not ruled out.

She died by strangulation. Buried in a shallow grave, a heavy stone placed over the loose dirt covering her torso. But the stone did not stop the wash of rain and did not stop animals from further unearthing her body. She was found in a tangle of cacti and green mesquite near the creek bed and just over the fence that separated the Schneider land from ours.

"Miss Merritt was at a party you also attended," Baker said, and made a steeple with his hands, tapped his index finger to his lips, and frowned. "On the night she was killed."

Maybe it was the way everyone at the station ran around like chickens with their heads cut off—understandably, given two homicides in one week would overwhelm any small-town department—or maybe it was Baker's performance, but my confidence in the investigation was shaken.

He leaned toward me. "Can you tell me who else was there?"

"My cousin and I joked the whole town would be there; it's not far off. Mix of Garnett folks our age and a little older, probably some high school seniors, too, and a group of older guys.

We, my cousin and I, left before it got too wild. That was a little before midnight. I thought to offer Victoria a ride since she'd been drinking, but she'd already gone off. My cousin said she saw her sitting on some guy's lap. His name was Randy," I said.

"Did you think that strange behavior from her?"

I blushed, shook my head no.

"Why not?"

"I don't know that. I just think." I shrugged my shoulders, unable to go further. What *did* I assume about Victoria? Baker's voice had changed from bad cop to after-school gossip. Face took on the *you know the type of girl* look that didn't need explaining. Randy and those men at the icehouse snickering, how they'd turned her into nothing more than a punch line, came rushing back. "I was distracted," I said, shifting in my seat. "I had to drive my cousin home."

Baker crossed his arms over his stocky chest, leaned back in his chair. "Can you think of anyone who might want to harm her? Anyone acting suspicious that night?"

"I don't know about that night," I said. What kept coming back to me was Sunday morning. The time I'd spent in her home not knowing she was dead. The museum-like stillness, the stale, sealed quality of the air inside the trailer. Or did it only seem like that in retrospect? Gravel crunching under bike tires, him appearing like an angry ghost. Flushed red skin, dilated eyes, *Don't fucking lie to me.* "Her ex seems like a jerk, but I don't know—"

"We've spoken with the husband, Brandon, yep. His mother too."

"Did he end up reporting her missing? He was looking for her on Sunday when he confronted me at her place."

"Let me ask the questions, okay?"

Sheriff Garcia sighed, clearly annoyed with Baker, and then

said, "He didn't. Was his mother, Glory, called it in. Not long before the girl's body was found."

As I was leaving the interview room I ran into Justin and his father. Bill Schneider was a tall man with a ruddy face, attractive in a bullish, alpha-male way. The cops must have interrupted them at work on the ranch, as the two of them were dusty, flecks of dry grass and foxtails stuck to their pant legs. Bill took off his cowboy hat, rubbed the sweat off his forehead, nodded at me, and went into the interview room with Chief Baker. Justin darted his eyes back and forth between us.

"Annie," he said, moving close to me as Bill shut the door behind him. "I already talked to the Ranger they had here earlier. You?"

"Yes," I said. The past couple of days I'd felt two ways: wanting answers, detached in my thinking, and yet my body ached—I couldn't control the physical chaos of my sadness. My hands shook. Stray tears wet my cheeks and I observed them without emotion, as if I hadn't realized they were my own.

The concerned yet mortified look some guys get when confronted with women crying flashed across Justin's face, and he hesitated before taking my hand. "You girls need to be careful. This psycho could be lurking anywhere."

"You think it was a stranger? Like a serial killer?"

Justin frowned, his face pale despite coming in from working outside. "This is Garnett. It's got to be some rando. Some pervert. You know another girl was killed about an hour from here not six months ago? Then Ashley said something about a guy she swears was following her the other weekend."

"I'm being careful. You should too. This person, this killer,"

I said, the word funny feeling in my mouth, "they could still be around. The killer might've been at your bonfire."

Justin nodded and bit his bottom lip. He clearly hadn't slept. Catching a glimpse of myself in the bathroom mirror earlier I'd seen the same blank eyes, the same deepening shadows.

"There were people there I'd never seen before. It got out of control. I feel terrible it happened at all, but especially to someone at my home," he said, and dropped my hand. "I should have been paying better attention. I feel sick over it. I—"

"It's not your fault," I said.

It's not your fault.

But what if I'd stayed and looked for her? I glimpsed the digital clock above the door and rubbed my eyes. It was just past noon but felt like three in the morning. Nikki, concerned, had told me to call her when I left the station. "I've got to get going," I said, and reached in my purse for my keys and phone.

"Wait." His face searched mine. "Can we get a cup of coffee?"

I dug deeper, realizing I'd left my phone on the charger again. I'd been so spacey the past few days. Part of me wondered if I subconsciously wanted to be inaccessible. Before we'd known what had happened, I was glued to the damn thing. Checked it over and over, waiting for a text, a call, a sign, never truly expecting any news to be this bad. And then it was. Maybe if I didn't greet the world it couldn't touch me. Maybe I could stay sealed in the past if I closed my eyes tightly enough.

"I don't want to be alone either. It's scary. . . ." I paused, noticing he reddened. "But I—"

"Dad and I drove separate so he could head down to the co-op after this," Justin said. "We could leave now and go to the café."

"God, no." Going back to work yesterday had been surreal— her apron still on the hook by the shelf, her handwriting on the schedule disturbing now with its wide, happy loops and hearts dotting the i's—and I didn't want to repeat the experience. Not yet. "Actually, I don't have that much time," I said, and pointed toward the vending machine.

The air outside would be thick with heat and gnats, but my arms had goose bumps and I couldn't stand the fluorescent-lit room a minute longer. I bought two Cokes and we sat shoulder to shoulder on a stone bench warm from the sun and lightly dappled in leaf shadow. Justin looked down at his work boots white with caliche dust and touched the back of his neck with the cold can. I could smell his smell of laundry starch and cedar, suddenly familiar again, and wanted to trace my finger where the can had left a trail of condensation on his skin and pull his face to mine. I wanted to forget—

A car horn made us both look up.

"Get in!" Mary-Pat called to me, her arm hanging out the driver's side window of Leroy's blue Ford as it idled at the light in front of the station. Leroy leaned forward and made a show of scooting into the middle seat and leaving the passenger's side door open.

Justin sat up straighter and nodded politely at the two of them as I stood to leave. "Be careful, Annie. Let me know if you hear anything," he said.

"You do the same."

He gave my arm a quick squeeze before I pulled away.

Chapter 12

Marty Santos, a drifter often down on his luck, was the one who had found her. Marty parked his camper in kind of a no-man's-land off the road that divided the properties. Technically squatting on ours, but it didn't bother Leroy. They occasionally got drunk together. Marty kept to himself—few even knew anyone lived in that derelict, windowless camper—but he had decided to move about that afternoon, feel the sun on his face. Maybe hitch a ride to town, see and be seen.

The fence was broken. Vultures circled overhead. He thought it could be dead or injured livestock, in which case he'd alert the neighbors. And then, the shoe: a woman's Western-style boot. Pretty, ornate red leather crusted with dried mud. He skidded down a short hill near the creek and saw a bluish bare foot sticking out from behind a bush, and closer—all he remembers is he retched in the dirt, turned, and ran. He stumbled and panted, the landline at the Schneiders' old hunting cabin impossibly far, sobs jerking his chest, his sweat mixed with tears, and by the time he reached the dusty phone he could barely see or breathe. The first person he called was Leroy, and when no one answered he had the presence of mind to call 9–1–1. There are few times in your life when time unspools so slowly and so clearly that you realize a moment is a crossroads. Maybe it was like that for Marty Santos, realizing he'd seen a dead body for the first time, someone's tragedy lancing through his life so unpredictably. Maybe—

"Where are we going?" I asked, turning to face Mary-Pat and Leroy next to me in the truck, knowing, deep in my bones, I, too, was running toward the dead.

"The place," Mary-Pat said.

"Are we allowed? Isn't it a crime scene?"

"It's my property," Leroy said. "And that young woman died on my property, so—"

"We need to let the law do their job. If I didn't think you'd try to drive up here either way I wouldn't be, what's the word? Enabling," Mary-Pat said. A rabbit darted across the road and Mary-Pat hit the horn with her fist.

"I only need to know what happened," Leroy said. "Why here? Why?" He shook his head and reached for a can of Budweiser from the ice chest on the floorboard cradled between my feet.

"So," I said, pulse quickening at the sight of yellow police tape shreds caught in the barbwire fence. Off the shoulder, a white wooden cross with *Chavez* scrawled across it was jammed in the dirt, a wreath of blue roses and several prayer candles propped against it. I hadn't realized before how close the scene of the hit-and-run was to the place, the bonfire, and the scene of Victoria's murder. I didn't believe in Spooky Sheila's nonsense about curses and bad energy, I didn't, but this area—something felt wrong. Gut-feeing bad. I willed the car to move faster, turned to face both their profiles. "Why do y'all need me here?" I asked.

"As I recall, little darlin', we hired you," Leroy said. It was

quiet, and almost under his breath he began whistling, the song unfamiliar to me. I followed his eyes up to the rearview mirror, tracked the faded yellow dashes on the long line of highway and the water tower slowly fading from sight. I sucked in my breath as Mary-Pat hit the accelerator. I could feel the vibration from us driving over the cattle guards in my teeth. Did I really want to get involved? Should I tell Mary-Pat I was tired, to take me home instead? Leroy would understand, I knew, but all the same I couldn't speak.

Once, at a lecture series in college, I heard a lawyer from the Innocence Project tell about the moment he knew he wanted to devote his career to overturning wrongful convictions. He explained that once, as part of a class assignment his final semester in law school, he spent an hour talking to the professor's client who was an inmate on death row. Explained to the audience how being in a narrow cell with that man changed the course of his career. Proximity to the underserved, I believe he said. That struck me as true. I'd be full of shit if I thought myself a moral crusader. That's not what I'm getting at. It's about being in the throes of the dark thing that calls you.

If I hadn't gone to the place that day, hadn't witnessed the place she'd lain, I likely would have done something entirely different with my life.

We drove along the fence line and passed a mustard yellow camper parked in the thin shade of a blighted oak. Marty sat on a wooden stepladder that didn't quite come up to the half-rusted door. He waved, unbuttoned shirtsleeves flapping open to reveal his pale, bony wrist.

"He's a suspect?" I asked, raising my index finger in reply. "Or a witness?"

Leroy laughed.

"Why's that funny? He found her body."

He laughed again and Mary-Pat smiled.

I felt my ears get hot. "But seriously, why's that unreasonable to think?" Leroy had always been like this—with the joking, the lack of explanation, the nonchalance—and it now struck me as condescending. Part of me wondered whether my dad would have quit the force out of sheer annoyance with Leroy even if he hadn't been in the accident.

"Contrary to your grandfather's assumptions, it's not," Mary-Pat said, probably sensing my frustration. "But he'd hitched to Colburn for a poker game at a buddy's that night. Driver verified it and men at the game did too. He didn't return to the trailer or the place until late the next day."

"So, what, the cops keep you in the loop on all this?"

"Begrudgingly, I'll admit. You know I only fully retired from the sheriff's department five years ago, so I've still got connections, and to be frank, they need our expertise at times." Mary-Pat motioned between herself and Leroy. "I had a chat with Baker and Garcia yesterday."

"I knew Marty didn't do it," Leroy said, and after a moment, "It's not in his nature. Pull over here, Pat."

The truck jerked to a stop and I lurched forward. "Is it in anyone's nature, though? Killing someone? That's unnatural, period."

"With the exception of serial murderers and sociopaths," Mary-Pat said, and unbuckled her seat belt. Leroy followed suit, not before finishing his beer and tossing the can on the floorboard.

"You think a serial killer did this?" I said. "That's what the gossip is."

"Judge, jury, executioner. Can be dangerous, but gossip's also a useful tool," Leroy said, and burped.

"Not likely a serial killer, yet no one's exactly ruled it out. But Marty Santos didn't do it." Mary-Pat got out of the truck and Leroy slid out behind her. "Drop that bone."

"I figured as much with the alibi," I said, and opened the passenger's side door. "Just making a point."

The air was still and the horizon wavy with heat shimmer. We were on the eastern edge of the place. The land spread before me, wide-open expanse only interrupted by scrubby stands of green mesquite and purple thistle and the escarpment to the north. Looking out across it always felt both familiar and unexpected. Like a moment of happiness can feel on an otherwise ordinary day. I'd been coming out here with my grandparents my entire life, but now? A familiar ring of old oaks seemed threatening, hiding danger, their black limbs poking at the sky as turkey vultures circled above. Like disembodied kites, the birds dipped and floated through the haze. Nearly to the Schneider fence line, we inched closer toward the low spot near the creek where Victoria had been buried.

"Over yonder," Leroy said, and pointed to the mesquite. The grass was flattened by tire tracks from the police vehicles, and yellow tape still ringed the perimeter. Someone had stubbed a cigarette and crushed a paper coffee cup in the dirt.

I looked around, back up the way we came in, unsettled by déjà vu—the day after the party Leroy and I nearly came to the very spot.

"Friday. We didn't check," I said. "Why didn't we check the fences?"

Leroy nodded. "I thought about that too."

Rationally, I knew it would have already been too late to

help Victoria, but another part of me felt as though I'd abandoned her. She'd been left outside. Left alone for three days, discarded. Shuddering despite the heat, I felt achy, chilled as though I had a fever.

Leroy motioned from where Mary-Pat had parked the truck up the hill and down to the creek bed. "Let's try and get this straight. Reconstruct, if you will."

"We think they came through the property this way. Up this way from the road," Mary-Pat said.

I followed them into the tall grass. "How do you know?"

"'Cause last time anyone saw her she'd took off thataway," Leroy said. "To the highway."

"But how do they know she didn't turn right, then wander over here? Meet up with someone here? We're probably a twenty-minute, give or take, walk west from where the bonfire was. She was hanging off some roughneck named Randy that night. What if he followed her?" I asked.

Mary-Pat caught up to us, her steps in sync with Leroy's. "Because her phone was found on the side of the road. Someone picked her up. The cops haven't made that much public—about the phone, how she must have dropped it while getting in a vehicle—that's their smoking gun."

"But maybe the killer tossed it after the fact," I said.

Mary-Pat shook her head. "Why, and, why somewhere so obvious? Why not turn it off? A wallet-type purse, a wristlet, was left on her person—if the killer thought to toss her things, why not all at once? The victim most likely dropped the phone."

"She wasn't killed here, not on the place," Leroy said, and stopped. He leaned his head back and closed his eyes for a moment. "Seems she was picked up by someone. They tried to have their way, or they had an argument. Things escalated. It's likely she died in a vehicle. The way her boot was off, some marks on the body, the way the underbrush was mussed—hard to say for certain, given the rain, but seems they drove out here and she was dragged to that spot postmortem. The killer only thought they could hide her body here. Sloppy. Most crime scenes are, unlike in the television shows."

I looked around, the chill I felt intensifying. If you didn't know, you would assume our family's property was a good place to hide a body: It was overgrown and unkempt, the gate unlocked. Only a broke cistern, crumbling foundation, and a dark, abandoned-looking camper to witness the burial.

"I offered her a ride home. What if I'd stayed? I feel like I owe her now," I said. "God. It's so surreal when it's someone you knew."

Leroy frowned. "When I saw her picture, the one they have up at the station, I knew that I knew her."

"Only twenty-two years old," Mary-Pat sighed, then looked at her wristwatch. "Shoot. I've got an appointment this afternoon. I'll drop you back at the station to get your car, Annie."

"Wait," I said, stepping in front of Leroy. "You knew Victoria?"

He looked up at me, nodded. "Seen her at that VFW bar turned honky-tonk."

Chapter 13

Leroy felt it appropriate he and I "pay our respects" to Victoria's in-laws, her only living kin. Glory—Brandon's mother, young herself at forty-five—led us into her family's seventies-era ranch-style house and I felt pricks of heat along my neck and chest. It was claustrophobic. Brown shag carpet, low, popcorn ceilings, and every inch of the room cluttered with dead animal: buck heads mounted on the walls, doves in static flight, bobcats, and a possum mid-hiss. A coyote with its mouth in a snarl stood sentry at the top of a narrow bookcase.

"We have a taxidermy business, me and my husband," Glory said. She wore her hair in a bouncy perm, had a pleasant, dimpled face, and talked with her hands in a flighty, distracted way, but her round eyes were focused and penetrating. There was something unnerving in her gaze.

"Your husband around?" Leroy plopped down in an armchair, shifting slightly to remove something poking him from under the cushion—luckily, only a Barbie doll.

"No, he hunts up in Canada this time of year. Takes a group of business executives. They pay him to be their guide," Glory said, again with that expectant stare. Sitting there felt like we were about to break the bad news all over again. Felt like my thumb was in the dam and the room would flood when I spoke. I looked at Leroy and he seemed uneasy too. I couldn't imagine it would ever get easier, talking to the next of kin. Glory sniffed and wiped a tear from her cheek as Brandon came into the room with Kylee, sat on the couch, and bounced the girl on his knee. Her eyes were puffy, her nose red from crying, but she seemed momentarily uplifted at the sight of her Barbie on the coffee table, which I handed to her.

"Thank you," Kylee whispered, and lowered her face. She favored Victoria: olive skin, dark hair, and black-brown eyes that tilted down at the corners.

"You're welcome, sweetheart," I said, thinking if I could've, I would've grabbed her and squeezed her tight. She danced the doll across the coffee table and sang quietly. Glory took a Kleenex from the elastic waistband of her track pants and dabbed her eyes. "I know y'all came to talk about Victoria. Don't let me forget I have something of hers to give you."

Kylee looked up. "Mommy?"

"Son," Glory said, and huffed, "I told you to put her down. She oughtn't hear this, and if she takes her nap too late, we'll be up all night."

"Come on, baby girl," Brandon said, and took Kylee's hand. "I'll be right back. Y'all make yourselves comfortable," he added, which was awkward since we were already seated. It was clear he was not head of the house, probably wasn't his father either. While we waited for Brandon, Glory offered Cokes. A girl, maybe seventeen or eighteen, hair in a messy bun at the top of her head, sat on the sofa and folded her legs under herself so she appeared to perch like a strange blond bird.

"Hi, I'm Annie," I said. I waited for Leroy to introduce himself but he just kind of saluted the girl with two fingers.

"Melody, um, Brandon's friend," she said, her voice high-pitched and nasally. She tilted her head, again reminding me of a bird. "I just want to say, no matter what everyone else is saying, Victoria was a good momma to Kylee."

Leroy leaned forward. "Who said she wasn't?"

"And what would make them say that?" I asked. Melody's eyebrows drew down as Glory came back in the room with two plastic cups, Brandon at her heels.

Glory sat next to Melody. "What's going on?"

"Melody was just saying some people felt Victoria was irresponsible with the baby," I said when Melody only stared back blankly.

"She loves Kylee. Loved, I mean," Glory said, and held her hand to her heart, which seemed, if not insincere, over the top. "Lord help us, but—and I don't mean to speak ill of her—she wasn't cut out for the responsibilities. It's not for everyone, being a parent."

Brandon nodded, tapped a finger to his lip in a pondering motion that made me want to smack him. "Victoria was probably going to leave town, leave us with Kylee, after things got settled with her granny and we finalized the divorce. It was what she wanted."

"It was always about what she wanted," Glory said, and then after a moment her face softened. "She was a kid herself."

"So, remind me, you took care of Kylee mostly?" I said to Brandon and Melody. She placed her hand in his.

"Yes," said Brandon and Glory in unison. "I help out when they're working," Glory added.

"It's a shame," I said. "We only worked together a few months, but I felt like we were friends. I don't guess I really knew everything going on in her life. Her death was such a shock to me—I mean, what on earth? Do y'all have any idea what happened?"

"She was dating," Glory said. "Other than that, I don't really know who her friends were of late. Her people's all passed or in prison besides us."

"Wait, what?" Brandon said, and jerked his head toward her. "I don't know shit about no boyfriend. Why didn't you tell me?"

"Babe," Melody said, and squeezed his hand. "Cool it."

Glory grimaced. "I told the law is who I told! She was at that VFW bar off Route Ninety drunk as a skunk. Hanging off some man. That's all I know. Didn't get a good look at him. Not that it means anything—least we haven't heard nothing."

"She liked that bar." I looked back and forth between Glory and Leroy, and Glory shrugged. "She went a lot?"

"She regularly escorted a lady I assumed was her grandmother," Leroy said.

"I stopped in for a drink a week or two ago and she was there when she should've been home with her baby. Flirting and cutting up with some men. One of them hugged her a little long. You could tell they was, oh, what's the word, intimate," Glory said in a confiding whisper.

"Never saw her with a date, per se." Leroy pointed at his arm in the sling. "But I haven't been out, much less dancing, since I took a spill."

"Interesting. You saw them just the once?" I asked Glory, hoping she'd say more. It seemed she wanted to, given the smug look on her face at the last revelation.

"Not my usual watering hole," she said, meeting my stare.

I heard a cry coming from the back of the house—Kylee, howling now—and startled so I nearly spilled the Coke.

"I'm sorry. Baby has bad dreams every time she closes her eyes," Glory said, and shakily stood. Kylee's cries sounded deep, guttural, and were growing louder. If I didn't know better, I'd have thought she was hurt. Poor Kylee. She wasn't only upset, wasn't only sad for what she'd lost too soon. She was terrified.

"We've got to get a move on," Leroy said.

"I'll let y'all know about the memorial service; excuse me," Glory said, then turned around quickly. "I almost forgot—hold on— Son, go see about that baby!"

Brandon almost imperceptibly rolled his eyes before getting up.

Glory reached behind a stack of *Reader's Digest* magazines for a brass figurine. "Here." She shoved it into my hands. "I don't think Vic had many girlfriends. It's nice you cared."

"Thank you," I said. It was a cowgirl, the length of my outstretched hand, and looked a little like Dale Evans. "Did this— did it mean something to her? It's just, maybe it should go to Kylee."

The girl howled again.

"Oh, honey, I think Vic used it as a bookend. Kept it on her desk when she stayed here. You can take it as a little something to remember her by."

I nodded, the weight of it heavy in my palm.

"So, how'd I do?"

Walking out into the bright sun was disorienting after the weak lamplight of the Barnes family's living room. I struggled with the latch on the chain-link gate and, when it swung open, hurried down the walkway. A dog tied to a post off the side of the house whined and yipped, envious of our escape. At least ten cars in varying states of decay sat parked at the far side of the rutted and weed-choked three-acre spread.

"When you interview someone, don't say too much. You want them to fill up the silences," Leroy said, following me at a slower pace.

"You don't ask questions?" I opened the back door and carefully placed the figurine on the car seat.

"Course you do. But don't lead them too much is all. Let them show their hand."

I thought about several times when I was a kid on the phone with him, telling him about my day at school, how mid-story I'd hear the dial tone and realize he'd hung up on his sweet little granddaughter. Likely bored. I was pretty sure his interviewing technique was more linked to antisocial tendencies than anything else.

"You don't ever think you can draw them out by acting friendly?"

"I'm friendly," he said.

"Practically chummy."

"You don't have something to say, why fill up the room with dumb chitchat?"

Behind the wheel I cranked up the air, and we rode out. I'd decided to head toward the VFW bar, thought maybe we'd take a look around. Silent, Leroy was writing something in the steno pad he kept with a mechanical pencil in the pocket of his work shirt.

"What did you make of them?" I turned quickly to Leroy, but he was still writing. A few moments passed. I turned onto Rural Route 90. I thought he wasn't going to reply, but then he laughed.

"Shoot. They can't even hide the fact they didn't care nothing for that poor girl."

"Yeah," I said. "I get the feeling Brandon wants custody for one reason or another—and Glory's resentful of being the *actual* full-time caretaker. Brandon couldn't take care of that kid, can barely take care of himself."

"Now what I want to narrow down is if they benefited from any assets Victoria had. They were still married," Leroy said.

"Unless she was hiding something, she wasn't wealthy. Just that land out to Cedar Springs, maybe eight to ten acres."

"People have been motivated by less. And either of them could have picked her up from the party that night."

"Do the police have cell phone records?"

"They will," he said. "And then there's the question of who she might have been seeing all those nights she'd stepped out."

"As far as I knew she was single," I said. "This is it? The VFW bar?" I slowed in front of a small, single-story building of blanched red brick. Low-slung red roof and an overhang to the side, you'd think it an abandoned Dairy Queen were it not for the black POW-MIA flags out front and the blinking Christmas lights and neon beer signs in the windows. A yellowed marquee with block letters and an arrow pointing around to the back entrance read: YESTERDAY ONCE MORE.

"Bar's open every night, but Thursday night is when there's music. They've got a country-western band that plays old-time songs," Leroy said. "Turns into a regular honky-tonk. We'll come back Thursday. Maybe ask some questions. Today I think we ought to go back to the office and organize our thoughts. Have a bite of supper."

"This place." I squinted, tried to see inside. "It's odd. Small. You'd miss it, if you weren't looking."

"I hadn't been to the post in a long, long time. Only just stumbled on it again a few months back when I was out driving one night, looking for something."

"Trouble," I said. The wind picked up, pinging the car windows with grit from the gravel lot and bits of dry stalk from the surrounding fields of maize.

"You do know me, little granddaughter. You do."

It made sense that Leroy would like this place—a barfly is drawn to neon—but Yesterday Once More was kind of a strange place for a young woman to frequent, and especially alone. Maybe Victoria had humored her granny by taking her, then kept it up after she passed as a kind of remembrance. I imagined Victoria crossing the lot, sidestepping broken glass in those red leather boots, and I remembered her favorite song playing in her car: "Why don't you mind your own business," she sang, her voice sly and sharp as Hank's. She meant it too, fixed me with those mean black-brown eyes.

"I seen her in here maybe four or five times. Don't think we spoke. You know I come more for the atmosphere," Leroy said. He ran his finger along the wound on his face. It was nearly healed but would leave a scar. He hadn't been out of the house much in the past few weeks, unusual for him, and I wondered if it made him a little weird. Feeling time pass, maybe. Just thinking it made me sad, and I reached across the console to squeeze his hand.

"You're still pretty quick on your feet," I said, remembering him dancing with me, twirling me around our living room when I was a little girl. He was a good dancer not because of any fancy moves, but because he had so much fun with it. You could tell he was really savoring the music. He had his favorites: the Rays (Price and Charles), Bob Wills, and Eddy Arnold. Weren't those old songs my favorites too? I thought about Sundays after church, how Momma and I did laundry to prepare for the week ahead while listening to Patsy Cline. To this day, the smell of sheets fresh out of the dryer will bring me back to her greatest hits, the particular melancholy of her voice, of Sundays. And there was something bright, tempting, in the heartbreak sounds. In music there was the passion I hadn't yet experienced in real life. There was intrigue, experience, love in those songs—pain, even—and I wanted that.

"Victoria. Did she dance?"

"Yes, I remember her dancing," he said, and I thought I knew why she went to the VFW bar. She went for the music.

Chapter 14

That night I came home to the little pink house and found some comfort in the familiar trappings of life as I knew it: the neighbor's orange tomcat sitting on our fence post, Nikki's blue Chevy under the carport, and the porch light, greenish, snapping with moths, my beacon. And yet I didn't feel safe. The pit of my stomach felt hollow—not dread, but something worse—I felt as though I'd lost control, that there was no real order to the world.

Nikki opened the front door and leapt off the steps to hug me. When her hand rested on my back, I felt it tremble. "Where have you been all day?"

"Out with Leroy. Paying our respects to Victoria's kin."

"Paying respects? Or nosing into something you shouldn't?" Nikki shook her head and started back toward the house. She kicked aside a phone book someone had thrown on the steps— over a week ago—that neither of us had bothered to toss.

I followed her inside, closing the door softly behind me. "What do you mean?"

"Don't go borrowing trouble, Annie."

I knew what she meant in a practical sense, but emotionally too: it was almost like I had gotten in deep enough to will the worst. If you go looking for darkness it will surely find you. Irrational as it was, both fear and guilt gripped me. Not that it had been a game before—though hadn't it, in some terrible way? All the nights we'd spent looking for ghosts, conjuring shapes from the darkness? But there was no looking away now. This was real.

"We only want to know what happened," I said after a moment.

Nikki spun around, her face red. "Ha-ha. That's maybe half of it."

"What?"

"You're bored," she said. I must have looked as shocked as I felt. She crossed her arms over her chest and stuck her chin out. "Go on, leave. Move to Austin, or New York, or L.A., or wherever, but don't kick up a hornet's nest here for the rest of us before you run off."

"It's not that I want to leave, not now."

"Some of us have fewer options," she said, and looked at me like she'd tasted something bad. "That girl is dead. What if whoever did it comes after you? You think you're so special that you can't get hurt?"

I shook my head. "I'm sorry I worried you."

"Whatever. Your dad's on his way over," she said. "You left your cell here and after about the tenth call I said 'fuck it' and answered."

Sitting on the back steps in the dark he looked smaller. Good, because I didn't think I could handle him looking down at me.

I took a deep breath, handed over a room-temperature Dr Pepper, and sat. "Sorry I don't have ice." The air was still and the concrete improbably warm against my thighs for the time of night. "You know we're not out to, like, have a showdown with the killer. We're trying to gather any evidence that might help the investigation."

He set the can on the ground. "Your grandfather is not well. If something were to happen, you think he could protect you, much less himself?"

I wondered if Nikki could hear from inside, if she was pleased. But, fair point: an octogenarian with his arm in a sling and a smallish twenty-two-year-old didn't make a formidable duo. Mary-Pat was more capable and more convincing, but she likely sided more with Dad on this one.

"You're saying I should pack heat," I said, and nudged his arm. The thought did cross my mind. I wasn't a bad shot. Hell, I'd hit a can on the fence post once. "Or at least my phone. I'm sorry y'all were worried. I got swept up and didn't make it back to the house to grab it. It won't happen again."

"I don't know why you think this is funny. And when you say you don't want a confrontation you better be sure the old man's on the same page as you. You don't know the kind of situations he's gotten himself into. It's a miracle he's alive today."

"I know it's not funny."

"You have no idea, Anne Louise. No idea the risks."

"Then tell me! Tell me what happened with you and Grand-dad. I'm not dumb. I know he's why you don't drink, and I know that the accident was more than just an accident. That your back injury isn't the only reason you quit. Tell me," I said, words rushing out before I could think better. "Tell me why you stopped caring."

Dad was quiet a moment, and I felt acid rise in my throat, knowing I'd made him angry. His anger could feel as though you were screaming at someone on the other side of thick glass. He would watch you flail, deaf to pleas or reason. But he put his hand on my shoulder, gently, and sighed. "No, honey, I'm not ready to do that. And I don't hate my father. I love him. And I love you. If something happened, I don't know what we'd do."

"Something could happen to me driving the car to the café, you know?"

"That's like the assholes who smoke cigarettes and say it don't matter 'cause you can get cancer from anything."

"Fair enough." I laughed a little. "But what if this is what I decided to do?"

"But why?"

"I don't know. Right now, this feels right. Is that stupid?"

"You're anything but stupid." He bit his lip and reached into his back pocket. "Here, I wanted to give you this. It's short notice, I know. Was going to go myself, but you have a better shot at standing out at this type of thing than I do." He unfolded a piece of paper, handed it to me. "They'll have all these big companies there; you just bring your résumé."

A flyer for a job fair in San Antonio, the paper was worn along the fold lines. He must have carried it in his wallet for weeks. Imagining my dad at the unemployment office, snatching a flyer off a bulletin board like it was a golden ticket, made me hot with embarrassment. Light through the kitchen window shone across the yard. I could see the breeze course through the grass but couldn't feel it.

"This says it's tomorrow at nine in the morning. . . ." I paused. "I don't have time."

"Check it out. You never know. I'll back off you working for him and Mary-Pat if you give it a shot."

"Fine." I kicked a pebble into a mound of dirt and watched fire ants scatter in every direction.

What would have been a two-hour drive took three, between rush-hour commuters and tractor trailers fishtailing in the high winds. Clouds darkened the sky like it was coming on night instead of day, looking some kind of beautiful. One thing I will always love about Texas is that you can see weather coming for miles. The sky is bigger here than anywhere else; I'm sure of it.

The storm broke right as I got off at the exit for the convention center. Driving through the parking lot, I wondered if there had been a fire inside the building—there were at least a hundred men and women shoving along the sidewalk getting their fancy interview clothes soaked.

Then I realized that it was the line just to get in.

"Screw this," I said, and parked in the only empty space at the very back of the lot, and considered which would be worse: putting my purse over my head and ruining it, or a rat's nest of wet hair. As if it mattered. I wouldn't get in, and even if I did, there was no way I was going to compete with all these people.

I should have expected this. Two weeks before, the cement plant in Parr City had fired half its people, same with Dickson Construction in Garnett. We were in a recession. Even out of my college classmates, only a handful had graduated with a job. Wealthy kids took the unpaid internships while the kids like me were in retail, waiting tables, or applying to grad school as an attempt to delay reality. Reality was the fact that despite a scholarship, I'd still needed to take out loans. I was thirty thousand dollars in debt. Thirty thousand. I could have been angrier. Everyone always said going to college was the ticket to getting a good job and I still hadn't seen any tickets, but I was thankful for those four years. My education was something no one could take away from me. Like an affair that had ended—better to have loved than not at all? It was also infuriating, that logic, even if I did believe in education for education's sake. I hadn't understood that concept until arriving; if not classist, the view was simply impractical.

There was something else that couldn't be taken away from me, something equally ineffable, and felt bone-deep. Law school, writing, the PI firm—whatever idea I'd had for myself, at its core, was rooted in this feeling. The night before, "purpose" was the word I had searched for and the thing I couldn't artic-ulate when trying to convince my father I could be a detective. That here, in Garnett, I had found purpose. It was in my blood and in the blood now spilled. It was simple, really: I wanted to uncover the truth. I wanted to make things right.

In fairness to Dad, I'd line up with the other job seekers once the rain lessened from monsoon-grade downpour to nor-mal. I kept the car running for the air-conditioning; the wiper blades barely kept up with the deluge. But I could still see the logo on the dually truck inching along in front of me: Artemis Oil and Gas. Boom and bust—we knew that cycle—but now, was there even such thing as a bust? Post-boom, they were still making money hand over fist. It was the shale, I figured. On those salaries you could be comfortable. That is, if you didn't get injured or killed on the job first. I was wondering if there were any female crews pulling wells when I remembered some-thing important.

Chapter 15

Breaking and entering was a little too comfortable for me I realized midway through shimmying Victoria's window up. Her place hadn't weathered the storm very well. The driveway was muddy, the patches of grass sunken, and her garbage can lay tipped on its side. Sun cut through the clouds, making rainbows on the oil-slicked puddles around her car. Anticipating the trailer being blocked off by yellow police tape, I hadn't actually planned on going in. I thought I'd peek through the window while balanced on the deck railing, close enough to read what I needed to see. But it was so easy to slip inside once I'd kicked off those pinching, interview-appropriate heels.

Someone had taken Oreo. Trash had been emptied and a few things looked tossed—I knew the police had to have searched—but the air was still and smelled faintly of Victoria's coconut-scented shampoo. I took two steps down the short hall to the bedroom, but the letter that had been taped to the vanity was gone. If Brandon hadn't interrupted, I'd have at least scanned its contents.

But Artemis's logo had been on the letterhead; I was sure of it.

Bold red *A* inside a blue hexagon that reminded me of a badge. They were hiring, after all, so maybe the letter was a job offer. But an offer to lease her land was the more interesting option. It must have been hard facing the estate aspect of her granny's death while still grieving. The business of tidying up a life was complicated, even if you had help. Maybe Artemis offered to relieve some of the burden, so to speak, if she made a lease. They paid good money up front—and then there were the royalties, which were ongoing.

What if she had other plans? Choked with cacti and mesquite, the land surrounding the trailer was not much to look at but went pretty far back. Victoria was a romantic, after all. The kind of girl who hung out in dark bars listening to country and western, she was the kind of girl who saw beauty in the shadows. I looked out the kitchen window. Some newish-looking shovels, a wheelbarrow, and a rake leaned up against the railing under the deck.

Once this local supplier had come and parked his truck behind the café. The old man had removed a blue plastic tarp from the flatbed to reveal crates and cardboard boxes overflowing with fresh-picked produce for Marlene to make her selections from. Victoria and I had come out to help haul it in—melons, tomatoes, peaches, peppers, and a mess of green beans—and when we were done decided to take our break. I sat on the back steps and took out my phone but looked up when Victoria approached the old farmer to stop him from leaving.

"This is nice," she'd said, running her hand along the tailgate, gazing at the remaining boxes. "So, where's the best place to start? Been thinking I might take up planting a few things of my own."

"I've been doing this a long time," the man said, seeming to puff up a bit. He kind of stared at Victoria, not quite sure if she was serious. "Pick something you like, start small, and you got to mind it. Takes time and patience. Water plenty."

"I inherited a few acres," Victoria said, a catch in her voice. Her granny had passed about a week before—I was afraid she might tear up again, as she had once or twice already in a quiet moment at work.

"I could eat these peaches every day," I said, coming to stand beside her. "How are they so much more flavorful than the grocery store's?"

"Shoot, can't give away all my secrets," the man said, and smiled. He shielded the sun from his weathered face and wiped it with the tail of his shirt. "You girls want some scratches and dents?"

We nodded and he filled a paper bag with bruised peaches. Barely overripe, they were sun sweet and heavenly. He left and we sat right on the back steps and ate them, letting the juice run down our wrists.

God, things could have been different. Standing in her kitchen, alone, pretending she'd just had me over for supper and was picking fresh basil and tomatoes from her garden to make a sauce the way Marlene had taught us to. I wanted so badly for things to be different.

A half-drunk bottle of wine sat on the top shelf of her fridge. I twisted off the top. It smelled okay—fruity, cheap pink stuff—so I took a sip. The sugar in it made my teeth hurt; the burn in the back of my throat made me shudder. Victoria had been buzzing that night; warm and happily dulled. Still, she would have panicked. Her heart racing like a jackrabbit's when she realized she was about to die.

Or had she felt nothing at all? Her body not her own, did she feel like she was floating? My own tongue had felt large and use-less, nearly gagging me. I remember the shadow on the ground in front of me (was that really me?) tumbling toward the back deck of the fraternity house, the buzzing of the floodlights at the top of the drive, my knee scraped and bloodied.

It doubles you over, remembering does. I slumped against the wall of Victoria's kitchen, my thoughts fragmented, cutting me like shards of glass, and took another sip of cold, sweet wine. What scared me was the feeling that it wasn't me having too much to drink, too little to eat. That it was no accident. That someone hurt me. Someone drugged me, made me im-mobile, unable to speak or to claw my way up, like an ani-mal bled out in a snare. I never wanted to think of myself as a victim. I've always been the person who would rather joke about things, who would rather move on. I never wanted to be a stereotype—the wounded woman, both vindicated and valo-rized for her weakness.

And, still.

I find myself dwelling on the purple scar across my palm, marveling at the invisible made visible, the past rupturing the present, the proof that I deserve something resembling sym-pathy, if not from others, then maybe from myself. Lack of control is still what I fear most. That our only option is to react, recalibrate, resolve—that's been the hardest part of life to learn.

Chapter 16

I tied my apron on. The static from Marlene's weather radio, snippets fading in and out, made the room feel like a combat zone. Sheila sat in her usual spot, mumbling, pouring packet after packet of Sweet'N Low into a to-go cup of water. The way she took quick sips from it made her seem like a deranged hummingbird at a feeder.

"She hasn't even bought anything," I said to Marlene. The café employed a loose no-loitering rule, emphasis on loose.

"Don't even care, honey. Keeping her happy so she'll quiet down. You missed it earlier—she told some pamphlet pusher they were destined to die today. Didn't go over too well."

"Tactless given what's happened," I said, loudly, though normally I'd have laughed. Sheila pointed at me and I swear I nearly snatched that sugar water out of her hand.

"I wish I could have done something," Marlene said, and dabbed at her eye with the paper napkin she had balled up in her fist. Sun slanted across the room from the picture window. It had become a pretty day, and Marlene, too, looked pretty in the way some people are pretty criers. Her face had loosened up, and washed of makeup, her eyes looked brighter.

"How could you have known?" I said, knot forming in my throat. I was the one who should feel guilty, not Marlene. I was the one who saw Victoria at the bonfire and did nothing.

Marlene sniffed. "What if I'd scheduled Victoria for the overnight shift instead of Dot? Or what if Fernando hadn't given her a ride? Would she have stayed home that night? Thinking these kinds of thoughts can drive you nuts, but I'm so upset."

"Wait, Fernando gave her a ride? The night she died?"

"Dot said so—said she overheard Victoria and Fernando making plans after work last week."

The hair on the back of my neck stood up. My first day back after we learned about the murder, he and I sat in the big booth and talked half the night about it, but also about lost people, lost time. Regrets we had. I told Fernando I'd seen her at the bonfire, that I hated myself for not giving her a ride. He'd only listened then, every few minutes giving a sad shake of his head. Why hadn't he said anything to me about also seeing her outside of work that night?

"If you hear anything about a service will you let me know? I went by her mother-in-law's house to return some things she left here, give a teddy bear to the little girl, but they were a bit short. Not that I blame them."

"It'll be at the city cemetery on Friday at ten," I said. "The coroner will have released the body by then."

Marlene winced at the word "body." Glory had called Leroy to tell him, "She didn't do a service for her granny. They wasn't church people, but it's important to do a service. You need closure." As if it were over after she was buried. In situations like this, wasn't it the cause that mattered more? The longer the case went unsolved, the longer the wound stayed open, no matter how lovingly we bid her farewell.

"I'll be there. Thanks, doll," Marlene said, and patted me on the shoulder.

A family claimed the five-top. I took their orders—cheeseburgers, all of them—and brought the ticket to Fernando in the kitchen. He didn't look up, just started flipping patties on the grill. I waited.

"What?" He finally turned around.

"You didn't tell me you were with Victoria after work on Thursday," I said. "I thought you hadn't heard from her."

"It wasn't, like, a big deal. Why? Do you think I hurt her?" His arms were rigid and his close-cropped black hair glistened with sweat at the temples.

I took a step back. "You talked to the police again?"

"Yeah, Ranger was in here yesterday."

"A Texas Ranger?"

"No, a park ranger. Jesus." His voice hardened. "I told him the truth."

"Which is what? Because I'm starting to wonder why you lied the first time."

"I didn't lie. You didn't ask."

"A lie by omission is still—never mind," I said, trying to sound calmer than I felt. "You can talk to me."

He took a deep breath. "That Thursday, not long after you and your cousin took off, Victoria and I go to clock out, same time. She's telling me about some honky-tonk that's only Thursday nights."

"Yesterday Once More?"

He nodded. "I kind of made fun of her about it—it's in the old VFW bar, you know? My old uncle calls bingo there. But she asks if I wanted to go dancing with her," he said, and turned red, blushing or from the heat of the kitchen I couldn't tell. "But later it was obvious she just wanted me to drive her."

"Why's that?"

"She was already drunk when I picked her up from her place. Maybe not drunk, but tipsy. Texting some other guy," he said.

"Who was she texting?"

"Troy Schneider," he said, disdain in his voice. I was surprised. Troy and Victoria surely didn't run in the same circles, but then again, they were two of a small group of young adults in Garnett. Those still here after high school, even if they weren't friends growing up, oftentimes ended up marrying. The field of eligible singles simply narrowed the longer you stayed in this town.

"She said change of plans, let's go to a bonfire at his place. I felt like a tool, so I dropped her off and left. She said she'd get a ride from someone else when I told her no way I was hanging out with those assholes," he said.

"You don't like Troy?"

"I don't care about him specifically. It's that whole crowd. It's just like—"

"High school," I said.

"Yeah." A smile flickered, then disappeared. It wasn't so long ago. We'd talked once, not long after I started, about how ambivalent we felt about that time, about this place. He and I weren't outcasts, yet neither of us had been popular. There were contingencies on acceptance into our respective cliques. I was a nerd—uptight, too, never sharing my homework or letting anyone copy my test—only invited places because I was Nikki Avery's cousin. He was talented at football because of his size, but tormented since elementary school for being fat. Was invited to the team parties, but on the rare occasion he went was ignored. Paid obligatory attention by a few cheerleaders, but never dated. "I had other plans, so whatever. I'd only gone because I thought—"

"You thought she was interested in you?"

"Screw you."

"Not saying she wasn't," I said carefully. "I just didn't know y'all talked."

"We didn't really. Thought we might have gotten to know each other. I wish we could have. It's terrible what happened." He flipped the spatula in his hand and laid the patties on buns, topped them with thick squares of cheese.

There, the first note of remorse from him, I thought. *Or tenderness.* Fernando was a hothead. I'd known that since grade school when he chucked a plastic shovel at Russell Jenkins for taking too long at the water fountain. But wasn't he rightfully angry and defensive? His life was on the line, it now seemed, whether he was guilty or not.

"Do you know who she was going to get a ride home with?" I asked.

"No. I don't. She called me later, I assume for a ride home, but I couldn't understand her, and besides, I had other plans."

"Plans doing what?"

He shook his head and slid the plates across the counter. "Here, order's up."

I was sweating and plucked at my shirt before I loaded the plates, balancing the tray on one forearm. Maybe I should be more cautious—what if he was lying? What if he— Was I confronting a murderer? I swallowed hard. "How was she when you last saw her?"

"Alive," he said, his voice choked. "I fuckin' swear."

"Okay, calm down—"

"You know me, right? I barely knew her," he said, crying now. "But you know me."

I nodded, but my stomach dropped. He had her in his car. He had been angry with her. There were holes in the story.

"It'll be okay," I said, hurrying toward the swinging door with the tray.

"She was alive," he said again, and turned from me, stifling a cry with his fist, his voice cracking when he said, "I think she was sad, Annie. She seemed really sad."

I left during what we called the dead hour: fade from blue dark to full dark, after supper, after the businesses shut their doors, before the drinkers and the strangers fanned out into the bars, then stumbled into the café. Cicadas ripped into the silence. The streets were empty of people, but the gutters and narrow alleys between the century-old brick buildings were clotted with trash. The stop sign on the corner tagged with black spray paint. It wasn't always like this—city services had been reduced recently due to funding—but part of me feared this was our new normal, a slow unspooling. Like a cat I sensed my eyes adjusting to the night, outlines of objects sharpening. Instead of going to the bullet I paced down the street. Was Victoria sad, as Fernando said? Her granny was gone. She was getting divorced and must have felt more alone than ever. Even though she loved her daughter, she hadn't chosen to be a mother, not yet, and that was its own kind of loss.

I wanted to know that her life and her experiences mattered. You can't treat someone like trash and erase all those lived experiences—the way the breeze that night felt surprisingly cool on her skin, or the way that first cold beer fizzed on her tongue, the pain she registered as he put his hands around her throat—not without facing consequences.

I looked up at the unlit window of Leroy and Mary-Pat's

office. We were meeting in the morning. They would be more clearheaded about Fernando. He was someone I'd known almost all my life and my brain wouldn't go there. Then again, imagining anyone killing was hard enough, so why not Fernando? Had he really not offered to pick Victoria up from the party? He was just mean enough to not and they weren't close, but who knows what was actually said, actually arranged. I thought of the pasture and of woodsmoke, remembering how fire lighted the dark sky. How crushed cans and cigarette butts had littered the hardpan dirt. How rowdy it got when the keg rolled and Troy Schneider had to heft it upright. Troy the landman—Victoria texted him, and the letter, too, I was sure was from the oil and gas company he worked for, a professional connection perhaps turned deeply personal.

Chapter 17

"Would it be weird if I invited myself over?"

"Not at all," Justin said. "But I'm about to head over to Mike's to work out."

"It's almost nine," I said.

"Too hot to run during the day."

"True."

"Anyway," he said, drawing out the last syllable. "Mind if—"

"I won't be long. I'm turning onto your road now," I said, and hung up before he could formally protest. It wasn't Justin I was looking to talk to anyway. Instead of taking the dirt road down to the pasture where the bonfire had been, I hooked left and met up with a long, paved driveway.

The best word I could use to describe the Schneider house would be "sprawling." Newish construction, ranch style, stucco with blocky limestone columns and arched limestone-covered entryway, it looked more like one of the McMansions you'd find in the suburbs of Dallas or Houston than something in Garnett. It was hard to tell what the primary structure of the house was; bay windows and turrets and garages and side porches seemed to crop up and spread from the impossibly green turf. It irked me that they must water daily. What they did with their well was their business, but still, we were technically in a drought. Green grass felt arrogant. A fleet of vehicles sat at the top of the well-lighted driveway like an assortment of shiny toys: a black Suburban and Troy's cherry red company-issued truck sandwiched between Justin's silver F-350 and their dad's Aggie-maroon Texas Edition.

I parked the bullet on the opposite end and went to the door. Knocked, but no answer. Rap music was playing inside; the bass actually made the door throb. As I was about to pull out my phone, a shadow flickered under the porch light and Justin tapped my shoulder.

"Didn't mean to scare you," he said.

"Yes, you did."

He grinned. He was wearing red basketball shorts and a tank top. I'm generally opposed to men in tank tops, but Justin had the biceps to prove he'd been working out with Mike, so I'd allow this trespass.

"Everything okay?" he asked.

"Fine. I was wondering if Troy was around?"

Justin made a pouting face. "Said every girl ever." The two could have been twins and Justin certainly wasn't wanting for attention, but I had to admit he didn't radiate the same confidence Troy did. Up until sophomore year, Justin was more of a loner, sticking with the FFA kids who, like their parents, mostly had droll conversations about cattle and the weather. Then he made varsity football, got as good an arm as his brother's, and kind of started acting like him. Both had that cool guy affectation down—unbothered, easy smile—but in Justin's silences you sensed things unsaid, that maybe he was quiet not because he didn't care, but because he was listening.

"Come on, you're my favorite," I said, followed him inside, and stopped. I remembered the last time I was here—white-carpeted staircase and two doors down to his bedroom, blue plaid sheets, my nervous excitement at being with him, alone—and my breath caught in my chest.

"So, what do you two have to talk about?" Justin asked. He stopped mid-stride and turned to face me. He leaned his body close so my back pressed against the door, reached over my shoulder, and turned the dead bolt. "We're being extra careful, these days," he said, and looked me in the eye. "Normally we just leave it open."

My face and neck flushed, stomach tightening as he lingered with his arm over my shoulder, propped on the door.

"I wanted to see if your brother remembers anything about Victoria Merritt. I think they might have been friends," I said.

"Troy's never mentioned her," Justin said, and stepped back. "And I think he would've said so, in this case."

I followed him into the hallway that opened up into a beige-carpeted family room with plush, gingham upholstered furniture, and breathed a little easier. On the wall amidst the calligraphy stencils of homespun sayings—*bless this nest* and *home is where the heart is*—were framed photos of Troy and Justin as kids. In one they'd been dressed as cowboys and posed in a field of blue-bonnets; in another, scarecrows holding hands in a pumpkin patch. Mrs. Schneider was the type that would buy matching outfits, hire a photographer, and send out cards, and not just at Christmas. Justin must miss her; I knew firsthand how you could be mad and still miss someone, how you could still ache.

"I'm helping her mother-in-law plan the service. Victoria didn't know many people in Garnett and I might be grasping at straws, but I think she and your brother knew each other," I said, and sighed dramatically. "Anything to help a grieving family," I added for effect.

As if on cue, the music stopped. Troy hurried down the stairs. His ash-blond hair was wet and his face flushed from the shower. He wore dark jeans, pale suede boots, and a button-down shirt the color of fresh cream was rolled up over his tanned forearms.

Justin whispered, "He's been going out every night since he and Megan broke up."

"So, what happened exactly?" I whispered back, but Justin had left my side to follow Troy through the house.

Troy Schneider and Megan Miller: Garnett High's homecoming king and queen two years in a row, on and off again sweethearts since middle school. Rumor had it this was the last time, though. Megan was starting a new job, moving to Houston after her sister's wedding in a few weeks. Instead of being happy for her, most everyone—her friends, even her own sisters—said she was acting high on herself. Funny, because when Troy was hooking up with other girls away at college the same people were pretty quick to look the other way. Funnier still was the way they now wondered what *Megan* must have done to lose him, though I don't think anyone was actually sure who had called it off. I followed Justin into the kitchen as he called after Troy.

"I have a date," Troy said, then turned to face us. He looked me up and down and smiled. "Hey, Annie. Good to see you the other night."

I blushed slightly—I didn't think Troy Schneider remembered my name—and cursed myself for being flattered.

"She's here to talk to you," Justin said, a note of teasing in his voice.

"To what do I owe the pleasure?" Troy smiled, but his nostrils flared and his eyebrows were raised. He rapped his class ring on the granite countertop. "Sorry to be rude, but—"

"You knew Victoria Merritt," I said. I wanted to be direct but wished I sounded less accusatory. Last thing I wanted was for him to clam up. "Her service is on Friday."

"No," he said, and his smile slackened. "Unfortunately, I didn't know her well. Damn shame what happened."

"Wait," Justin said. "You told Dad you didn't know her at all."

Troy ignored Justin and looked back at me somberly. "She was an acquaintance through work. We'd been having conversations about her land, formerly her grandmother's. Artemis was looking to lease and, well, I won't bore you with the details. I think we talked maybe three or four times."

That confirmed the letter. "Not boring to me. The details, I mean," I said.

Troy rolled his eyes. "Artemis is seeking to route the new pipeline through the back of her property and also a service road. I can see why she'd be nervous, all the stuff you hear about toxins or leaks, but come on."

"Wouldn't you worry?" I asked.

Troy shrugged and went to the fridge for a water bottle, not offering one to either Justin or me. While the rest of the house appeared untouched since their mother's departure, the kitchen looked more like a bachelor's: uncluttered, the matching dish towels and napkin holders gone, only pizza boxes stacked on top of the stove. "Like I told her, that's all hippie bullshit," Troy said, and took a long drink.

"There's room for debate," I said. "Least that's what I've heard."

"Annie likes hippie bullshit. She went to a liberal arts college." Justin laughed and leaned forward, inserting himself ever so slightly between Troy and myself.

"Seriously, done right, all this is safe," Troy said. "You know I know that side of it too. There are plenty of regulations."

"Anyway," I said, barely resisting the bait. Troy was in the same fraternity as a politician's son. That's how he'd gotten his first job at the Railroad Commission, which everyone knew was awfully friendly with the industry it was supposed to be regulating. I also doubted Bill Schneider's reaction if Artemis tried to lease his pristine ranch would be so favorable. "You think she wasn't going to accept?"

"No. And it was my job to tell her they'd be getting what they wanted sooner or later, so better to take the first offer," Troy said, tossing his empty bottle into the can. "The company would pursue condemnation and eminent domain next. That was our last meeting."

"What does that mean? 'Eminent domain'?"

"The pipeline will be a common carrier—meaning other companies can use it too—and so Artemis says they've the right to pursue it because it's for the greater economic good. It's the same thing with public utilities like power lines and roads."

"That doesn't seem right since it's her property. Private property." I understood what he was saying, but there was something wrong about it. What was drilled out of the Permian had to make its way to the gulf refineries somehow, I knew that. I drove a car that used gas. We needed jobs. So, okay, I got it. But what protection did we really have if something went wrong? I bet Victoria's reluctance went even further than safety. Landownership meant something here. Maybe it was the mentality of staking your claim and all the other macho bullshit people romanticized. Maybe it was that Texas-sized sense of pride. But if it were my family's land, we'd fight too.

Troy shook his head. "It'll be underground, totally safe; she'd never have noticed it. Plus, the offer was very generous."

"You met at your office?"

Troy raised his eyebrows. "What's with the interrogation?"

I needed more info, so I bluffed: "Just curious because I thought I might've seen you two out—"

"Out? Our relationship was professional, not personal."

Justin sounded impatient now, having been ignored. "Dude, why didn't you tell me you knew this girl?"

"Why does it matter?" Troy said.

Justin's eyes widened. "What do you mean why does it matter?"

"Sorry, Annie." Troy hung his head. "You said the memorial is Friday? I can't. Work's pretty busy."

"Guess I thought you were friends. You invited her to your bonfire," I said.

Troy's mouth opened and closed like a trout's. "Oh, yeah." He nodded after a moment. "We were texting—about Artemis—and I said have a good night or fun weekend, something like that, and she tells me she doesn't get out much. Hinting pretty hard. I was trying to be nice. No idea any of this would happen." His face drew down again and for a horrifying moment I thought he might cry. "Annie, I'm sorry, but you'll have to excuse me," he said, and looked toward the door.

"Right. I know y'all were fixing to leave."

Justin touched the small of my back and led me toward the door. "You want to go for a drink after I get done at Mike's? Meet up at Mixer's?"

"I'm kind of tired. Rain check," I said, and smiled sweetly. "Troy, good seeing you."

"Night," Troy said, then quickly turned and picked up his phone. I was certain the scope of his duties for Artemis didn't expand to texting after hours, but maybe he really was just being courteous. There were a lot of Artemis people at the party

I'm sure he didn't know personally. Why, then, did he seem defensive?

The door closed shut behind me and I heard the click of the dead bolt.

Eminent domain. The words rattled around in my head as I drove down the dark ranch road, the cluster of lights that was Garnett shining in the distance. Victoria had had no choice. No say in the matter. The ground beneath her feet had shifted.

Chapter 18

Looping roads that once seemed as imprinted on my memory as whorls on my thumb were somehow less familiar. Darker, more twisted. I turned on some music. A throwback, bit of a joke—a country classics playlist Victoria made—that stung my heart. Certain songs had seemed as indelible to me. I don't know when I first sensed it, this slight shame, but sharing this music had felt like a secret exposed. I loved it so much it almost ruined it. Victoria had liked what she liked and didn't care, so I wondered what was wrong with me when the road sign I'd been chasing flashed past.

After leaving Justin's all I wanted was to think and drive, and I'd ended up nearly an hour west. Up near Parr City, where the new drilling and pipeline layout had started. Instead of turning around and back toward the farm-to-market I was pretty sure some of the Andersons still lived down, I saw a service road cut into the trees off the side of the highway and decided to try it. It appeared like a fresh incision; sprays of dirt fanned onto the asphalt where big trucks had gunned it back onto the highway, and it was still soft. Dust clouded the windshield making it hard to see, so I slowed to a crawl until finally I began to make out the lighted tower on the horizon. It would be fenced off, unsafe to enter, but I wanted to get as close as I could while it wasn't busy during the day. See for myself what Artemis offered.

These were not like the pumpjacks I'd seen before. Two vertical towers shot up into the sky. Spotlights dotted the red and white sides and lit the yellow safety scaffolding so it appeared neon. The flare at the top burned hot white, blue at the center. The fence was topped with rolled wire and the security lights bathed the area in a dull orange glow. Trucks, tankers, and skid-steer loaders sat parked around dark, empty-looking portables, no people far as I could see, but the steady hum and whoosh of the machinery carried over the flatland.

There was a dog in the middle of the road. I waited a minute, but it stayed prone in the headlights, likely dead. There was a small house to the right off the road, and I worried it was their pet that had been hit. I turned the engine off and pocketed the keys. Left the headlights on, the warning beep fainter as I shut the door and drew closer. As I did, a gust of foul air assaulted me. Sulfurous and so thick it had a taste. I pulled my T-shirt over my nose and waited for it to pass or for my nose to acclimate, but it lingered on the breeze. It was not a dog dead in the road, but a small coyote. The headlights illuminated the silver in its hair, and there was no blood and no sign of impact that I could see. If I hadn't known better, I'd thought it was asleep. Its mouth was open, its black gums bared and teeth frozen in a snarl. Eyes flat and yellow. Nothing had attacked it yet, not even the flies. It was still a coyote, not a carcass.

A branch snapped behind me. Then, soft, low—could've been a frog, but it sounded human, like throat clearing. A shadow crossed the beam of the headlights and I ran in the opposite direction, not daring to turn around, and jumped off the road into the weeds. The house up ahead had lights on inside, so I took my chances in that direction, cursing myself for leaving the bullet. My jeans snagged on a branch and I crashed into a thigh-high chain-link fence. A porch light flipped on. The yellow bulb illuminated the yard and sharpened its shadows so it appeared stage-like.

"Who's there?"

A thin, fifty-something-looking woman came out of the house. Loose strands of dark hair trailed out from under a shower cap and a blue housecoat was knotted high and tight around her waist. As she drew closer and before she beamed me with her flashlight, I could see her beady eyes and the hard line of her jaw and tell she was an Anderson.

"Hey." I put my hands up, in case she was armed. "Lillie? I'm Annie McIntyre. William's daughter." Lillie was my father's second cousin, maybe first-once-removed; I wasn't sure—and hadn't done the math on what she was to me.

She drew closer and beamed me with her flashlight again. "You favor your mother. Lucky you." She laughed but quickly frowned. "Is Leroy okay? Scared me to death when he took that fall. I called, but he hasn't picked up."

"He's much better, thanks. I saw something in the road and worried it was your dog. Got out and thought I heard someone behind me. Didn't mean to frighten you like this. I know it's late."

"You might've heard someone. Think they're gone now, but used to be a man and woman stayed in a tent hidden down yonder," she said, and motioned with the flashlight toward a tangle of dark brush just over the road. "He'd gotten a job with the company and they were waiting on his first check to come through. Some men are sleeping in their trucks. Dangerous, you ask me, but can't blame them exactly. I do tell my daughter to keep her eyes peeled. One man was hanging around, strutted up in my yard once and tried peeping in the window."

"Wow, that's crazy," I said, my stomach tied in knots. "Hey, mind if I borrow your flashlight? I can bring it back by later."

"Don't worry about it. We got several," she said, and handed it to me. "Those trucks race down this road. You said something got hit?"

The flashlight was solid metal, warm where she'd held it. "Coyote. Don't think so. I wasn't even sure it was dead at first."

"Neighbors lost a hog yesterday. Dropped dead." She looked down and kicked at the dirt with her pink moccasin. "Something in the air."

"Is the smell always this strong?"

She raised her eyebrows and laughed.

"No offense, I just—"

"Since they started about six or seven months ago. Think it's the storage tanks. We seem to be downwind. It's not just that one." She pointed ahead. "Further north, blows right down here. You can't tell, but it's a little lower here. We're in a bit of a sink. My daughter—you know Britney, right?"

I shrugged my shoulders. Her name rang a bell, but I couldn't picture her face. We weren't close with this side of the family. Years before I was even born, Leroy had arrested Lillie's brother for something petty like selling stolen copper wire, which kind of soured any reunions. Oddly, Leroy was the only one who'd made amends and now kept up with their side.

"Brit's got migraines. Her little boy's got to wheezing now too. I talked to the company and they sent the state inspectors out. Ran tests on the air and the wells and said it's fine, all normal levels, so I don't know what to think."

Goddamn Troy—you'd have to be willfully stupid to think this wasn't bad. Whether or not the drilling made them sick, it spoiled this land. "Levels of what?" I shook my head. "And what does 'normal' even mean? When the company sought your consent, did they warn you?"

"Consent? They didn't ask me a thing. Down there's not my land. It's the neighbor's, technically."

"But it's basically your backyard. You don't at least get paid?"

"They paid him, some . . . ," she said, and paused, her chin trembling. "I don't get a dime."

"What will you do? Move, or—"

"If I were fixing to sell, who on earth would buy this place?" Lillie said, sweeping a hand across the horizon of her world: dry, nearly grassless yard with a busted trampoline, mesquite at the far end of the property, the wavering flare peeking over the tops of the trees, a boy's white undershirts pinned to a metal clothes-line fluttering in the wind like tiny ghosts.

"Maybe the company."

"We're not going anywhere." Lillie shivered and looked back at the house. "I left something on the stove. You all right? Need to come in?"

"No, ma'am. Thanks for the light," I said. "One more thing: That man who came around Britney—what did he look like?"

"Maybe six foot, wore a ball cap. Didn't get a good look. He didn't come up again, probably 'cause he saw she didn't live here by herself. You be careful getting home, Annie. Tell your folks hello—don't you touch that coyote! I'll get a shovel out in the morning."

The back door closed behind her. I faced the overgrown, dark stretch of brush between Lillie's yard and the dirt road and tried not to think about what critters and discarded crap from the company I might step on. I gripped the base of the flashlight, prepared to swing if need be, and ran. It didn't take me long to reach the bullet, but I panted getting there, my heart racing.

Seeing no one in either direction, I sidestepped the coyote, got inside, and locked all the doors.

Those flat yellow eyes felt burned into my skull.

The radio roared to life, louder than I remembered having it on, and I floored it. Dust and gravel flew—I didn't care. The last song I remember listening to with Victoria, and one of my favorites, "Crazy," picked up at the chorus. Sitting in her car on our break—antsy, a little pissed-off feeling—we'd been waiting out a mid-shift, another endless day bleeding into night.

"Screw, marry, kill. Those three," she'd said, sly smile dimpling her cheek. She wagged her fingers over the steering wheel in the direction of the café window. Two tables who'd both settled up. A young, good-looking man we'd never seen before, and a teacher from the high school grading papers. Fernando, his back turned, jotted down a phone order.

"We called it kiss, marry, kill when I was in school," I said. "Maybe we should play M.A.S.H. next."

"Me, I'd definitely do it with that one." She pointed to the younger man first. "But I'd marry Fernando. He plays tough, but I figure he's a softy. The makes you breakfast in bed kind. Course I'd kill that bastard always tipping me, like, five percent." She pointed to Mr. Harvey slurping on his fourth or fifth free refill of Diet Coke.

"Same, but marry the hot one instead. He seemed sweet— best of both worlds, right?"

"Not allowed!"

"You can't sleep with the one you marry?"

"I don't make the rules." She pointed at the dashboard clock before reapplying lip gloss in the mirror. "We better go in before Dot gets her panties in a twist."

"So, that's what happened with your ex?"

"Wow." She laughed. "Guess we're playing truth or dare now."

"I have a feeling you'd always choose dare, though."

"Maybe." She shrugged. "You're the one who'll have to choose careful. I'm good at coming up with both."

She never did, of course. Wind moved through the branches hanging over the side of the empty road. Was I out of the sink? I rolled down the window, breathing, thinking I was mad enough now to choose dare.

Chapter 19

"But it's not fair," I said lamely. "What recourse is there?" I spooned powdered creamer into my cup and stirred, noting the now empty coffeepot—like most things in that office—needed a deep clean.

"You could take an eminent domain case to trial, but there's no precedent of the landowner winning," Mary-Pat said. "But back up a minute, who told you about Fernando?" She looked between me, standing in the center of the room, and Leroy, seated at a rolltop desk cluttered with handwritten notes, receipts, and takeout napkins.

"Fernando. He's not stupid, knows he's in hot water," I said. "Why didn't you tell me if you already knew he was under investigation?"

"I saw the file only yesterday, in confidence. It's not like this is an official case for us," Mary-Pat said, pacing. "I've been busy with a paying client."

"If Annie's our apprentice, we ought to keep her in the loop. On everything," Leroy said, and propped both feet on a metal filing cabinet.

McIntyre Investigations was on the second floor of a red-brick building on the courthouse square. Directly below was a law office, and because the building was old and its walls thin, I could hear the murmur of their conversations, a copy machine warming up, doors closing and opening. Coming here as a girl—usually with Mamaw to drop off Leroy's supper—I was both awed and intimidated by the view of the courthouse, the pebbled-glass door, the service awards and surveillance photos tacked to the blackboard. Wanted so badly for Mamaw to let me stay, to let me help Granddad and his buddy Pat round up the bad guys. I looked around the room, at the old oakwood floors, the windows wavy with leaded glass, and again felt that queasiness of being thrilled and afraid at once. Soon I'd have my own desk, my own files.

"Okay, okay," Mary-Pat said, and sat at her desk, messy as Leroy's. She dressed nondescriptly most of the time and today was no different: white blouse, jeans, and steel-toed boots, a single braid, no makeup, and no jewelry. On the blackboard behind her head remained traces of both her and Leroy's handwriting: his draftsman-like, hers neat and slanted. Contrary to some cowboy attitudes and a few habits, both were methodical, orderly in most ways. A heavy wooden frame hung on the wall next to the blackboard. It was a clipping from the story *Texas Monthly* did on the two of them after the cold case solve. I was in sixth grade at the time. My memories of that year, my teacher, what boys I liked, and what I learned in school were all mixed up with my imaginings of Leroy and Mary-Pat's hunt for the Hayes' killer. The day after it was announced and for months afterward, people stopped me at school, the grocery store, the library, to nod and say "give Sheriff McIntyre our regards." Say how proud I must be of my grandfather.

How could I not romanticize it?

Mary-Pat took out her notebook and clicked her pen. "Here's what I know, per my intel from Sheriff Garcia's office: The working theory is that Fernando did decide to pick her up from the party. Once she was in his car and clearly drunk, he decided he'd pull off into a wooded area and have his way with her. She put up a fight, and in both fear and rage he strangled her. He probably didn't know what he was doing until she was already dead. He panicked, decided he needed to hide the body, and drove down a little ways to Leroy's land where the gate was unlocked."

"How are they sure it was him and not someone else?" I asked, finishing the sludge that passed for coffee in one jittery gulp.

"They've got cell phone records. They've got a search warrant for his car. He has no credible alibi," Mary-Pat said.

"Let me say this: They need to make an arrest. They're not ill intentioned, I don't think, but are there blind spots? Prejudices? Sure. Prosecutor with a prime suspect—it can be like a dog with a bone; they won't drop it," Leroy said. "And they're overwhelmed with the other homicide, the hit-and-run."

"So, you don't think Fernando did it?" I said.

"Didn't say that." Leroy shrugged. "Shit, it looks like he might've."

"I do think the truth is sometimes hard to uncover. It takes time. Sometimes more time than is politically convenient," Mary-Pat said. She slid her finger under the lid of the box of kolaches she'd brought us, seeming to struggle with the temptation to eat another. I'd inhaled three already.

"If they've got cell phone records then the police know that Victoria texted with Troy Schneider that night. That he's the one who invited her to the party, that the two of them discussed a large sum of money. He might've offered her a ride home."

"That doesn't explain her phone by the side of the highway. I think someone picked her up at the road. Plus, Bill says both boys' trucks were in the driveway the whole night. He's a light sleeper; they have a motion light—he would've known if someone came or went," Mary-Pat said, sighed, and went for the pastry. "Lord. One more to finish my coffee with."

"You ought to cook more often," Leroy said.

"Don't count on it."

"Anyway." I sat back down in the creaky metal folding chair they set up for me in the corner. "You're saying Troy never left the bonfire?"

"Not in his vehicle, presumably. Though of course Bill could either be mistaken or lying."

Leroy took a sip of the supersize fountain drink he'd asked me to run get him from the café, swirled the ice with his straw. He was quiet for a moment. "Who benefits from the pipeline through her yard?"

"Artemis. But like I said, they were going to invoke eminent domain. They'd get what they wanted with or without her consent. . . ." I paused. "Oh, but royalties. Her daughter? And by extension Brandon and Glory?"

"They hadn't officially divorced yet, so directly Brandon. Might've he picked her up had she called. And another thing I want to know is why Glory was watching her at the dance. She herself said it's not her usual spot. Was she following the girl? There's more to that. We might learn something if we go to the places she frequented. Get a better feel for her life," he said. "Little darlin', we still going out tonight?"

I nodded. It was Thursday—the night Yesterday Once More had a live band.

Mary-Pat turned to me. "Were you friends with Victoria or her ex? On the Facebook?"

"She didn't have one. Or any other social media from what I could find," I said, though Victoria had already told me as much.

"Too much drama," she'd once said. "So-and-so sees you checked in at this bar, sees you tagged in a photo with somebody's ex, and before you know it people are talking crap."

Windows rolled down, cigarette dangling from her fingertips, I was in the passenger seat and fiddling with my phone, probably texting Nikki. "There's no such thing as privacy anymore. I should probably delete mine."

"You little priss. As if you have something to hide. As if you've ever done anything remotely 'risqué.'" She made air quotes and laughed—not noticing how I sat up straighter, how my face flamed—and I almost told her. Almost let her see I, too, could be vulnerable. But I didn't. I kept it hidden, a morsel of pain tucked under my tongue.

"It's hot out here, come on," I said, and turned off the stereo. "And have some of this gum. You'll smell like smoke to your tables."

"I don't give a damn 'bout my bad reputation," she sang.

"Come on. Everyone does," I said, forcing a laugh. "Care, I mean. About what people think."

"Nope. I only want people to leave me and my kid be."

I think she meant to sound flip, but there was a defiance, a weight in her voice. "Is someone bothering you?" I asked.

"Only everyone," she'd said, and waved me off.

"Brandon's account is private, but we have mutual connections," I said to Mary-Pat and Leroy. The coffee left a burnt taste in my mouth, so I walked across the room and reached for Leroy's Coke. "Mind?"

"Go on."

"That's strong," I said, and handed the cup back to him.

"Found a treat in my desk," he said, and held up a half-empty bottle of Wild Turkey. "Good thing too. I needed a slapper." That's what he called liquor mixed with Coke. I was pretty sure he was the only one who called it that.

"A slap or a slapper?" Mary-Pat grinned. "Y'all, I've got to get down to San Antonio."

"I'll get going too," I said. "Maybe I can look into—"

"Anything you do will be after you finish up here. Filing and office upkeep is what I'm paying you for, remember?" Mary-Pat pointed to a fat stack of manila folders on the floor. The whole office was a mess. It would take me an hour, at least, to even make a dent. Leroy shook his cup, snickered.

"Right," I said. "Maybe I need another drink."

Leroy leaned back in his chair and looked out the window. "Let it loosen up your memory."

"You're reliably shaken and stirred," I said. As I wrenched open an ancient file cabinet, Glory's gift, the brass cowgirl, flashed through my mind. The cowgirl resembled Victoria—her spirit, rather—a bold, chin-up kind of fearless. Was that a clue? After we left their house, I'd examined it, turned the cold metal over in my hands, tried prying off the felt base though I knew there was nothing hidden inside. That it was simply a gift. A token. I was still learning a remembrance could be its own type of clue.

Chapter 20

Leroy needed to feed the dogs, do his business (whatever that meant), before we went out again in the evening, so after we left the office I dropped him at home. Drove to the river, pulled over, and got out. Looked over the stone bridge into the clear, spring-fed waters. Green grasses swayed in the steady current and the glint of sun on water reminded me of silver dimes in a wishing fountain. I ought to have gone home, rested before our night out.

But it was so damn hot. The short and violent rain didn't do much to alleviate the dry heat and I felt as desperate as the weeds pushing through cracks in the concrete. Girls around here know to keep a throwaway swimsuit in the car during the summer—I made a kind of cover with my car doors and changed into a Walmart two-piece I'd stashed in the glove box. The water was cold and the contrast between the slippery river rocks and the hot dust at the bank stung the bottoms of my feet. Water raced through my hair as I leaned back and let the current carry me on my back, half swimming and half floating.

I didn't pass the usual rowdy groups of kids and drunken State students since school was in session, but a family was barbequing at Rio Vista and a handful of tiny kids, some still in diapers, splashed in the shallow water by the concrete steps. Around the bend and farther down it was quiet again. Underneath a railroad trellis, I shivered in shadow until I floated out into the blinding sunshine. A man cut across the current to block me.

"Annie? You okay?"

"Hey, Wyatt," I said, and planted my feet, digging my toes in the cold mud. "Just floating."

"Usually people use a tube. Although the other day I saw a kid on an air mattress with speakers and a six-pack."

"Where're your water wings, then?"

He smiled. "I'm checking on the rice."

"Huh?" The water only came up to my waist. A light breeze made the hair on my arms stand up.

"For class. It's a rare, wild rice that only grows in the Geronimo River, so the department acts as a kind of steward. There's even an endangered salamander native to this river," he said, and plucked a Coors can from the thick strands of what I previously assumed was grass. Waving under the surface it reminded me of green mermaid hair. "Man, I was awful upset to hear about Victoria."

My face felt hot. "Be honest with me. Were you two seeing each other?"

"No." Wyatt looked genuinely surprised. "Why would you think that?"

"She said . . ." I paused, not sure how much I should reveal. "Well, it's just that the other night you were looking for her—"

"I wasn't interested in dating her," he said quickly.

I raised my eyebrows.

"Victoria was a pretty girl. It just wasn't like that. We'd been talking about her land. About the Artemis pipeline. She had some concerns, and actually, so do a lot of people. My department chair has been involved with some environmental groups," he said, and crossed his arms over his chest. "But why are you asking me this?"

"Just curious," I said. "And I'd have to agree with you on the pipeline. Have you been out to where they're drilling? Too near people's homes."

"Yeah, I've seen it." He nodded. "It's a shame. But what about you—were you close with her?"

"In a way," I said. "Work friends, you know?"

Surely, he knew. The person you can't imagine a shift without, telling them things about yourself you wouldn't normally share, bonded by the endless hours spent alongside the other, and in your "real life" you might not hang out, but maybe one day. Everyone had this person at their job, if they were lucky.

Wyatt nodded again. "Talk's going around about Fernando; I'm sure you've heard. You think he really did it?"

My shoulders felt tight. Maybe that was why I didn't want to believe he'd killed her. Whenever workplaces insisted on calling employees "family," I called bullshit. And yet, at the café, we were tighter than most. Fernando hadn't been charged with anything. Whatever happened to innocent until proven guilty? In a town like ours there was no escaping the court of public opinion. Whether he was actually guilty wouldn't matter; he would carry this forever.

"That's what we're trying to figure out," I said.

"'We'? Are you working with the police or something? Your grandfather is retired, isn't he?"

"Gosh, no. And Leroy is retired, yes," I said a bit too fast. I didn't want him to know I was helping Leroy, or anyone really, not yet. "I'm curious. Involved by association whether I want to be or not. Did you also see her at the bonfire?"

"A little before I saw you, yeah. When I talked to the cops, I told them I thought she was looking for someone, but her words were slurred. Hard to understand what she was saying."

"You talked to her?"

"She pulled on my sleeve, but when I turned around, she said something like, 'I thought you were someone else.'"

"And you didn't see her after Nikki and I left?" I asked, my stomach in knots. I looked down at the blur of my pale feet under the rushing water, unable to meet his face. "I keep thinking I could've found her then. It's terrible because I should know better, but I—now I need to know what happened."

Wyatt's voice softened. "Annie, you can't think like that. And no, I didn't stay much longer after y'all left. Justin broke up that fight your cousin caused and it was getting kind of wild. That point of the night where you've either got to sober up and drive or take two shots. After Justin and his brother got it upright, these guys started doing keg stands and one threw up."

Even if they all were wasted, how was it that with that many people there, no one had seen anything? Maybe they had and didn't know it. I'd combed through any photos posted from that night, but all I discovered was the dramatic lighting Ashley, Macy, and Sabrina considered flattering for selfies, their long hair dangling awfully close to the fire. I paddled under the water to stop from shivering and felt myself drifting. The afternoon was waning and I felt I ought to get home, but I wanted also to spend the afternoon with Wyatt, talk about wild rice, anything else. A purple dragonfly skimmed the water and landed on his shoulder. He stood still and we were quiet until it flew off.

"That's good luck," I said.

He splashed me. "I'd tell you my wish, but it'd embarrass us both."

"Hey—what were you going to ask *me* the other night?"

"At the café? Probably for a refill." He grinned. "And if I could call you. See if you'd go to a movie with me." He squeezed my fingers under the water. At first, I registered it as him stopping me from drifting in the current, but even in the cold water, even though it was fleeting, I knew it was more.

"You might find my number in an old yearbook," I said.

"It's a date then."

I laughed. "I don't know, Wyatt."

"What?"

"Think I'm nervous."

"Don't be nervous. It's just me," he said. Wyatt, who'd been in the back of my mind for a long time, the Wyatt I'd known forever. Not quite déjà vu, not quite a dream. An inner vibration: I remembered one of the last nights we spent together before he left for college.

"You're not mad, are you? I just want to know what's going on," he'd said, and reached over to touch my face, hand brushing my cheek.

"I'm pretty good right now, us just being together," I'd said, and parked off the road behind his parents' house at the back of the property to drop him off. We'd been to the movies and, after, the café. The engine ticked and we sat for a long moment in the dark, neither reaching for the door.

"Want to hang out some more?" he asked. I said yes and he led me outside to the far side of their yard, behind a row of pecan trees where the family had set up a picnic table, some Adirondacks his dad had made himself, and a firepit with chalky heaps of ash. I sat on the arm of Wyatt's chair and we started kissing, touching.

"Annie, is this—"

"I want to," I said, covered his mouth with my free hand, then reached for the metal flask. I wanted part of myself to stay private from him, so I didn't speak, just took a pull of whiskey. Wyatt was smart, but it seemed in certain ways he was more innocent than I was—I already knew, I think, that we would break up—despite our age difference, despite him not being a virgin. I opened my palm. A tremor ticked through my fingers. We sat in the dark and I felt totally in my body then, and different than I had before. Heavier, like my bones were steeled. His body was warm and smoother than I thought it would be, the soft middle of his stomach tender, pale in the thin light of the moon. There was a scar the length of his right forearm where he'd held a lit Roman candle the wrong way a couple of Fourths back. I wondered if he felt nervous too, a feeling like someone standing over your shoulder. But I opened my eyes, looked at Wyatt, and that was it. The weight of him was somewhere between being held close, loved even, and being pressed like a leaf in the pages of a book.

"Stole it from my brother and he obviously can't call me on it," he'd said afterward, taking a thin joint from his pant pocket, and I laughed as he made a show of filling up his lungs, his chest widening. I hugged his waist and wanted to cry not because I was hurt, or unhappy, but because I was exhausted with being so cavalier. It mattered; it did. Tomorrow it might be different between us, I'd thought—good or bad.

I ducked underwater and the cold current moved my hair back from my face. When I surfaced, Wyatt was still there smiling, and for a moment the world seemed clean and bright and safe again. I stood and kissed his mouth.

"It's just me," I said. "You know me."

Chapter 21

I had the feeling of waiting so long for something exciting to happen. Maybe I am only remembering the buzzing under my skin and the tightness in my chest now, now that I know. Yesterday Once More didn't seem quite real. Like I'd imagined it, called it up after a lifetime of blue Sunday nights listening to country and western, dreaming of spinning out on the dance floor in a bright turquoise dress and white cowgirl boots. I heard the music first: fiddle, steel pedal so sharp it cut the air.

"Little darlin'"—I hear his voice and my heart cracks wide open.

The barroom was dimly lit and smoky. At the door Jimmy Ryland took our cover, three dollars apiece, barely looked up from where he was sitting in a foldout chair with his cane propped at his side. There were other vets Leroy's age and a handful of younger servicemen and -women. Some I knew; most I didn't. And then there were the even more lonesome-looking folks nursing whiskeys, not talking, closing their eyes when a song they liked came on. It was early—there would be a country band in an hour; in the meantime the jukebox played oldies. There were happy-seeming folks practicing their two-stepping and their western swing, showing off their moves.

It had a mysterious charm. Like you had stepped into another time, removed from everything else.

Leroy sat in a chair at the perimeter of the wooden dance floor while I went to get us beers. The bartender was a stranger to me, middle-aged, but I felt as though he could have been a friend—he had the eyes, I suppose, a way of looking at you that made you feel like you and he had inside jokes. I walked through a haze of his Newport smoke and leaned my elbows on the bar.

He unabashedly looked me up and down. "Hey, girl, what's good?"

"Two Shiners, please." Framed and faded photographs of service members intermixed with velvet renderings of western landscapes and a Texas flag hung on the wall behind him. There was no tap, just a big ice chest with beer, Cokes, and a bottle of Barefoot wine. Setups but no liquor. I put on my best smile, asked, "Remember a girl who used to come in here, about my age, with long hair, darker than mine? Victoria?"

He pulled out two longnecks, hesitating. "Girl who got killed?"

I handed him my card. "Did you ever talk to her?"

"Cash only, doll."

I pulled some bills from my wallet, put a little extra in the pickle jar he had set out.

His eyes lit up, but his mouth was still set. "You don't look like a cop." He pried the beers open with the metal rim of the bar top.

"That's 'cause I'm not. In fact, I don't know the cops are doing all that great a job. She was my friend and I'm just trying to get some answers."

"Can't understand it. Girl was a pistol, sure, but she was real nice, not loud, not out borrowing trouble far as I could tell. Took Granny out every week until she passed."

"You knew her grandmother?"

"Rita was married to one of our veterans. They came here a lot when he was still alive, for bridge, bingo. The post was special to her. Shit, I was sad to hear about that lady, and now this? The girl came herself a few times. You could tell she wasn't taking it so well," he said, turning his gaze down. "Drinking too much."

"She ever bring a date?"

"She had a lot of dates," he said.

I raised my eyebrows.

"Now, now, I don't mean that in any kind of way. Just she was pretty and had lots of attention," he said, and held his palms out.

"Do you remember the last time she was here?"

"Yeah, a couple weeks ago. She talked to the guy in the band, can't remember which. And some blond guy, I remember. There was a bit of an argument. Nothing serious, no fists."

"You know who he was? Why they were fighting?"

He shook his head and shrugged. "Hadn't seen him before. They didn't stay long. You asking these questions, I just don't know," he said, and slid his eyes away. "This other lady was also asking questions about her and I said to mind her own business. I'm not much of a bartender if I can't keep anybody's confidences."

"Me? Come on," I said, leaning on the bar top. "Which lady am I like?"

"You're not like her." He snickered. "Know Mike Barnes? His wife, Gloria, I think."

"Glory," I said. He nodded, but a group came up to the bar

151

and started shouting orders, edging me aside. "I'll be back," I said, but he didn't hear.

I took the beers with me back to the table. Leroy was no longer sitting. He'd left on the table the car keys and a couple of empty glasses, no idea who he'd gotten them from, and was dancing with some lady. I watched him move across the floor. The arm in the sling didn't seem to bother him or affect his balance. His two-step wasn't as much a count as it was a fast shuffle, like how good dancers seem to float.

"Annie, right?" A young man came up and offered his hand. "Want to dance?" I took his hand and he placed the other on the small of my back. It was a fast song and at first I couldn't find the rhythm. But then I looked up at the lights, soft pink and blue, and all the smiling people. Relaxed and let the drumbeat lead me.

"I recognize you from Marlene's," he said.

"Sonny, yeah, I remember you."

He'd been in basic with Marlene's son, Travis. He came in one day as I was leaving, Marlene cooing over him, giving him extra pie, and asking after the son who never called or wrote. I'd felt her loneliness so keenly that day and think for that reason Sonny was forever endeared to me. He'd been sweet to Marlene, had stayed over an hour to visit with her, long after he'd finished eating. The song ended and I motioned back to the table where I'd left my beer. We sat and Sonny reached over to the table next to Leroy's and mine, grabbed a bottle of Jack, then measured out two fingers into the plastic cups on our table.

"You home for a while?"

"Ended my last tour with some injuries," he said softly so I almost couldn't hear him. "Three surgeries and almost a year driving back and forth to the VA for rehab, I'm home for good."

I nodded, not sure quite what to say. After a pause, "You ever hear from Travis?"

"Not since he left overseas. I'm sure Miz Marlene is missing him."

"She does; I know that," I said, and, silently, a prayer for Travis. Sonny, unlike Travis, seemed unthreatening. He had traditional good looks: strong jawline, symmetry to his face. Light eyes and eyelashes, his hair pale and close cut, gave him a kind of blurred look. The scar tissue was hardly visible, a shiny patch of pink skin at the base of his neck. Did it extend down his back, his chest? He wore long shirtsleeves buttoned at the wrists despite the heat. "Sonny," I said, "you come in here a lot?"

"I can't dance as well as some." He laughed. "I like it, though. The post is good."

"Did you know the girl who got kill—"

"Victoria? Damn." He looked off for a moment. "Yes, but not well. Sounds stupid, but I just keep thinking about how I never got up the nerve to ask her out; well, then again, she seemed to want to be alone."

"What makes you say that?"

"She flipped out that one night. I understand it—you girls got guys hounding you, maybe you're not looking for that—I get it. Anyway, some men come in here, drunk, loud, hitting on her. Then I hear her yell, and I mean yell, '*Mind your fucking business! Stay off my land!*' I thought one had tried following her home."

The hair on the back of my neck stood up—the bartender had also mentioned an argument. "Did you tell the cops this?"

He shook his head. "Never asked."

"She's fighting with someone—loudly, in public—then ends up killed."

"Well, when you put it that way," he said, and rubbed his chin.

"But it was probably no big deal, right? It might've been nothing, guys being guys. But I'll go in tomorrow, if you think I should."

"Might be a good idea," I said. *Damn.* She'd been upset with a guy in here; somewhere along the way Glory got involved; then she wound up dead. I needed to figure out how, and if the events of her last time here equaled murder. Then again, maybe the answer had already presented itself: Fernando looked guilty as hell. Why did something nag at me? The night she died was a Thursday, and on Thursdays she went to Yesterday Once More. She'd mentioned it to me at the café too, I remembered. This was where she was supposed to be the night of her death, not the bonfire, I thought, noticing the way the room was more shadow than light, how the families had left now that it was after sundown. She'd hardly known anyone at the bonfire. This, this was her place.

"You look pretty tonight." Sonny tipped his chair back and took a drink. "Hope you don't mind me saying."

"First time seeing me without a stained apron and smelling like fryer grease." I laughed, but I did feel fancy in the dress and boots. Getting ready I'd sat at my old-fashioned vanity, once Mamaw's, and thought about how she used to say, "Go on, play pretty," while I dug through her case of old Avon products. How I'd smear waxy lipstick across my mouth and paint my lids blue and long to be some fancy, grown-up lady. There was a grown woman in the mirror now, but still, that longing—she wasn't quite who I'd expected to see.

"I'm getting you another beer," Sonny said, and pushed his chair back, just as Leroy called out to me, motioned for me to join him on the dance floor.

We'd danced—him, my mother, Dad, Mamaw, and me—

countless times before in the living room at home to all their favorite records: me a little girl standing on the tops of his boots, then later, as a preteen frowning, gawky, my ankles cracking with each step. That night at Yesterday Once More was the first time I'd danced with him in public, and I could see concentration but also joy on his face. The song was one of his favorites, "Fraulein": "When my memories wander away over yonder . . ." Leroy sang along, his heels greasing the floor, me spinning. The steel pedal and fiddle cried, and he seemed moved, his face watery from a mix of sweat and maybe tears.

"Your grandmother. She liked this one."

"I miss her."

He nodded, but his eyes darted away. He watched the other dancers swinging out around us, smiled, and winked at a young man nervously escorting a date onto the floor.

"Granddad, I heard something might be important; if you want to go sit, I'll—"

"Oh, in a bit," he said, and spun me with his good arm. "The first step in any missing person, any homicide, investigation is to identify the victim."

"Okay, but we knew Victoria. I knew Victoria."

He looked at me, halfway smiled. "Did you? Really?"

He wasn't even investigating, I realized; he just wanted to drink and to dance. But I'd come along for this too: to indulge Leroy, to see him in his element. Before this was Victoria's favorite place it had been his. Most of the other dancers knew him, waved and smiled when they saw him. The song ended, and after I let go of his hand he swung back out again. I saw Sonny sitting with my beer out of the corner of my eye and went to join him. Leroy paired up with someone else, taking breaks at the bar for swigs of beer or whiskey. Sonny and I drank more too, made up stories about the couple under the disco light wearing elaborately embroidered boots, he in a blue polyester suit and she in a rhinestone-studded vest.

"Decades ago, they robbed banks, got rich, and spent it all one wild weekend in Vegas," I mused.

Sonny laughed. "Bet they're swingers." Really, they were wrinkled and kind of sweet looking, someone's grandparents. But I knew they must have secrets, shame, drama shared between them. I dreamed once that my mamaw was sitting in the plastic-covered rocker-recliner on the porch and one by one reenacting all her major fights with Leroy. Yelling at him—"You're sick. An alcoholic. Foolish and impractical!"—while a long trail of blood browned and dried down the front of her housecoat. The dream frightened me, and I never told anyone for fear it was either inappropriate or bad luck, since not long after the dream Mamaw got sick and passed away. I wondered if Leroy felt like that—like all he could do was replay, rewind, repeat.

For me, for many people, wasn't the past the thing you wanted to escape?

But of course, Yesterday Once More wasn't real. This room, this music, the cotton candy feel in my head from the drink, this was the pretty past. All lit up in soft pink neon, rhinestone rainbows popping on the ceiling as the disco ball turned.

The band was taking their time setting up on the stage at the front of the room. Leroy made a beeline for the vacant jukebox, the fluorescent light from the catalog illuminating his ruddy face. "Another on me. I insist," Sonny said, taking his hand and making a drinking motion, then moving his head all sloppily. I nodded, acknowledging the obvious trajectory of the night. But it made me uncomfortable. *A night can go up, up, up before it crashes*, I thought, watching the dancers spin like tops.

Beer in hand, Leroy came to our table.

"Sheriff McIntyre." Sonny stood and offered Leroy his hand. "Honored to meet you. And I'm an army man myself."

"Thank you for your service." Leroy smiled faintly and sat.

"You once saved my mother's life. The bank robbery in Parr City, when you—"

Leroy waved his hand in the air. "Shoot, that had to have been thirty years ago. Only doing my job. I'm glad she was okay."

Between my pride and the drink hitting my bloodstream, a feeling of warmth washed over me. I'd of course heard about it. Many times. Ten people and three tellers had been held at gunpoint, one shot and critically wounded, when Leroy and his deputy, a fresh-faced rookie named Mary-Pat, snuck in the building through an air vent in the ceiling and ended the stand-off. Both robbers lived but were doing life in Huntsville.

"You're a real legend at our house."

"Thank you, son."

Leroy's song came up on the jukebox, the last one before the band started. He had chosen "The Tears of a Clown," and he alone got up and started on a strange dance that involved hip movement (to my horror) and a sway that was not altogether under his control. He did a hop-step-spin to the shrill, calliope part of the music, like a circus elephant on a tightrope. There was a syrupy sadness to his cheer—the frown upside down!— but the minstrel was well received by the others, who then proceeded to join him in a conga line that snaked around the floor.

Later, he went out the back door to vomit in the dirt.

"Let's go home," I said. "Do you need to go to the hospital?"

He laughed, widened his eyes, and shook his head as though I'd suggested we fly to the moon. A zip of irritation shot up my spine. It was his lack of control, the way you could be having a good time and then he would take it too far. Nikki could be that way too, but she and I could at least call bullshit on the other. I couldn't tell Leroy no. Anyway, he'd drink more at home, only alone. And if honest, I was too buzzed to drive.

"Relax, darlin'. If you don't relax you will miss things," he said.

I looked at the sliver of neon light under the door. Wondered if he knew how he'd struck a chord, such a long-held anxiety of mine. Relax, lighten up—I'd always felt a little on the outside of things as they were happening. Watching instead of experiencing. That night, though having fun, I had had this feeling. Mourning a moment that hasn't yet passed. A soft-sided sadness I now understand as love. Constant fear of losing the ones you love. Leroy stood and wiped his mouth with his shirtsleeve and I walked him back across the barroom.

The rest of the night is fuzzy in my mind. The band played—they weren't great, but no one seemed to mind because you could dance to it. There were a couple more dances with Sonny, surely, because I distinctly remember my arm hooked over his strong shoulder, my chin resting in the soft spot between his collarbone and neck that smelled dusky, private, and his hand guiding the small of my back as we moved across the floor. Plastic cups sweated in people's hands and a man sitting alone by the window absentmindedly drew stick figures in the condensation that glowed every time a car turned its headlights on in the lot outside. The click and rumble of the shoddy air conditioner finally coming on was enough to get a small cheer from the floor.

It was around this time that the men from Artemis came in. Three men in the thick denim and red company-issued shirts, they hadn't changed their boots from the work site. A man with blond hair, lanky and tan, was Randy, the one Nikki and I had talked to at the icehouse the other night. He had also been at the bonfire, Victoria in his lap. My head spinning, I stepped into a dark corner and hoped he wouldn't recognize me. I wasn't sure what he would think—I was afraid they would still be mad—and was nervous. I hated that. Hated my heart hammering against my rib cage, a fight-or-flight response. Maybe them being older made their looking seem leering. Made their desire too naked, too raw. Tall, blond—I pictured Randy, hazy like a nightmare, coming up a dark dirt road after work to peer into a young woman's bedroom. Could he be the one who'd startled Lillie Anderson at her home one night?

Randy and his crew watched the stage, and when the band took a break between sets they came closer, ribbing the drummer. Long, ropy arms covered in ink, gauges in his ears, the drummer was familiar. I realized then he had been at the icehouse too. Steve, I remembered. Randy pulled some folding chairs away from the wall and made a semi-circle facing the crowd instead of the band as they got back to playing, then pulled out a bottle of tequila and passed it around.

"Sonny," I said, "are those the men Victoria argued with?"

He shrugged and squinted his eyes, red rimmed now and glassy. "Maybe. Yeah, sure."

"She talked to the drummer? Or the other man, the tall one?"

"There was a group of guys she was talking to. One was a blond guy, tall, wore one of those red polo shirts I seem to remember. Knew him from somewhere. I wasn't with them, though, you know? I only really paid attention when she started hollering and they started leaving."

I tried to locate Leroy. Of course, I was not thinking clearly—Sonny's bottle of Jack was nearly empty—but it was like a buzzer sounded inside me. Maybe I could get one of them alone, if I worked up enough courage. Not seeing Leroy, I made like I was going to the restroom and slipped out the back door to the parking lot. My feet were unsteady and I skidded on the loose gravel. The bright red and blue of the Artemis logo on the white dually made their truck easy to spot. I don't know what I thought would come of going out there, but I had the brilliant idea I should set up a kind of surveillance. Or maybe I wanted to rest my head. I don't remember. Parking the bullet across from their truck, I sat in the driver's seat, watching the door, waiting for them to come out.

I woke with my neck craned weirdly against the window and dried drool on my chin. Leroy was leaned back in the passenger seat, his cowboy hat tipped over his face to block out the rising sun.

"Crap, crap, crap," I muttered to myself, and reached for the keys that had fallen onto the floorboard. When I lifted my head it hurt so badly I had to close my eyes again. The men from Artemis were of course long gone, as was every other car in the lot. I turned the key and the dashboard clock said six.

"Morning," Leroy said, and sat up straight in his seat. "What do you say we go to Walmart. You know I'd like some powdery donut holes."

The thought of walking through fluorescent-lit aisles made me nauseated. "You don't want to sit somewhere? Order real food like bacon and eggs?"

"A little something sweet will be fine."

"Sorry I made you sleep in the car. Wasn't planning on having so much to drink."

"That's okay," he said, and looked in the rearview, lightly touching the stitches on his face. "I had a fine time."

"It's not fine. I feel like crap and I've treated you like crap by not getting you home." I moved my tongue across my dry lips and wished for water. "This thing with her land and these oil company men—something's wrong."

"What happened to her will come to light." He buckled his seat belt and motioned for me to get going.

I started backing out and onto the highway. "Will it?"

"In a way the truth usually comes out."

"It's just that *everything* feels wrong." My head throbbed and the sun in my eyes nearly brought me to tears. What had happened in the nighttime? I hadn't been awake and I had missed it. I felt like a child wondering the exact moment dew had beaded on the grass, what spider had spun such a glittering web. Both awed and made fretful by the long dark.

"I guess you're looking for advice," he said.

"I guess I am."

"Take Ranch Road Thirty. It's faster and less bumpy."

"Good talk."

He was quiet for a moment. "Don't fear the mystery, darlin'. All I have to say right now is don't be afraid."

Chapter 22

Victoria was buried next to her grandparents in the city cemetery on the east side of town, adjacent to the railroad, and beyond
it the interstate. Trucks whizzed past on their way to someplace
else and I imagined these souls shooting up from the ground
like sparklers and leaving just as fast. I didn't think Victoria
would linger here. I didn't feel her here.

"Let us pray." The minister looked over his glasses at us, per-
spiration gleaming on his upper lip.

When I was sure everyone else's heads were bowed, I looked
at Brandon and Glory, each holding one of the little girl's hands.
Glory didn't have her eyes closed. She dipped her head in my
direction, embarrassed perhaps. The minister was one from
Glory's church, the Garnett Church of Christ. Victoria didn't
attend service anywhere when she was alive, to her mother-in-
law's apparent dismay, hadn't even wanted a church wedding,
or any wedding, for that matter. Victoria said it had been Glory
wielding the proverbial shotgun at Victoria and Brandon's wedding, and in some ways it seemed as though her funeral service was more about what Glory wanted. "I'm paying for the

whole thing. Not like I mind. I don't," she'd loudly whispered to the minister's wife as she helped her place one of several wreaths wound with pink ribbon and sprays of baby's breath at the stone. The decorations were gaudy, frilly, and did little to remind me of Victoria.

We milled about the parking lot before heading to Glory's home for a small reception. There weren't many others in attendance: a cousin of Victoria's late mother had driven down from Abilene, a couple of high school friends from Parr City, staff from the funeral home and Glory's church, and I'd driven Marlene. No one had been able to reach Victoria's father. No one had either seen or heard from him since his release from prison four years ago—Victoria once told me she assumed he was dead—and so little effort had been made to find him. She hadn't spoken much of her mother in the time I knew her, but once during one of our listening sessions in her car she'd told me that she was only thirteen when her mother had been killed in an accident on the way home from a bar.

"Where are Dot and Fernando?" Marlene looked around. "I told them to lock the door and put a sign up. People will understand."

"Maybe they'll meet us at the reception. Maybe they got the time wrong," I said, wondering if Fernando forgot on purpose. Did he feel like he wouldn't be welcome, given the suspicion? It seemed to me like not coming was more damning. Marlene didn't seem to know that Fernando was being investigated. How she managed to not was beyond me, given the gossip mill that was the café. Maybe she willfully ignored it—it would be hard, especially when you lived upstairs, if you considered one of your employees might be a murderer.

"I suppose we better go to the house with the family. I wish to God this hadn't happened to that little girl. To grow up without your momma is a hard thing," Marlene said, and pulled some Kleenex from her purse. *Or to be someone's momma*, I thought. My mother used to say she was still her own person, but her heart—me—simply beat outside her chest. I watched Brandon hand off his daughter to his girlfriend. And Kylee, red-faced in a black yoke dress that looked tight at the neck, squirmed so she nearly fell out of the woman's arms. She tugged at a matching bow barrette tangled in her baby curls and whimpered. It was so unfair. All of it, unfair.

I remembered the day I walked in on her in the bathroom. Victoria had stood in front of the mirror with her work shirt bunched under her armpits and was examining her stomach. "What are you doing?" I asked, not able to hold back my laughter.

She'd worn a red bikini underneath her clothes. I noticed then that the top button of her pants was undone and an open bottle of liquid foundation rested on the sink. "I'm supposed to meet this guy at the river and don't have time to drive home," she said, and pulled her shirt down, but not before I realized she'd been applying the makeup over her cesarean scar.

"Won't that just come off in the water?"

"You're so damn nosy. Just get out," she said, and pointed at the door. Her voice was hard, croaky with tears at the same time, and she wouldn't look at me.

"Sorry," I said, standing beside her so we both faced the mirror. "But I think you look great, and if this guy doesn't like all of you, if he's so dumb to care about your kid or—"

"I said get out." She stared straight ahead. "You don't know shit."

We followed the family out of the cemetery. The noon sun was bright and the air dry. My shoulders burned in the high-necked but sleeveless navy dress I wore, the one I'd bought for Mamaw's funeral and never looked at again until that day. Just as I was about to unlock the bullet, Marlene and I saw Dot's brown minivan come down the narrow lane to the cemetery and careen into a spot by the gate. "She must have realized she was late and tore out; her apron's still on," I said. Dot slammed the car door and hurried past Glory, Kylee, Brandon, and his girlfriend toward Marlene and me.

"What on earth is the matter with you? You missed the service," Marlene said.

Dot was bent over, hands on her knees trying to catch her breath. "They came into the café and took him away," she said, her voice shaking.

Glory came closer. "What?"

"Fernando," I said, my chest tightening.

"The cops arrested him for—for her," Dot said, pointing toward the freshly tilled earth, her face pale. The handful of guests who hadn't left formed a circle around her.

"Oh my. That Ranger said they'd be making an arrest soon. Thank God," Glory said to Brandon, who'd come up alongside her. Brandon bit his lower lip and looked down. Glory embraced him, but he stood stock-still.

His girlfriend, Melody, patted Kylee on the back, cooing, "They got him, baby; they got who done the bad thing to your momma."

I took Dot's clammy hand, felt a rapid flutter in her wrist before she shook loose. "We were cleaning up, had already closed for the funeral, when the Ranger and some state troopers come with weapons drawn. Yelled at me to open the door and get down, they've got the building surrounded." Dot started to cry. "I was so scared. They slammed him hard against the counter and cuffed his wrists. Broke a glass."

"Why?" I said, and wiped my sweating palms on my dress. "He's not a damn fugitive."

"Surely this is a misunderstanding," Marlene said, verging on tears.

"Fernando didn't say anything, just got this terrible, blank look on his face," Dot said. "It was like something in him completely shut off."

The arrest happened in time for Sheriff Garcia and the Texas Ranger assigned to the case to deliver a press conference at the five o'clock news hour. Stations in Austin, San Antonio, Houston, and Dallas all picked up the story:

> An arrest has been made in the investigation into the murder of Victoria Merritt, 22, of Garnett, Texas, who was found strangled in a wooded section of private ranchland off State Highway 125 on September 10th. Fernando Garza, 21, also of Garnett, has been charged with her homicide after cell phone records were obtained by law enforcement and DNA evidence belonging to the victim was recovered from inside Garza's vehicle.

Sitting upstairs in Marlene's apartment, she and a still-shaken Dot on either side of me, I heard the words, and that night I read them over again. Scrolled through each posting of the story on my news feed and read every comment ranging from grief to bloodlust. There it was, over and done. There would be a trial, yes, but the uncertainty, the fear of an unknown killer on the loose, was put to rest. Fernando killed Victoria. A shovelful of earth tossed over her grave.

Chapter 23

For the first time in nearly ten years, Marlene closed the café for the rest of the day and night. People banged on the windows. People called. People hung out in the parking lot behind the building, unsure where to go. So, Marlene opened again in the morning with Dot and me waiting tables. Save for the high school football field, there wasn't a community space in Garnett. The café was the beating red heart of our town. It was hot inside, thick with dread, and I didn't want to be there, but I was needed and it felt good to be needed at a time like that.

Sheila sat in her usual booth. The ranchers and the old men sat by the window. The cops sat in their usual spot by the door. Stony-faced, they let their radios blip and buzz without turning them down—adding to people's alarm—while they refueled on coffee and pie. More drivers off the highway than usual; they'd heard murder on the radio and come out of morbid curiosity. Reporters came, people I hadn't seen in weeks, months, came to eat and swap gossip.

"Pretty little thing, kinda trashy."

"He had his way with her."

Marlene sweated through her apron. The dishes piled up in the sink and the trash needed to go out, but still, after lunch she told Dot and me to go home. Both of us offered to keep working, but she shook her head. Her cousin from Haskell was coming down to stay for a few days, and the two part-time high school kids committed to more hours, despite their parents' concerns that they, too, be tainted by the strong stink of death in this place.

"Fine," I said, guilty for leaving, but relieved to escape the refrain.

"Mexican that worked in the back, the big one."

"Choked her with his bare hands."

"Thought he could get away with it."

God damn these people and this place. I sat on the bench outside the café and looked across the street to the redbrick building. Mary-Pat's Silverado was parked out front, but the shades were drawn upstairs. A thin, hunched-over lady with dark hair wound into a tight bun and wearing a blue velvet tracksuit tried the door to the stairwell. Hustling to catch her, I nearly got clipped by a pickup truck—the driver honked and the lady turned around.

"Are you going to the law office?" I called, coming closer.

"McIntyre Investigations," she said. Her eyes were puffy and red rimmed, and a scribble of hastily applied lipstick pilled at the corners of her frown. She was older, maybe in her seventies, and I'd met her a long time ago, back in elementary school, when she'd brought a box of pink and yellow *conchas* for a class party.

"You're Fernando's grandmother."

She straightened her shoulders and nodded. "Fernando didn't do it."

"I'm Mr. McIntyre's granddaughter, Annie. Let's get you inside."

As I closed the outer door behind me, I heard a tapping on the stairs. I looked up to see Mary-Pat drumming her fingers on the railing.

"What are you doing here?"

"I saw Mrs. Garza outside and I decided to escort her in," I said, and helped the woman up the last of the steps, pointed toward the open door to the office.

Mary-Pat sighed and took her elbow, directing her toward a chair. "Ma'am, I hate that you came all the way here. I was just fixing to call you back."

Mrs. Garza opened her purse, took out a wad of cash, and silently handed it to Mary-Pat.

Mary-Pat shook her head. "The investigators have physical evidence. Put that toward a good lawyer."

Mrs. Garza pushed the money into Mary-Pat's hand anyway. "I can get more later. I need you to prove he didn't do it. His lawyer isn't listening. She doesn't even care. . . ." She paused, her eyes searching Mary-Pat's. "My daughter-in-law can't handle the stress, is bedridden, and my son is offshore for another month. It's up to me to fix it." She straightened her shoulders. I knew Fernando's mother had lupus or something autoimmune related and his father, while still financially supporting them working on a rig in Louisiana, was never home; the elder Mrs. Garza had been the primary caregiver as long as I'd known Fernando.

Mary-Pat sat down heavily in the swivel chair. "It's not only about money. Listen, you need to get on the same page with the lawyer. She works for him. She's a public defender, and I know sometimes they get overworked but—"

"She wants him to plead guilty!"

"Do you know he didn't do it?" I said.

It got very quiet for a moment. Both women stared at me.

Mrs. Garza blinked. "You think I don't know my own grand-son?"

"Help us then. Tell us something," I said, and looked at Mary-Pat, for approval I suppose, but she had her gaze fixed on Mrs. Garza.

"He says he was with someone at Estrella Club, a young woman. No one's been able to find her and I think the lawyer thinks he's made her up," she said.

"What's the woman's name?" I asked.

"He doesn't remember. He says maybe Maria or Marina. It started with *M*. He hadn't met her before that night, but he bought her a drink and they talked outside, sitting on the tail-gate of someone's truck, he says, in the parking lot for over an hour. He'd been drinking too."

"Did he say what she looked like?"

"Bleached-blond, nearly white hair pulled back. A line of scrip-ture tattooed right under the collarbone. A mole." She touched the skin above her upper lip. "A beauty mark, he said, dark lip-stick, and dark skin. She was tiny but stout, and pretty, he says."

My hands felt tingly. A picture flashed through my mind, but I couldn't bring it back. Who did I know who looked like that in Garnett? Where was I?

Mary-Pat finally spoke. "No one else saw them? His lawyer asked around?"

"I don't know; I don't think so," she said, her chin trembling. "That's why I need help. I thought I could trust Mr. McIntyre."

"Okay," Mary-Pat said. "We'll do our best to follow up on some loose ends we don't think have been fully investigated and present it to his lawyer, should she need it."

"Thank you, thank you," she said. Her whole body seemed to relax, if only for a moment. "Fernando is everything to me and to his family. He is a good boy. Really, he is."

Mary-Pat nodded, and I resisted saying anything more until Mrs. Garza had walked down the stairs. I watched from the window as she exited the building, then crossed the street toward an old sedan with sun-faded Garnett Steers Football bumper stickers. Her grandson really had been a standout on the field. Powerhouse, they called him, or by his jersey number, sixty-six. "Look out, here comes Sixes," people said, both teasing and with pride. Mrs. Garza had seen her boy suffer blow after blow—his knee, his scholarship, and his future—and now his very life. She looked up at the sky before getting in the car. The sun was on her face and she clasped her hands together. Moving her lips, her eyes shut tight as she stood rocking on her heels. Praying, I realized.

"I don't want to get her hopes up and take all her money," Mary-Pat said. "Fernando is going to be convicted. His lawyer might at least be able to get his sentence reduced."

"He says he's innocent."

Mary-Pat looked like she wanted to shake me. Instead, she took a deep breath and stood, putting her hand on my arm. "Listen, Annie, I stand by my word. I promised to follow through. I want you to lay low, though. I can handle this."

"My granddad says I'm his apprentice and yours. And now we have a paying client. It's an official investigation."

She stepped back, wagging her finger. "He is supposed to be retired, and you don't know what you're getting into. I was thinking of training you on simple surveillance, not a murder investigation."

I paused, weighing what I said next.

"The name on the door is McIntyre. As in 'Leroy McIntyre,' as in 'Annie McIntyre.'"

She narrowed her eyes. I couldn't tell if she was angry or a little impressed that I'd pulled rank. I immediately regretted it, though—I knew the place might as well be hers.

"You're right. It's not on me," she said, and reached for her laptop bag. Pointed to the extra chair in the corner. "We have work to do."

"Thank you," I said, breathing a sigh of relief.

"I said we have work to do. Sit your ass down."

Leroy's ears must have been burning. He showed up at the office right before I got the chance to call him. It took him forever to climb the stairs, and I felt a twinge of guilt: maybe Mary-Pat was right and I should have kept Leroy and myself out of this.

But it was too late now. We had a client.

Leroy did a double take when he saw me. I hugged him and he sat, letting out a long breath. His face was red and he started scratching at his arm in the sling.

"How did you get here?" Mary-Pat asked.

"Hitched a ride with Marty Santos."

"Marty Santos doesn't have a car and that camper hasn't moved in a decade," I said. "What're you talking about?"

"I said we hitched. I had got a ride with the neighbor over to the place, saw Marty, and we got to walking down the road and thought we'd hit town. Some hand gave us a lift."

"Good Lord."

"You heard about Fernando Garza, I'm guessing," Mary-Pat said.

"I did."

"His grandmother was just here wanting to hire you."

Leroy nodded. "Thought she might. I've known Rosie a long time. She's a good person. Don't know her grandson, but maybe he's in over his head."

Mary-Pat stared back at him, unmoved. I was beginning to learn that was her assessing, thinking, but damn she looked angry.

"He looks guilty as hell," Leroy added.

"Mary-Pat was filling me in on what she's learned from the sheriff before you came in. Tell him about the blood," I nudged her.

"Basically, Garcia acknowledged she didn't bleed. She was highly inebriated and there wasn't much of a struggle after their hands were around her neck," she said. "And it should be noted that no DNA could be recovered from the victim's body—the rain and the elements took too much a toll. The evidence obtained is *only* from Fernando's vehicle."

"The DNA is probably hair, or fibers," I said, feeling hot, antsy. The late-afternoon sun beamed through the sides of the drawn shades. Cheap shades poorly fitted to the big old windows. "And we know—Fernando admits—she rode in his car to the bonfire."

"The D.A. seems to think whatever they have is enough, but I can see it being not nearly enough." Mary-Pat paced. The more she walked, talked, the more animated her face became. "Mrs. Garza did say there's a possible witness the law hasn't been able to locate. A girl he was with in the Estrella Club parking lot."

"We've got our work cut out for us, then," Leroy said.

"They don't know who she is," Mary-Pat sighed. "Dang, it's already five. I don't know what we'll do, other than go to the club and ask around. He doesn't even remember her first name."

Already five. Dust motes floated in a stream of sunlight. I thought for a moment. "But I might."

Chapter 24

"Don Juan's?" Nikki looked at me. "You're sure?"

"Yes. It was when I brought the spare that time you locked your keys in the car," I said.

"That hostess gig was the worst, not even the hardest, just the worst. Manager made me wear heels and wouldn't let me sit down the entire shift. Couldn't talk to the servers, either, 'cause he thought they'd persuade me to give one person more tables than the other."

"What's that joke customers always made?"

She rolled her eyes. "'Sir, will you sit in the main restaurant or in the tapas lounge?' I'd say, and this old fart—always an old fart—would chuckle, say, 'There's a topless lounge?' Every damn time."

I couldn't help but laugh. "Sorry."

I knew she didn't want to go inside the restaurant—a popular "date night" place in Colburn she'd worked at for about six weeks before getting her chair at the Beauty Shoppe—but I realized back in the office that this was the place I'd seen the mystery woman. Standing next to Nikki's ex, Bobby, had been his cousin Monica. "It's already five," she'd said. "I need to go." He was her ride, and he wanted to wait with Nikki in the parking lot for me to get there.

"She has the same tattoo, same hair. And a Monroe piercing," I said. "Not a beauty mark. But I'm almost certain she's the woman Fernando was with. It's worth checking, anyhow."

"Yeah, I remember her," Nikki said. "But Bobby, ugh. Note to self: never date a coworker."

"You said she's a dishwasher?"

"Back then, anyway." She bit her lip. "There's a lot of turnover."

We were in front of a run-down but surprisingly busy strip mall near the county line. Don Juan's anchored one end of it and was next to the China Palace Buffet, Nails 2003, and a tanning salon called Bottoms Up. The whir of industrial-sized fans on the restaurant's empty patio mixed with the highway sounds and the bicker of families shuffling to and from their cars. I got out and motioned for Nikki to follow. I thought it best we enter behind the building at the kitchen so we might catch Monica without her manager, but as we walked across the expanse of parking lot, our heels sinking in ribbons of soft tar, my sense of unease grew. The world seemed to me flattened, dulled from a long day of ceaseless sun and blacktop. It was dusk and maybe my eyes were tired, but I felt as though I couldn't see as well as if it were fully dark, as though the half-light blurred my vision more.

Realizing I was alone, I turned back. Nikki lingered by the corner of the building, stood on one leg and fiddled with the strap of her sandal. Nikki, excited when I'd phoned to tell her what was going on, chatty when I picked her up from work, now hesitated—why? My thought was that if I involved her in the investigation, she would be more supportive, because part of me wondered if she wasn't so much afraid as she was sore with me for leaving her out. Her messy bun was coming loose and she moved a piece of hair behind her ear over and over again.

"Still mad at me?"

I kicked at a soggy cardboard box and jumped as a roach skittered out from underneath. The dumpster behind the building overflowed, and a strong smell of rot leached out. This place made me grateful for Marlene and the café. The café was old and tired, but at least it was old and tired and scrubbed clean.

"Mad? A little," Nikki said, and shooed a fly from her face. "This is dangerous, despite what your crazy granddad says."

"What I recall, Monica's like five-one, so guess I'm not intimidated."

"Don't." She made a noise like a growl. "Don't act like I'm not right. I know you're *always* right, but—"

"No. You're right," I said, knowing I should have said so earlier. We never went this long without making up. And she'd had a point when we'd fought: Getting involved with Leroy's firm, never mind a murder investigation, was dangerous. And seemingly out of the blue. One day I was looking for copywriting jobs at PR firms and thinking about the LSAT; the next I was a private investigator's apprentice. I couldn't quite explain to her that an unnamed desire had been building for a long time. Like a tight coil inside my chest now sprung. "If you don't like it," I said carefully, "why'd you agree to come?"

"Someone's got to mind you," she said, smirking. "It's just that I know you're going to do it. Try this out. You're nosy, stubborn. I know you better than anyone, that you can't stand this town, so I also kind of wonder what your long game is."

"Yeah, sometimes I can't stand it. But I don't hate it. I love it. I'm beginning to think you just don't want me here. And by the way, you've never minded me. You act like you never left, but you left me first," I said in a breathless rush, my chest constricted again. An image: Nikki, eighteen and packing her dad's truck for her move up to Austin, so happy, and me, seventeen, tears running down my cheeks and into my mouth as I watched from inside the house. Maybe she didn't care. Maybe she simply didn't need me like I needed her, and never had.

My fists were balled, and before I could think better of it I said, "You would've stayed gone if you could've hacked school."

As soon as the words left my mouth, I regretted them.

Nikki stood quietly for a few moments, and her face crumpled. "Guess we all can't be as smart as you."

"It was hard for me," I stammered. "And even with a degree—that I'm majorly in debt for, by the way—I haven't found anything else, so who's the smart one? Even if I applied to law school, I wouldn't get in, much less afford it."

"Yeah, well, shit's not fair. Shut your mouth and let's get this over with."

"Wait." I reached for her arm, but she pushed ahead of me and banged on the rusty back door of the restaurant, sticky trails of garbage juice running down from the handle. Someone on the other side of it yelled for us to hold on.

Bobby opened the door.

"Oh, hey." Nikki turned scarlet. "Uh, my cousin has something she wants to ask you."

This was not our plan. I had wanted to watch the place, feel the situation out, and then find a way in. Not roll up like the cops. I suspected Monica—or whichever woman Fernando had talked to that night—didn't want to be found. Why else would she not have come forward already? Why else would she not talk to Fernando's lawyer?

Bobby wasn't likely to blurt out her location either. He looked at both of us blankly, his mouth a flytrap. Either he was stoned or he was, as Nikki once said, an attractive idiot. He had soft brown eyes and fine features not quite square with his bulked-out frame. "You never called me back," he said to Nikki, blowing past what she'd just said. With his arms crossed over his chest, wearing the black polo with the Don Juan's logo emblazoned over his heart, I was reminded of that time I came to pick her up, and the time I'd seen Monica. How he'd stood the same way—stance wide, limbs poised and ropy with lean muscle—and, again, I felt a quick twist of fear in my stomach.

"Is Monica working tonight?" I said, instinctively inching closer to my cousin. "I need to talk to her."

He shook his head, leaned on the doorjamb. "She doesn't work here anymore."

"Can you give me her number, then? Or tell me where I can find her?" I asked.

His eyes narrowed to slits. "She in trouble?"

"Come on. Do I look like trouble?" I forced a smile. He shook his head and walked down the step so he was directly in front of us.

"Don't be a dick," Nikki said. "She still stays with you, doesn't she?"

"Why don't you come over tonight and find out," he said, and with one quick motion grabbed her wrist and pulled her to him. With his other hand he stroked the underside of her jaw. Thumbed under her chin so she was forced to look up. This was why Nikki lost her nerve. I didn't even consider it could be Bobby.

"Let her go," I said, heart thumping.

Nikki tried stepping back, but he tightened his grip. She wiggled her fingers, now dark red, blood pooling at the tips. "Stop, you big silly," she said, and smiled, but her voice was shaky. A black bag of garbage sat at the base of the dumpster, half of a rotting onion peeking out from the top. Choking on the smell, purple bulb slick in my hand, I aimed, then fired.

"What the—"

Bobby retreated, letting go of Nikki to wipe his face. I looked down at my hand, the hand that had just hurled an onion at Bobby's face.

Nikki ran back beside the dumpster.

"Tell us where she is or I'll tell the manager what you do with the till on the nights you close."

"That really hurt!" He blinked back the sting from his eye and kicked the onion down the steps.

"Come on, Nik," I said, walking backward. "We'll call the manager from my car."

Bobby shook his head. "You'd really rat me out? Jesus, fine, she stays with my sister and her kids. River Oaks, B-15."

I squirted hand sanitizer into my palm and hers.

Nikki rubbed her hands together. "Are we going there? To River Oaks?"

"Not now," I said, and put the car in gear. "Had Bobby been rough with you before?"

"A little," she said, turning her face to the window. "Not really."

My heart sank.

"It was nothing. Don't worry about it," she said, smiling weakly, and I could have died from shame. I had put Nikki in harm's way. I was such an idiot.

"Sorry," I said, looking at the road. I wondered what all she kept from me, and why. Again, the terrible sense we were not as close as I thought. But we all kept ugly things hidden, didn't we? I'd never told her about senior year, or any of the other daily small yet searing humiliations I suffered at a college out of my league in so many ways. Drawing it out into the light meant it was real and that you could be hurt by it. Maybe Nikki was afraid I would judge her. *Goddamn Bobby.*

"Let's focus on supper," Nikki said. "There's still beans and corn bread in the fridge."

"I don't want that again," I said, already driving toward the place I knew would cheer both of us: the Whataburger on the far side of Colburn, close to the university. Going there after the game had been a treat for us growing up. I made the turn onto the highway and she knew without me telling her. I pulled into the drive-thru lane after riding most of the way in silence.

"Two number twos, both with Dr Pepper. Oh, and cut the onion on one," I said into the intercom.

Nikki laughed, and then I started, and by the time we got up to pay my side ached and tears were streaming down both our faces. The kid at the window rolled his eyes. I had to pull over and park we were laughing so hard. "The look on his face when you hit him," she snorted, and reached in the bag for a fry.

I grinned. "So, what's he doing with the cash at night? I think he crapped his pants when you said that."

"No clue."

"What, you were bluffing?"

"I was right, though." She laughed harder. "He's such a shit."

We made up. The way we always had, by moving on. A shared understanding that we were bound no matter what—by blood, by proximity, by the weight of all our shared days—and might as well get over it. Truces depended on humility, on openness, but when we got back to the house I lied. Said I was going to bed, but instead waited for her to take a shower, knowing she'd change into pajamas and fall right asleep. Turn her back long enough for me to slip out. I didn't want her to know where I was going when I opened the door and stepped out into the blue-black night, alone.

Chapter 25

Window down I could smell the river water and hear it rush. It was black as pitch leading to the apartment complex, the roadside dense with cypress, tangles of live oak, and tall grass. When it flooded, this was the place people drowned. They died in their cars, unable to see black water sweeping over the road. Black, deadly cold water frothing with debris.

River Oaks—Garnett's sole public housing—was redbrick, blocky, and wide. Building B was mostly full and I circled the lot before finding a spot. Most of the windows were open; it was starting to cool down at night. I didn't want anyone to see me coming, so I walked up the side of the building, winding between hulking air compressor frames and metal clotheslines before stepping onto the short concrete porch of unit 15.

I knocked. Waited a few minutes and then knocked again. It was nearly ten at night. Maybe I'd come again in the morning. As I was about to leave, a little boy opened the door.

"Pizza?" He looked up at me expectantly.

"Sorry," I said, and before I could ask, a woman in a low-cut black top and matching miniskirt came to the door. Bottle blond, tattoo peeking out underneath a bra strap, short and curvy, she touched the piercing over her painted red lip.

"Monica, I'm Annie." I extended my hand. "Mind if I ask you a few questions?"

She raised her eyebrows in response but kept the door open a crack.

"I hear you party at Estrella out off Highway One-Twenty-Five," I said with a mixture of forced casualness and false confidence.

Monica halfway smiled as she grabbed a sweater and walked out onto the porch, the little boy pushing her waist from behind. "Sure. I get out." She patted the little boy on the crown of his head. "Javi, go brush your teeth. And you better not wake your mommy up."

The boy huffed and spun around, screen door slapping behind him. She didn't ask me in but motioned to the white plastic chair on the porch. I shook my head and stayed standing. The porch was swept clean and clay pots of rosemary and thyme made a border at the edge. An open bag of damp potting soil made the air smell like it had rained, and I took a deep breath of it. The television was on inside and the source of thin blue light coming from the window. Monica leaned against the railing and pulled close her lacy cardigan. She looked me up and down and I self-consciously tugged at my ratty running shorts. My legs were pale and spindly looking in the dark. "Are you married?" I asked.

She shook her head.

"Do you have a boyfriend?" I asked.

"I don't date women. No offense."

"I'm not asking you out," I said, glad she couldn't see me blush. "I wonder if anyone might be angry you spent a night—a night another woman was killed—with Fernando Garza, who is now accused of murder. I wonder if that's why you aren't coming forward to defend him."

She frowned. "Who are you again?"

I wasn't sure if saying you were an investigator without a license was lawful, or smart, so I said, "You knew my cousin Nikki from Don Juan's when she was the hostess. Bobby told us where to find you." She rolled her eyes; whether at the mention of her cousin or Don Juan's I wasn't sure. "You and I met once, briefly—anyway, I know Fernando. He and I work together, have known each other since we were kids," I said.

"Okay, so?"

"I heard you were with him that night. If what he's saying is true, then maybe he didn't kill that girl. See why I'd want to know?"

"I don't know what my idiot cousin told you, but—"

"Monica, Fernando's grandmother is how I know. Can you just tell me what happened?"

She stared angrily. "Only if I can talk, like, off the record."

"Okay," I said, not quite sure how to respond. "I'm not a reporter, definitely not a cop, but I am here for Fernando, just so we're clear. His family hired my grandfather, who's a private investigator."

She fiddled with her lip ring for a moment. "Fine, but can you sit? You're making me nervous."

Nervous myself, I nodded and perched on the edge of the chair. She focused her gaze over my shoulder at the shimmer of light on the small section of river visible through the trees. "I was about to leave," she said. "I watch the boys when my cousin works and she was going in early, so I shouldn't have been out late, but you know. I was getting in my car as he was pulling up. I waved and came up to the window, because actually I thought he was someone else. Had a couple beers in me so was running up and hugging this poor dude! I figured out pretty quick he wasn't the same guy, but we laughed about it and talked. Just shooting the shit, you know? Think we smoked a cigarette. I don't know how to explain it, but we had, like, this connection."

Maybe embarrassed, she looked down at her feet.

"I can understand," I nudged. "How you can click with someone."

She looked up and maybe it was the way the light fell, but her eyes looked wet with tears. "We sat on a tailgate and talked for, like, two hours." She smiled quickly, then frowned. "He didn't even try to pick me up."

"Two hours? Do you know the exact time?"

"Almost midnight when I left the bar. After two, about two fifteen, when I checked my phone, because I remember I was shocked. I told him I had to get some sleep."

"He never even went in and got a drink," I said hurriedly. "That's why no one else saw him. He was with you the whole time."

Given the time frame, Fernando wouldn't have been the one to pick Victoria up. She left the bonfire before midnight—no rational person would think she waited by the highway for nearly three hours. He was with Monica when Victoria was killed. Monica was Fernando's alibi. He didn't do it.

The truth seemed neat, so contained. So why did the thought of it sink in me like a stone down a well? Monica chewed her lip, watching me.

"What did he do after you told him you were going home?" I asked.

"Got in his car. Last call is around then, so he probably left," she said.

"Do you remember him at any point on the phone or talking about a woman named Victoria?"

"His phone rang once and he answered it. I don't think he could understand the person he was talking to. Kept saying, 'What? What?' Then hung up. This was not long after we started talking. And he got a text, maybe a few minutes later, but don't think he replied. Mumbled something about this chick had been a bad date."

"You should come to the sheriff's station with me. Tell them all of this," I said.

Her mouth opened. No words, only the weird choking noise when your throat is clogged with tears, came out.

"Why not?" I said, the sinking feeling intensifying.

"I won't talk to any cops," she said. "I shouldn't talk to you."

"You realize he'll go to prison and the real culprit, the person who murdered a woman, will go free," I said.

Monica cried, openly now. "We're Salvadoran, okay? That's where we came here from. I won't; I can't—I just can't talk to the cops. You can figure something else out with what I've told you, but I won't go to any cops."

There it was, the reason why she hadn't come forward, and perhaps the reason Fernando seemed reluctant to mention her even to his grandmother, much less the investigators: Monica didn't have papers.

"I'm sorry." She sniffed. "He called me again, but God, I just ignored him."

"I know the sheriff. He'll work with you."

"No. I've had trouble before."

I reached out and lightly touched her arm, but Monica jerked back. She paced in circles around the small porch with her head down.

"I'll go with you," I said. "We could go right now, tonight. You'll feel better."

"Who do you think you are?" She wiped her eyes and stared at me. "Feel better? Really? He got himself into this mess. I barely know him. They might not even believe me."

"He will probably do life in prison, if not worse."

"No."

"What if it were you?"

"Jesus Christ. I know you're not going to leave me alone about this, are you?" she said after a few moments and more tears. "Let me put the kids to bed. Tell my cousin what's up. I'll come out and find you after I've had a minute to think."

I nodded and she went inside the apartment, locking the door behind her.

I waited over an hour. The parking lot was dim, quiet. Once a man walked outside and looked curiously at the bullet, but my lights were off and he didn't approach. My eyelids were so heavy. I jerked my head up and checked for Monica every few minutes, but she still hadn't come outside. The blinds were drawn and not even the television light seeped through. Maybe her cousin had convinced her to stay put.

Sitting on that porch in the dark, I had sensed in her an intense fear: a memory undulating behind her eyes, a black wave at the wall of a dam. It can be nearly impossible to know another person's life. There are the private intensities, the experiences we never bear witness to. Dark chambers in the heart yet sealed. And for Fernando and Monica, hardships I'd never face. My jaw ached. I'd been grinding my teeth, my mouth set in a tight snarl.

I knew it was time for me to go. I drove the moonlit road with my window down, wind rushing in my face so I'd stay awake, radio up loud to drown the sound of things unseen—a car, I was certain, tailing some short distance behind with its headlights off, trill of cicadas, yowl of hungry coyotes—and my sinking sense of despair. Monica would not come forward. If I returned to the apartment at the break of day, to try yet again, she would be gone.

Chapter 26

Leroy cracked open a can of Budweiser and threw his empty into a paint bucket on the floor. "If we can't show he's got an alibi, we simply have to prove someone else is guilty."

"Simply?"

I sat at the kitchen table beside Leroy, moving a stack of newspapers and magazines, a pistol, and three Buck knives to do so. Tired of every place in town, we met for lunch at Mary-Pat's house. Leroy had suggested Richie's BBQ, but no one wanted to drive that far, and besides, I was curious—hadn't been to the Zimmerman place since I was a child, not since Mary-Pat's parents were living. The 1890s farmhouse, built of white limestone and shaded by a trio of live oaks, was known as the Christmas house because for years the Lutheran church held a bake sale here and every December elementary school classes took a field trip to see it. The big, beautiful house would be decked with bright red winterberries, sprigs of evergreen, pinecones dipped in gold paint, and an electric train set chugging around a lighted tree nearly as tall as the twelve-foot ceilings. It had been like Santa's workshop: smelling of cinnamon and cloves, the white-haired Mr. Zimmerman used to hand out ginger-bread or a handmade ornament, other years bouquets of candy canes tied with green ribbon.

To say things had changed would be an understatement.

"Provide reasonable doubt, rather," Mary-Pat hollered from the stove, her back to us. The pink bric-a-brac-embroidered apron tied over her stiff work outfit was oddly discomfiting, like she'd come down in her nightgown. She spun around and waved a spatula in her hand, grease dripping on the hardwood floor. "We went with Mrs. Garza and talked to the lawyer and she agreed she needs our help."

"Then we went to that Tejano bar, Estrella. That was a wash," Leroy sighed. "Hardly a soul would talk to us. The few that did say they never seen him. Reckon the law's been breathing down the owner's neck ever since the hit-and-run, 'cause the man who was killed had been drinking there. The spot of the accident is less than a mile away. They were thinking someone was coming from the club, or maybe had seen the vehicle at least."

"Damn shame." Mary-Pat shook her head.

"There's thousands of white pickup trucks registered in our county alone. At this point the law's just praying the driver grows a conscience and comes forward," Leroy said.

"Is it a coincidence?" I asked. "Two violent deaths in the same small town—a few miles on the highway apart—on the same night?"

"Sometimes it happens that way," Leroy said, but I could tell he wanted to say more. He didn't talk when he didn't need to, though; he didn't speak before he knew the answer. He was unsure of something.

"Well, I don't know either," Mary-Pat said, reading my mind. "But lunch is ready."

I got up to help her carry over the platter of sliced ham, a pan of corn bread, greens, potatoes, and some beautiful, thick-sliced red tomatoes and fragrant hunks of cantaloupe. She had set out some of her family's pretty dishes—bone china painted with yellow roses, so delicate it was nearly translucent—at odds with the scratched and mismatched silverware.

"This looks mighty tasty," Leroy said. "Little darlin', you want a beer?"

It was only half past twelve, and yet I reached into the mini ice chest by his feet. Leroy had been teasing Mary-Pat about cooking for him more often, but it really was a fine meal. I spooned a generous helping of spicy chowchow on my plate, Leroy cut his melon into bites, then salted and peppered it, and Mary-Pat brought out fancy honey for the corn bread. I startled when a fat brown tabby cat jumped right onto the table, inched closer to my plate, and licked his chops. I snapped my fingers, but he didn't budge. "Is he allowed up here?" I asked, and tried to ignore his unnerving stare along with my suspicion that her animals jumped everywhere, including the spot where she'd just prepared our food.

Mary-Pat shrugged. "I don't care. Do you care?"

"I don't care," Leroy said.

I shook my head—it was like that story I'd heard: Her first Christmas alone in the farmhouse, Mary-Pat decided she'd keep up the family tradition and welcome the community into her home. When the first class of second graders came for the annual field trip, they were met with boxes, newspapers, and magazines in haphazard stacks nearly to the ceiling, large tufts of cat fur in the corners, case files strewn about, and a full trash can of empty liquor bottles by the door. Still, the teacher bravely led the children through the maze of it. The kids sat in front of the tree—decorated, at least, but shining a little less brightly—and as Mary-Pat launched into the history of German and Czech settlers in Texas, the ritual of hiding a pickle in the tree and whatever odd bits of trivia came to her mind, there came a low growl and rustling of branches: one of her old toms had brought in a maimed bird that was taking refuge in the tree. Cat and bloody bird burst forth, leading to multiple children with scratches and a vow from the school to never bring a group again.

"Okay," I said, and took a bite of ham, guarding my plate with my other arm. "If it wasn't Fernando, who killed Victoria?"

"Hell, if I knew that"—Leroy smiled—"I could go home and watch my programs."

I rolled my eyes at him.

"I've a mind to try her in-laws, her ex," Mary-Pat said. "You two already spoke to them, but I'm going to see if I can get a clear answer on their whereabouts the night of the murder. Victoria did call Brandon in addition to Mr. Garza."

Leroy nodded and patted my shoulder. "You and me, we're going to the patch."

"The patch?"

"Oil field. Artemis's closest work site, rather—we aren't about to drive out to the Permian."

"Right. You still owe Lillie Anderson a call, that reminds me."

"Maybe we'll have a look at where those boys are staying. They're strangers in this town. We believe they had a questionable encounter with Victoria earlier, at Yesterday Once More. Might've been they slipped away from the bonfire before or right after the young lady and no one would've missed them."

"Seems likely," I said. "Those guys are sketchy."

"You two sound like everyone else in this town. Those strangers are simply folks looking for good-paying work. Not the boogeyman," Mary-Pat said.

Leroy took a swig of beer. "Fair enough. You know I keep an open mind."

"Good." Mary-Pat cleared her throat. "Doubt is all the defense needs; just indicate the investigators didn't do a satisfactory job or that there are other worthy suspects."

Victoria stormed my thoughts. Angry, mean mugging, heady with the smell of citrus perfume and tobacco, all hipbone and swagger. I could see her. *Now where do I figure in this?* I heard her say—a phrase she used every time the schedule posted—her voice clear as a bell. Fernando wasn't the only victim. At the very beginning, there was Victoria. At the white-hot center of all this pain and suffering was a life—*her* life—cut short. No, I wouldn't forget Victoria.

"Not just reasonable doubt," I said, my voice halting. "I mean, I know that's all that matters for Fernando's defense, but I really want to know who did it. We have to find the killer."

"Yes." Mary-Pat met my gaze. "Yes, of course."

Chapter 27

"Get off the highway at Herzog Road. Turn off Farm-to-Market Three-Twenty. That's out to where they've been drilling," Leroy said.

"I remember how to get there, nearly over the county line. Come to think of it, the site is a straight shot west from Victoria's land," I said. "Must be why they'll route pipeline that way."

"Yep." Leroy opened his ice chest and fished for a beer.

"You mind waiting? I really don't want to get pulled over. It's one thing driving around Garnett." It was less that I thought we'd get pulled over, more the sense he was already too drunk. Earlier he'd farted, loudly, and at the disgusted look on my face had shrugged his shoulders and said, "Oh, I didn't think you were listening."

"I can talk us out of a ticket." He cracked the can. "I know people."

"Your reputation does precede you."

Around the bend in the road and over the last rise before the open flatland, I saw the odd green glow of a flare stack and a metal tower shooting up from the ground. Beyond it and for miles were the familiar black and yellow pumpjacks like a mass of ants spread over the horizon. Traffic picked up closer to the site, mostly diesel trucks and water tankers. Potholes half as wide as my car marred the road and I had to slow down to veer around them. It was after four and close to a shift change, so most of the men at the site were gathered together around several pickup trucks when we pulled up in the bullet. Looking us up and down, they seemed confused by our presence, and not one person said hey to us, just stared, wary looking and dead tired.

"Do any of y'all know where we could find one of your co-workers by the name of Randy?" I asked. "Or Steve? Both are white, slender, blond hair and blue eyes. Steve is shorter, maybe five-seven. Randy's about six foot."

"Who're you?" one of the men in grease-stained coveralls asked. Sweat and dirt coated his face, and the rag he wiped across his forehead wasn't much cleaner. The hot wind changed direction and filled my nose and mouth with that same noxious smell that nearly gagged me the other night.

Leroy stood slightly to the front of me. "Name's McIntyre. I'm a private investigator, licensed by the state of Texas, and this is my assistant, Annie," he said, and pulled a card in a plastic sleeve from his back pocket. I could hear someone snicker; another pointed at Leroy's arm in the sling.

"Private investigator, sure," one of the men said, and poked the man beside him in the ribs. "Grandpa, you sure you didn't escape from the home?"

"You're hilarious," I said, not looking at Leroy. "Either of them in there?" I motioned toward a row of trailers that seemed to serve as break rooms or offices.

"What do you want with Randy and Steve?" One of the men looked over to me, jutting his chin and his chest out as he came closer.

"Just to talk," I said, needles of heat pricking my skin.

"Neither's got cause for concern," Leroy added, his voice softer sounding. Leroy didn't have a big ego—never had—but I imagine he was wounded by their banter, knowing he did in fact appear old, frail even, for the first time in his life.

"Yet," said one of the men. They snickered again, one meeting my eye and winking. Taking two slow breaths through my nose, I fought the urge to turn and run.

"Fine then, boys, where's the boss?" Leroy said.

"Over in the office." The man spit in the dirt as if the words had literally left a taste in his mouth. He pointed toward the smaller of the trailers in a semi-circle. Leroy and I walked toward the office, the air eerily quiet, slowly, calmly, aware we were still being watched. The rumble of machinery and diesel trucks pulling in and out of the site drowned out whatever comments I imagined they were making.

"What's going on out here?"

A middle-aged man leaned out of the open door we were about to knock on. He was paunchy, red in the face like a drinker, and wore sunglasses that looked expensive. He was cleaner than his crew; dark, slim-cut jeans, his shirt starched and white.

"We have a couple questions to ask you," Leroy said, and edged himself inside the door. The trailer was cramped and stale smelling, like wet cardboard and day-old coffee. Banker boxes were stacked on each side of the man's metal desk and on the wall hung several black-and-white maps dotted with red push-pins. As Leroy moved toward the man, I squished between the wall and a leather desk chair. The map was right at my ear and I turned to read it, wishing I could step back and see the whole of it, or take a picture with my phone. What I could make out were lot and tract numbers and the outline of the highway near Cedar Springs.

"Listen, unless you have a warrant, I can't let you ransack my work site," the man said, and moved behind his desk.

"Really?" I turned. "Ransack?"

"We're not cops," Leroy said, and again produced his PI license. "Name's McIntyre. We just have a couple questions about some employees, Randy and Steve."

"McIntyre as in the former sheriff of Garnett County?"

Leroy moved his shoulders back. "The same."

The man smirked, shook his head. "You know my brother-in-law worked for D.A. Turnbull back then; he told me about the crazy shi—"

"Let's get back to Randy and Steve," I interrupted. "Twenty years ago doesn't have much bearing on this."

"Naw." The man chuckled and crossed his arms over his wide stomach. "I don't know a Randy and a Steve."

"You sure? Both work for you. We have reason to believe they might have information on or even have been involved in a recent murder," Leroy said.

"So? Listen, for all I know you're working for Vernon Smith."

"Who's Vernon?" I said.

Leroy turned to me, a sly grin at the corners of his mouth. "OSHA representative." He turned his face to the man. "You had some injuries at this site?"

"Nope." He frowned. "You work for Vernon? Or some insurance company?"

"Don't know Vernon personally." Leroy shook his head. "And we're not hired by the insurance folks. But I'll make a note to call the TCEQ office when I get back to mine. Thought I smelled something funny out there. You notice that, Annie? Fumes."

"TCEQ?"

"Environmental regulations."

"We've passed every air quality test, have pulled all our

permits. I don't know what your game is, but I'm tired of it."
The man opened up the top desk drawer, and from where we
stood, we could see a handgun atop a stack of papers. "You
ought to get going."

"I reckon he's right. Come on," said Leroy, and lightly touched
my shoulder, but I was steaming.

"What's your problem? All we want is to talk to them," I said,
and as I said it I could hear my voice go up two octaves, could
see the man's eyes roll. But I tried to stall—I wanted to take out
my phone and snap a picture of the map, but he was right on me.

"Go on, get," the man said as if we were stray dogs, and closed
the door behind us before we were even down the steps.

"That didn't go like I thought it would," I said. "Damn."

Leroy walked ahead. The land was flatter out here, the wind
made restless. A dust devil danced on the ground before me,
dissipated as it crossed the concrete pad. Most of the men we'd
spoken to were getting in their trucks and pulling out. A white
dually with a company logo on the door kicked up an even bigger cloud of dust as it peeled out from behind the semi-circle
of trailers. I ran forward a few steps, waving for them to stop.

If they saw, they didn't care.

"I think that's him. That's the truck I saw at the bonfire and
at Yesterday Once More."

Leroy sighed. "Seems everyone's feeling a little hot under the
collar."

"What should we do?"

He frowned and pointed to the bullet. "I don't know. I'm
tired."

I bought tacos from the stand behind Texaco, and we stopped
to eat at the rest area across the river. We were near the place

and not too far from where they found Victoria's body. How it pained me—forever, the place would be known to me as the site of Victoria's rough-hewn burial. These same trees and tall grasses witness to evil. Leroy seemed melancholy, as he often seemed coming out here, but talking to the Artemis employees and getting nowhere had made him more so. The sun was low in the sky and he wouldn't talk about the case.

He talked about the past, his mood shifting like a waltz through time. About living out here. Riding out before dawn, trekking through the open country eating dust. How he took his favorite ponies across the river to get to school in Garnett, playing on the school football team, some nights staying with family in town but usually making the journey back across the river again. How he liked the solitude and the rush he got galloping across the flats. About how he left school to find work on a road construction crew when he was still a boy because his father drank his way through what little money they had. How he'd enlisted and had to leave my mamaw behind.

It was different—he was different—when he came home.

I always thought of him as someone of both the past and the present, here, only drawn deeply inward. But part of me now thinks that his past was quicksand. He was reckless, avoidant, his thoughts and his actions dulled by booze and dance halls. I think about these things—his life and his ghosts so often—and so often find myself spending an entire day winnowing through my memories of him, both good and bad, never quite grasping all the faces of his enemies.

We finished eating. Leroy pointed to a rusty pen and a broken-down barn far across the highway, at its decrepit boards painted to resemble the Texas flag.

"Even when folks don't have much, they have pride. Even if you're poor, having land is something to be proud of. This girl,

Victoria, that land of hers isn't worth that much, isn't much to look at. But you know it was probably important to her and her family. Being a proper landowner means you give back to the land more than you take from it. You honor it."

"Think you're right," I said.

"But if you're wanting for a thing, you'll compromise," he said.

"I know. Don't think I haven't ever thought about all that— some of the kids I went to school with had so much. And I wanted that. Want that. Money changes everything. People who say it doesn't are liars," I said, and felt a flush on my skin.

"Indeed . . . ," he trailed off, reached down, and took a beer from the cooler. "Whenever I walk the place, walk the same dirt and breathe the same air that my people did, I feel a certain way."

"You miss when you were a boy?"

He cracked the can. "Want one?"

"No thanks." If I squinted, I could make out the gate to the place and, next to it, the Schneiders' fence line. Being out across the river made me nostalgic too, though I had no concrete reason to be, other than what I'd thought of as my inherited memories, so badly had I wanted to belong to the narrative he spun. And that's what it was, a romance. Why in our family was the past so vivid and the present merely a distraction? The thing about nostalgia, though, was it made us hopeful. My family didn't move back to the land. They didn't rebuild the house. They didn't save the money to buy horses. But maybe, one day—in Leroy's garage was a beautiful leather saddle, price tag still on, propped on a sawhorse.

"I sometimes think about how I could eat a sand rock. If I had to again, if a drought came bad enough," he said after a moment.

"What's a sand rock?" I tossed our trash into a bin and walked over toward the edge of the overlook. Could smell the sun on the dry grass, sweet and mellow.

"What it sounds like. A bite you can hold in your mouth to suck on." He leaned back and took a long drink, then said, "One day—not long, maybe a week or so, before I left to find work—the younger ones and me were standing there in the kitchen waiting for Mother to get home. My father had been gone weeks, and there was no food. But Mother walks inside with a sleeve of saltines and a can of Pet milk. She divvies up the crackers and pours a little of the milk on each, sprinkles the last of the sugar on each cracker, saying, 'Sweets for my sweets.' I kept my cracker between my cheek and tongue and let it dissolve. It was so good. Her face was long and pale, her eyes kind of deep set in her face, more than ever, and I know then that she must be starving, but she just sits there and lets us eat it all. Reckon it was later that evening when it came a short, hard rain. The land was washed clean, dust down, but still looking lean and sparse.

"Mother stepped out into the yard and took the mud between her palms to eat it. I followed her out to try it. It was a fine taste, I suppose, thick and wet, but mostly, well, I don't know." He covered his face with his hand and wiped his nose with his shirtsleeve. "It tasted like dirt. Hard to describe."

I imagined it was bitter. Bitter with the sourness of want—an aftertaste that lingered all his life.

Chapter 28

I went back to the house and took a hot shower. My skin felt feverish, achy, and knowing I was exhausted, I nearly went straight to bed. But Nikki nosed her way into my bedroom closet, hangers clicking against each other as she sighed and searched.

"Don't bother." I stared at the ceiling. "I'm staying in tonight."

"I don't want to go to Ashley's alone. It'll be weird. Just come," she said. "Dang, next weekend we're going shopping."

I yawned. "Aren't you and Ashley and Macy fighting over Cade Johnson?"

"We talked about it and decided it was definitely Cade's fault."

I was so tired I had only put on my underwear and lay on the edge of the bed wrapped in my pink chenille bedspread—like most of my bedroom furnishings, it was a hand-me-down, had been either Jewel's or my mamaw's; whose exactly I couldn't recall—and pulled at a loose seam. "How about I find us a movie and you pull some cookie dough out of the freezer."

She spun around and yanked on the blanket. "Maybe Wyatt will be there."

"How did you know we were talking?"

"So, I was right." She beamed. "I didn't know, but then yesterday he liked that picture of you at the fairgrounds I tagged you in, what, maybe a year ago? And at two in the morning? Obviously creeping on you."

I pulled the blanket tighter, cocooning myself. It must be going around the Beauty Shoppe now, which meant Aunt Sherrilyn knew, which meant my mother knew. I sat up. "You think I should go out with him, right?"

"Why wouldn't you?" She held out a strapless top and denim skirt I hadn't worn since high school.

I shook my head, trying to articulate this pull-cord sensation I had when thinking about him. "I wonder if I shouldn't try and meet someone new," I said. There had been a time when I would have done whatever Wyatt asked me to, would have stayed and waited for him forever. Our breakup felt like my heart was a rag that had gotten wrung out. I didn't want that kind of pain again; maybe that was the source of my recoil.

"You've both dated other people. You've both grown up. It's not like things won't be different. Worst case, it doesn't work out. No big deal." Nikki laid out a short black dress with a low back. It was jersey knit I'd bought at Forever 21 but looked kind of slinky on—not a bad thing, but Nikki chose cutoff denim shorts and an orange tank top.

"Don't you think that's a little much for Ashley's?"

"Jesus, Annie, wear what you want, but let's go!"

"Fine," I said, and pulled the dress over my head. She was right. If Wyatt was there, I wanted to look good.

Ashley lived in a new apartment complex over near the city limits heading toward the college. There had been a lot of new development over on that side of town; half of it sat unfinished:

wooden frames like sun-bleached skeletons and newly paved roads dead-ended into empty fields. We passed a telephone pole with a large, handwritten sign stapled to it advertising FRACK WATER for sale. I thought again about how disruptive Artemis was—how they ripped up everything around them—and reminded myself to stop clenching my jaw. But Artemis had folks trying to sell their well water even though we were in a drought. What else could they convince us was fine to do? What else could we exploit for money?

"What's the matter?" Nikki poked me. "Your face is all scrunched up."

"Everything. Just everything." I took a breath and counted back from ten. I would tackle the case first thing in the morning. Try to find Randy or Steve. Maybe without Leroy, I thought, and rolled down the window for air. We were in Nikki's car—a Chevy Cobalt she called Bluebird—formerly her grandmother on her dad's side's car. For unknown reasons Mrs. Avery had taken a bunch of those toilet seat covers that are like carpet and fastened them over the seat backs, and even though Nikki had since ripped them out, the car smelled strongly of talcum powder and slightly of mildew.

"Here we are," Nikki said, and punched in a gate code for the complex's parking lot. "Oh, shit, isn't that them over there?"

I looked where she pointed, toward a small, kidney-shaped pool. The area was decorated to look like a tropical tiki bar, or maybe a cabana, and was gated and surrounded on all sides by asphalt parking lot. Ashley, Sabrina, Macy, and some other people from our class and a few I didn't recognize were in the water. Red SOLO cups ringed the sides of the pool. "How lovely of them to let us know this was a pool party," I said. "Good thing I wore a damn dress."

"Bitches." Nikki yanked the parking brake. "Hey, y'all." She smiled as she got out of the car and waved.

Ashley stepped out of the pool and wrapped a towel around her waist. She wore a highlighter yellow bikini that flattered her tan. "You girls get yourselves a drink. Did you bring your suits?"

We shook our heads, smiling stupidly. My spare was in the wash after my impromptu river float the other day.

Ashley frowned cutely. "Wear one of mine! Apartment's open. Three-Twenty-Five. Top drawer of my dresser."

"That's okay. We'll just dip our toes in," I said, and went to the cooler for a beer. There were twinkling string lights along the pergola and Mike—one of Wyatt's former teammates—was tending kielbasa on a charcoal grill. He and I made eye contact before he got his phone out, and I wondered if he was going to text Wyatt to tell him I was there. Nikki and I shared a big lounge chair beside the water and watched as Ashley and Macy played chicken on some guys' shoulders. They pulled at each other's tops so that they nearly came off, then pretended to be embarrassed. I laughed as Nikki rolled her eyes so hard I thought they'd stick.

"There's Justin," Nikki said, and waved.

Any nerves I had about seeing Wyatt multiplied when Justin rounded the corner and smiled at me. I took a long pull of the beer in my hand. Justin didn't get the memo about the pool either; wearing jeans and boots, he carried a six-pack of Shiner and a bottle of scotch likely lifted off his dad. "Hey, girls!" he called, flashing that megawatt grin.

I pulled on the hem of my dress, goose bumps breaking out on my exposed skin.

"Come sit," Nikki said, and scooted a chair out with her foot.

"That's terrible about Fernando," he said, face sobering as he looked at me. "I just heard."

I wondered when people were finally going to bring it up. It was scary to talk about, and yet wrong to not acknowledge that someone we all knew had been arrested for murder.

"I played football with Fernando. Dude's been to my house. I'm glad they got him, but I just can't believe it." Justin looked so sad, like he might cry, and I felt so odd then. The light in the air was wrong—greenish from the pool's reflection and the parking lot lamps—and Justin's face was searching mine for re-assurance I didn't have in me.

"I'm not so sure," I said without thinking. "There's reason to believe he didn't do it."

"Then why did he get arrested?" Justin asked.

"Because they've got to arrest someone so everyone can feel safe again. Because this is a small town and they've had two ho-micides at the same time. Fernando is a big guy with a temper; he's Mexican; he's—"

"I heard there was DNA, phone records," Justin said.

"You hate to believe it, but they wouldn't arrest him if they didn't think the charge would stick," Nikki said.

"All I know is that something doesn't feel right. I was close to both of them—I feel like the truth's owed to me," I said, then finished my beer in one gulp, felt it slosh in my stomach as I shifted in the chair.

"I think we're all angry and confused," Justin said. "But—"

"I don't want to talk about this anymore," Nikki stopped him. She stood quickly, grabbed the bottle of scotch from Jus-tin, and went to the table for three plastic cups. I watched as she measured out three very generous shots, but felt Justin's eyes on me. The scotch burned going down and tasted like old smoke.

"Fine. Here's hoping justice is served," I said, and poured us each another. Nikki squinted her eyes at me, opened her mouth to say more, then shook her head. I think she couldn't decide whether or not to scold me or encourage me. She knew I was still investigating with Leroy. The burn of the scotch wasn't as bad as the first round, but still my eyes watered. The outline of objects—people's faces, the pool—softened.

"I needed that." Justin shook his arms out and scooted closer to me. I felt a pull inside my stomach. It had been just like this before—he and I at a lame house party, sitting closer, closer.

I rolled my shoulders, the knot in them loosening. "I know y'all are tired; it's just, being here with everyone again I can't help but wonder if someone at the bonfire saw something. Maybe they even don't realize it," I said.

Nikki bit her lip, looked at me. "Yeah, well, funny you should mention that. Today I was at work when Sabrina came in. We talked about tonight, but then we get to talking about the bonfire and what we told the cops. Sabrina says she thought Victoria came *back* to the fire and had another drink. Said she was going on about leaving for the VFW bar. Maybe she decided to come have another while waiting for Fernando? But then she was gone again."

Justin shook his head. "To think someone could—"

"Wait," I said, my pulse quickening. "You're saying Victoria came back to the party a second time, after everyone saw her leave already?"

Nikki shrugged. "That's what Sabrina says, but this is Sabrina we're talking about, so who knows."

Did I have my timeline wrong? Not to say Randy couldn't have waited around for her. "I thought no one had seen her after she got up from that roughneck's lap and left the party," I said.

"That's what I thought too. Sabrina was a little unclear," Nikki said, trying to downplay the information. Probably so I wouldn't be mad she hadn't already told me.

"And Victoria was asking to be taken to Yesterday Once More?"

"That's the VFW bar?" Justin asked.

I raised my eyebrows. "Turns into a honky-tonk on Thursdays. Yep."

"Oh, wow. She said something about wanting to go to Yesterday. It didn't make sense at the time," Justin said. "She stumbled into me and Steve saying something about it. God, I should have helped her then. Taken her up to the house. Instead, we got distracted—it was kind of crazy—shit."

"Justin." I touched his arm. "You know Steve? Blond guy that works for Artemis?"

"Pruitt, yeah. He was one of Troy's fraternity brothers. He was gone by the time I rushed. Think he dropped out," he said, smirking. "He's still in a band apparently."

"He and Victoria might have had a thing. He plays at the VFW bar," I said, heat rising in my face both from the scotch and from my impatience. "Was she alone when she left the second time?"

"I don't know. Honestly wasn't paying attention—I didn't even know there was a first or a second time she came and went. I'm sorry," Justin said, his forehead creased with worry. "You think she and Steve hooked up?"

"Maybe," I said, heart racing. "Let's have another of those." I motioned to the scotch. I needed to slow down, calm my nerves, and think.

Nikki shook her head and frowned.

"Give me that, you weasel," I said, and took the bottle. She raised her eyebrows and Justin shook his head no, but I didn't care. No burn going down this time. "Now then, I better say hi and be social," I said, and got up.

Ashley was taking pictures of us. I ducked my head and crossed my arms tight across my chest. I'd stood too quickly, the effect of the alcohol hitting me at once. I needed to talk to Sabrina alone, see if she remembered anything else, and get her exact account. On the other side of the party, she danced, swaying her hips by the side of the pool. She was rarely far from Ashley and Macy, so maybe they'd seen what she had seen. It wasn't surprising that people's drunken recollections of a rowdy, crowded party—outside, in the dark, at that—were blurry. But someone should have seen *something*. If Victoria had come back to the party after wandering off the first time, didn't that change things? She changed her mind about wanting to go to Yesterday Once More—why? Was she meeting someone? Or was she simply happier there? We might not ever know, I thought, but damn it, we should know how it is she didn't make it.

My sandals felt floppy and large, and I was dizzy, but kept moving forward, much faster than I should have, and the moment before I hit the water, knowing there was no way I wasn't going in, time seemed to stand still.

Pushing myself up to the surface, spewing over-chlorinated water from my mouth and nose and wiping it from my stinging eyes, I was only grateful I hadn't hit my stupid head. There was a heavy splash behind me and two strong hands gripped my waist.

Justin pulled me to the shallow end. "Annie, are you okay?"

I looked at him, looked at the others with their mouths hanging open, and at Nikki kneeling by the water's edge. "Call me

Grace," I said, waving to the group, and concern turned quickly to laughter. I only wanted them to look away.

"How's my outfit?" Justin came out of the bedroom dressed in Ashley's biggest T-shirt, tight and stretched over his arms, and a pair of gym shorts left by an ex-boyfriend who must've been rather husky. Both our clothes were in the dryer. I wore an old sorority T-shirt and airbrushed Soffe shorts likely bought on some spring break trip to Port A.

"A little mismatched. Thanks, by the way," I said. "You didn't have to jump in."

"Aw, come on." He laughed and opened the fridge for a beer.

The room was spinning, so I sat on Ashley's couch, thinking about how I always managed to embarrass myself in front of Justin. That's how the thing between us had started: a slip, a glimpse of my soft core. Only later had it been too much, my vulnerability turned liability. But that first time, it had been raining and the school parking lot flooded. Late for the bus and trying to hop a puddle, I lost my balance and dropped my books, hit a slick of grease, and would have landed on my ass had he not caught my backpack from behind. I'd both twisted my ankle and missed said bus, so we sat in his truck and talked, laughing and fogging up the windows. I've never in my life played dumb or weak, but there was something, something about our dynamic—I was crushing, and hard—and I easily played the part of the girl rescued, let him carry me up the driveway to my house that night.

Justin mussed his hair with a towel and sat beside me on the couch. Ashley's apartment looked like a girl's dorm room in a Target ad: everything in matching shades of pink and orange like swirls of tropical sherbet, vanilla-scented candles, a fuzzy white wing chair, and a bunch of plastic stackable storage containers, her monogram stenciled in a chevron pattern above the mantle. Comforting in its bland familiarity. I let myself relax but felt a trill in my spine as Justin leaned closer—

It hadn't been so different, then. The night at the stock tank we lay in the bed of his truck to look at the moon while he moved his hands over me, held me, and I remembered thinking I never wanted someone so badly. How the next night, at his house alone in his room, I'd straddled his lap and felt him hard beneath me. Nerves fluttering as he whisked his hand under my skirt. My cell phone had started ringing—I ignored it, at first—but it kept ringing, so I slid off his bed, remembering my parents had only bought it for emergencies. "Sorry," I said, reddening. "It's probably my mom."

I knew the number on the screen by heart and so drew my breath in sharply.

"Everything okay?" Justin peered over my shoulder.

I should have put the phone away, turned it off, but I faltered. There was a text. *I want to see you*, it read. *I miss you.*

Justin tried taking the phone from my hand. "You're talking to some other guy."

I should have lied, said of course not, but I shrugged. "It's nothing."

"Yeah, right," Justin said, and put his shirt back on.

"Justin, I'm not interested in anyone else," I stammered. "Wyatt and I are—"

"Wyatt Reed? You're still together with him?"

"No. We broke up. See, I don't even have his number saved."

"I don't play games, Annie."

He turned on the television set he had in his bedroom, not speaking or looking at me until I'd told him at least five times it was over between Wyatt and me. We made up by making out and then he drove me home. We sat next to each other the next day at school, not talking any more or any less than normal. But was he distant? He was definitely being distant, I worried, but I must have been forgiven by last period, because on our way out of class he pulled me aside and kissed me. Told me there was going to be a party at his brother's fraternity at State that night and that I should check it out. Not *go with me*, not *I'll pick you up*, I thought later, but that I *should check it out*—I hadn't learned there was a difference. And I learned the hard way, didn't I? Yet here we were again. Alone in Ashley's apartment, some kind of energy building, building—

Justin picked up the throw pillow wedged between us and tossed it on the floor. Put his arms around me and lifted me onto his lap. I touched his face, then moved my hands to the soft whorl of hair at the nape of his neck, but the scotch was still coursing through me, so when my lips met his they were slightly numb, my aim sloppy. I heard the flap of someone's sandals coming up the stairs and a peal of laugher under the door. I pulled back. The footfall continued past to the next apartment and the laughter grew more distant, but I rolled off his lap and stood to leave. Nikki would be looking for me. Ashley might walk in. And, Jesus, this time I really did have a date with Wyatt—what on earth was I doing?

Justin reached for my hand. "Don't be a tease."

Don't be a tease. I still didn't know what to say to that.

My head full of old half dreams, that night I lay in bed and thought about how things might have been different. What if Justin hadn't thought I lied? Would we have gotten serious? Maybe I would have stuck around, gone with him and our classmates to State. I wouldn't have minded that, back then. I thought I liked him, but it's hard to say if I just wanted him.

My desire hadn't gone away. It only morphed, muddied with shame.

After the text from Wyatt, Justin simply wouldn't listen to me. I pinned it on that—people only hearing what they want to hear. I thought about this time Victoria and I were working and a man had come and questioned aloud—to the room, to anyone who'd listen—about entering late into the Parr City rodeo that weekend and she was telling him about how her friend did, the contact person and all that. The man interrupted her to ask her for more coffee, then started repeating the question to another man in a cowboy hat sitting at the table next to his. She'd stood right next to the man's ear, telling him exactly what to do, and he still kept saying he would have to figure it out, talk to the guys he'd seen out at the feed store. And she got so flustered she threw her hands up and walked away. I thought then how often that had happened to me. That no one listened.

Chapter 29

A man and his son sat in the booth by the big picture window. In full view was the courthouse and, beyond it, McIntyre Investigations, the high noon sun illuminating its empty interiors.

Writing down the boy's order of steak fingers and fries, my hand shook. I gripped the pen harder and tried to focus. Hungover and still slightly mystified—I'd sent multiple drunken texts rife with typos to Sabrina to ask if she'd truly seen Victoria come back to the bonfire, and if we could talk again, and gotten no reply—I felt overcome with dread and wished to be anywhere but in the café in front of all these people.

"More coffee, sir?"

The man shook his head. I was about to turn toward the kitchen when a flash in the window caught my eye: a truck, company issued and cherry red, parked in front of the land survey office across the square. Troy Schneider's, I was certain.

"You need to cover my tables real quick," I said to Dot.

"Why should I?"

"I'll be right back," I said. "Promise."

Dot pursed her lips and took the ticket, muttering something bitchy, I assumed, but didn't pause to care. I ran out the door and down the sidewalk, crossed the street, and cut across the courthouse lawn. But the truck eased off the curb. "Wait!" I waved and ran faster, but by the time I reached the other side of the square it had turned off Main. Troy was the exact person to talk to—he might have seen Victoria the second time, and I now knew he had been a friend of Steve's—and I'd missed my chance. When I got back inside, I'd have to text Justin to ask for his brother's number, another sure to be awkward moment.

If only I had been sharp, sober, last night. My mouth was dry and my head hurt. My mind shot off in a million different directions, none productive, and Troy's truck was now a speck on the horizon.

Stopping mid-stride, the second-story window of the McIntyre Investigations office above me like a watchful eye, I realized what was really bothering me: I wasn't good at this. Hell, neither was Leroy. The way people laughed, his reputation for being an irresponsible drinker seemingly unchanged. The worst part was that at the Artemis site yesterday I'd felt superior. Believed myself an untapped resource. Leroy's better angel, the granddaughter who'd inherited only his talents. But I was wrong. Dormant in my cells and now awakened to brutal, roaring life were all his trademark weaknesses. Mary-Pat, bless her heart, babysat us both—the firm had always been a post-retirement vanity project for Leroy, and for her a chance at some extra cash, their landmark case a lucky break—and I was being humored until I grew up and ventured out of Garnett again.

Hadn't everyone warned me?

I looked back at the café. Watched Dot clear plates from the table along with my forfeited tip, then wipe the blue-checked tablecloth, but hearing two familiar voices behind me, I spun back around. Victoria's husband, Brandon, exited the basement of the courthouse, his mother at his side. The two of them appeared like a mirage in the desert, the only other people on an empty stretch of street.

Was this some sort of sign? At the sight of them I felt a surge in my chest. Maybe instead of bemoaning our failings I needed to try harder. Do better.

"Glory! Brandon!" I called. "Wait up!" I called again.

Glory turned around, touched Brandon on the shoulder, and looked unsure of whether or not to meet me halfway. They had been coming from the title office as well, and I realized that it was not a sign or even a coincidence: they had been meeting *with* Troy.

"Hey." I caught up to them in the narrow parking lot at the side of the building. "Is this about Victoria's place? The pipeline?"

"What if it is?" Brandon said. "What do you care?"

"Just asking," I said. "I know it was a big deal to her and that she was conflicted. Feel like I owe it to her to ask."

Glory took her sunglasses off and stared at me for a moment. "We're doing what's best for the little girl; it's now her inheritance. Those folks are offering good money for mineral rights and a pipeline easement."

"Would Victoria have wanted that?"

"No." Brandon looked at the ground. "Probably not."

"Don't matter. They're going to take it to court on eminent domain and then we really wouldn't see that money. That man Schneider said so. Said he tried telling Victoria the same frigging thing but that she wouldn't listen." Glory rolled her eyes.

"You're probably right. . . ." I paused. "But have you talked to a lawyer?"

Brandon shrugged, slack-jawed. Glory put one hand on her hip, motioned with the other to her son. "No, and he ain't about to. Not like it's your business. Excuse us."

I stepped in front of them. Pulse pounding in my temple, I tried to focus, think of the exact right question, but all that came out was raw feeling. "She didn't want them on her property. That acreage was in her family for I don't know how long. I'm sorry, but when I saw you coming out of the office, I had to say something."

Glory looked about ready to light into me if I didn't move out of her way, and quick. I looked toward the vehicle: a slate gray F-350 with dealer tags. God, they'd probably already banked on the first royalty check from the land, Victoria not even gone a month. "Nice truck," I said, not bothering to conceal the edge in my voice.

Brandon shrugged. "Yeah, we got a pretty sweet deal—"

"Hush, son," Glory said, then wagged her finger in my direction. "I've had it up to here with you and your weirdo pals. That Zimmerman woman comes knocking on my door again yesterday, asking questions all accusatory. Like they haven't done arrested the man who killed her. Stirring up our feelings, it's plain disrespect."

I wasn't sure whether or not Mary-Pat mentioned we were hired by Fernando's family. They deserved to know. I paused, said, "We care about Victoria, all of us. I'm afraid we've gotten off on the wrong foot. Come on in to the café and I'll get you a cup of coffee so we can talk." I motioned for them to follow me across the street. "All I want is to do right by her."

"Do right?" Glory clicked her tongue and shook her head. She turned, clicked the key fob to the truck, and Brandon followed dutifully behind.

"Please wait," I said.

Glory looked over her shoulder at me one last time. "Do right. If she had wanted to do right by us or, hell, do right by her kid, that girl shouldn't have been out drinking like a fish. Out hooking on the side of the highway in the middle of the night."

The next morning Leroy called me. Told me he had set up a meeting with Rob Bullock, an old friend of his who worked as a landman. "If anyone knows any dirt on Artemis or their guys, it would be Rob. Also want to see a map of that pipeline. He's coming over and we'll have us some breakfast," Leroy said.

When I saw his name flash across the screen I'd hesitated. I'd felt so down about him and his abilities, along with my own role in this mess. Hearing his voice was uncomfortable—like seeing someone after you've had a vivid dream about them—and I blushed, feeling as though I'd betrayed him by my thoughts alone. But Leroy wasn't deterred when I told him what happened at the pool party and on the courthouse lawn. Said that we'd try a new angle. At least we now had a tidbit: Victoria likely came back from the road. We'd figure out a timeline, nail down Sabrina. Pieces were shifting, he said, and thinking he might be right, I squared my shoulders. Today was a new day. At the mention of breakfast, I could almost smell the ham I knew he'd be frying for Rob, hear the pop of a can of biscuits being opened, taste Mamaw's red plum jelly, tart and bright on my tongue.

"I'm going to the vet's," I said, deciding on the spot.

"You got a pup I don't know about?"

"Brandon. Dot told me he has a part-time job at the animal clinic minding the dog runs and cages. Does some janitorial work. Victoria told her when he got laid off at the cement plant this was the only place that called him back. I think if I can talk to him alone without Glory he'd dish." I poured coffee into a chipped blue mug and stirred milk in, careful not to clink the spoon against the sides, quiet so as not to wake Nikki. She'd been a good sport and helped me with Sabrina last night, calling her from the salon phone. Though Sabrina hadn't even remembered exactly what she'd told us, only that she *thought she might've* seen Victoria come back a second time. "Guess you'll let me know what you hear. I think this Steve guy, especially, might be the one," I said.

"I plan to. Be good, little darlin'."

I finished my coffee, then dug out some low-rise, flared jeans from the bottom drawer of my dresser—God, I hoped those never came back in style; we'd all seen enough muffin tops and butt cracks to last a lifetime—ones it wouldn't matter if dirt or slobber got on them, and my Garnett Steers track-and-field finals T-shirt. Dressed and out the door, I paused in the middle of the sidewalk. Stomach twisting, I considered the fact that I wasn't on the schedule at the café. I could go back to bed for an hour, recharge my batteries before shooting out again. But I kept moving, ignoring the tinny sound in my ears like distant sirens.

The Geronimo Creek Animal Clinic is out in the country, off a crumbling asphalt road that ends at the Johnston family's land, a large animal hospital with a fenced-in stable and pens, a main office for pet care, and a dog kennel off at the back of the property. I went inside the office and rang the bell. Smelling of disinfectant, shampoo, and slightly of urine, the clinic was dark and empty. A woman with red hands and a face that looked equally over scrubbed came out behind the desk.

"I only unlocked the door for a delivery. We don't open till ten. This an emergency?"

"I'm here to see Brandon."

She rolled her eyes. "Oh, him. He's out cleaning the kennel. Just go around the back," she said, and pointed.

I could hear music and the hiss of a spray nozzle as I walked out back, and the dry grass made a faint crackling noise under my feet. Kennel cages were on a concrete pad inside a large, fenced-in area full of anthills and half-eaten rawhides. "Brandon?"

"What now, Nadine?" he called from one of the back cages without turning around, drawing out the last syllable. He was listening to Linkin Park.

"Not Nadine," I said, and nearly gagged at the smell; I'd just stepped in and smeared dog mess on my shoes. About half the cages were full, dogs whining and rattling the chain link. Brandon turned around and sprayed me with the hose.

"Sorry," he mumbled, and turned down the music.

"It's fine," I said, resisting the sudden urge I had every time I saw him to kick his shins. I stuck out my foot. "How about you get the bottom of my shoe."

He laughed and sprayed most of the mess off. When he lifted his finger off the nozzle the spray slowed to a dribble. "What's up?"

"Just checking, double-checking—you said you didn't hear from Victoria Thursday night? Night she was killed? I heard from someone that she might not have gone with Fernando. That she was looking for a ride after he turned her down."

"She did call me, okay?"

"Go on."

"What?" he said. "Y'all really think it was me. Please. I told the cops and that old lady I was with my girlfriend. It's been verified."

"Brandon, I'm grasping at straws here," I said too loudly, unable to control the desperation in my voice. One of the dogs whimpered in response.

"I'm grieving too. She was my wife." His face drew down and his eyes brimmed with tears.

"I know and I'm sorry."

"If anyone understood how much I cared for her, they would know I didn't do it," he said softly.

"You still loved her?"

"We had Kylee. That changed things, good and bad. Before the baby, things were different, mostly better, but of course I did."

I nodded, watching him blink hard and bite his lip. Trying to repair the crack in the façade, and failing.

"You know, I used to watch her in the hallway between classes. She was into theater and I went to all the shows just to see her in them. They were so bad." He laughed. "Vic, though, she kind of shined. Figured a girl so pretty and smart wouldn't ever talk to someone like me. But she did. She was quieter, real easygoing back then. It was a long time coming, but when we split up, she did a one-eighty. I mean she just kind of went wild. Used her granny as an excuse to move out and not be around. She was living her own life."

"She and your mom didn't get along, did they?"

He half laughed, half sighed. "No. My mother has always been a control freak. When Kylee came it ramped up. Mom grabbed the reins so much Vic eventually just said 'fine' and dropped 'em in her lap."

"Who do you think killed her?"

"Not my mother, damn." His face turned red. "Guess I'll have to trust it's the fucker they've got behind bars."

"I had to ask . . . ," I said, pausing. "I should probably tell you that Fernando Garza's family hired us. They say he didn't do it, and I have several reasons to believe them."

"Well, shit. I don't know what to say to that." Brandon's eyes watered again and he rubbed them furiously. "Honestly? I just want all this to be over. Hurts like hell."

"I'm sorry for your loss, Brandon."

"Yeah, yeah. If you're gonna just stand there, staring at me . . ." He shook his head, spit in the dirt. "Can you turn that hose off behind you? Nadine said I have to walk this one on the leash. I have work to do, okay?"

"Okay," I said, and reached for the spigot behind me. He opened the cage and a big dog that looked to be part shepherd and part pit, dark haired and muscled, growled as Brandon reached for its collar. Its yellow eyes fixed on me, and I instinctually stepped back off the concrete pad onto the grass, nearly tripping over the slack hose. The dog bounded out of the cage and out of Brandon's grasp. It raced toward me, and just as my body seized, the dog stopped short and circled me. It growled at me with teeth bared.

"Just be calm," Brandon whispered. "I think they can smell fear."

"You dumbass," I said, standing still and sweating bullets. "Call it off."

Brandon clicked his tongue, tried baby-talking it, but to no good. I kept still. A leg bite, okay, but if it went for my face or neck—"Brandon, go get some treats," I said, my voice shaky. The dog was on me now, sniffing me. Definitely part herder, it nudged me with its snout and nipped the hem of my shirt. I stepped very slowly toward the building and then, teeth. Hot, wet, needle-sharp sting as the skin broke. It yanked my arm back. I closed my eyes through the intensifying pressure, until finally, a high whistle and the sound of chow filling a bowl.

The dog opened its mouth and I sank to the ground.

The dog ran toward the bowl and Nadine clipped a harness onto its collar and tied it to the cage. Brandon looked at my arm and his face went white. "Uh, doc's not here, but Nadine's training to be a tech. She can fix you up."

Having reassured me that all dogs they board are up-to-date on shots, then cleaning the wound and bandaging it, Nadine offered me a painkiller that she said was basically Vicodin, but for dogs. I declined and felt pretty sore driving off in more ways than one. The thought crossed my mind that Brandon had let go of the dog intentionally. But wasn't that too risky? How would he have known the dog would attack me, not him? He also might not have gone to get Nadine if he had really wanted to hurt me. I came to the stop sign entering the highway. I felt like I was being punished. And the deeper I dug, the less clear everything seemed. My cell phone rang.

"Howdy."

"What did Rob allow?" I asked, my voice climbing two octaves. I didn't want to tell Leroy about the bite. I didn't need any reason for him and Mary-Pat to pull me off the case, and honestly it freaked me out to look down at my arm. Already blood blisters streaked down my arm from underneath the gauze.

"Thing is"—Leroy sucked his teeth—"Randy, Huber's his name, is out and Steve Pruitt is out."

"What? How?"

"Rob knows 'em. Says they came out to that rough old icehouse—what's it? County Line I think it's called now. Came out around midnight and they played pool. He remembers it was that night 'cause they smelled like woodsmoke, said they'd come from some rich kid's bonfire."

I swallowed hard. "They wouldn't have had time. Rob's sure it was midnight?"

"He was pretty certain. And you were right about the easement. They're starting construction next month."

"Taking the goddamned dirt under her feet whether she wanted or not," I said. "That was her inheritance." A glint of metal caught my eye—a big truck with a shiny silver deer guard rode my bumper. I checked the speedometer, clocked fifty, fast for this road. I waved my arm out the window for the jackass to pass, but he stayed. A cold shiver shot down my back. "Hey, Granddad, thanks for letting me know. I'm driving, so let me give you a call later on."

I dropped the phone, looked in the rearview, and tried to identify the driver. Their windshield was tinted and my back window dirty, but I figured it was a man for their size, for how they leaned over the steering wheel. I turned right onto the first street and they did too. I felt cold, clammy with sweat. The truck's engine revved, and certain they were going to hit me, I braced for impact. Black smoke jetted from the exhaust pipe as they swerved hard and sped around, maybe an inch from clipping my mirror, disappearing down the road.

I pulled to the shoulder and parked. Hot tears rolled down my cheeks. The driver was just a jackass being a jackass. Like that jackass dog. Like jackass Brandon, jackass Glory, and that jackass oil company. I let myself cry and it worked; I'm not sure how long I sat parked, but after some time my tension eased. At one point an older woman pulling a horse trailer slowed to make sure I was okay. I gave her the thumbs-up, waved, and ignored the pain in my arm—it was fine. I was fine. We would figure out a plan. We would, eventually, seize upon a clue and discover the truth. Me, Leroy, Mary-Pat, we would keep trying. We had to, didn't we?

It was so quiet, so still, and thinking I was alone, I relaxed and rolled down the window. Looked up from the dashboard to the sky. Hundreds upon hundreds of grackles sat perched. Birds featureless as shadows, black dots trembling on the telephone wires, in the trees, in the tinderbox fields of dry maize, as far as you could see in every direction. The din—a shushing sound, a hiss and murmur—grew louder. The whole of them were like a black shudder, a thousand eyes watching my every move.

Chapter 30

It was dusk, the sky peach when the dimming marquee light switched on. Wyatt waited as several people milled about behind him, now first in line at the ticket window. He wore a State ball cap, his hair in need of a trim and starting to curl at the ends, just brushing the collar of his white cotton shirt. But that was how I'd always liked it.

When I came up and hugged him, he pulled back and paused—I thought to kiss me—but an older man, a substitute teacher our class once cruelly nicknamed Junk Bucket for his sizable rear and whose real name I couldn't recall, stood behind us and cleared his throat. Said move out of the line if we weren't going to hurry it up. Wyatt shrugged and bought our tickets, then led me inside to the snack bar, a quiet, satisfied smile on his face. Guilty about Justin Schneider and the pool party, my stomach lurched—but why? It wasn't like Wyatt and I were—well, were we? I was nervous. Not in a bad way. Edgy with anticipation, maybe, like the way you feel blowing out birthday candles, or with a sticky plastic cup of sparkling wine in your hand on New Year's Eve, counting down. Wyatt leaned against the counter and swept his hand through the air. "You can have whatever you'd like."

"Popcorn and Junior Mints, please."

The popcorn was usually fresh, delicious if a bit over-salted, but for some reason their chewy, fruity candies were always stale. Eat a Red Vine and you'd risk ripping out a filling. It was chocolate all the way at the Lone Star. I smiled as I took in the hand-stenciled movie reels and film canisters painted on the walls, and the worn, multicolor-flecked carpet now peeling away from the baseboards. Walking through the lobby was like being greeted by an old friend. I'd spent a lot of time here as a kid. In Garnett, there aren't things to do after dark besides go to the late show—7:00 P.M. at the Lone Star—sit in a booth at the café, or get into trouble.

"Aren't you hot?" Wyatt asked, tugging the sleeve of my cardigan.

"It's always cold in the theater; you know that," I said, though I was actually quite warm. I didn't want to explain the purplish bruise extending down my forearm or the thick gauze.

We hurried inside, unnecessarily, for the theater was not half-full. A large new Cineplex opened in Colburn that year and had hurt the Lone Star mightily. We sat toward the front, Wyatt's seat not cooperating with his body. Plastic snapping, cushion whining, I realized when we sat how he'd grown taller and sturdier since high school. The floor was tacky with spilled Cokes and, like usual, the song "Pretty Woman" played on a loop against a backdrop of poorly formatted ads for the local dentist, Mixer's Icehouse, and the Garnett football boosters. "Prrretty woman don't walk on by," over and over.

"I'll scream if they play it again," I said, shifting in my own thinly cushioned seat.

"Have to admit it's catchy."

"Don't fix it if it ain't broke," I said, hating myself for thinking that might be true in more ways than one.

Mercy.

The lights dimmed and the real previews, the movie studio ones, began to roll. Five minutes in, one of the two teenage ushers walked up and down the aisle with flashlights, looking for contraband candy bought at the Texaco instead of the snack bar, tallboys smuggled inside big purses. The usher stopped before a couple getting friendly across the aisle from us. An older man, maybe in his thirties, and a girl I recognized as a high school cheerleader who often came into the café after practice. I remembered her because with her long, dark hair and the way her mouth was set, her nose straight and narrow, I had thought she looked like Victoria. When I had pointed this out to her, Victoria shook her head and sneered at the purple bow the girl wore high on her head, her snug cheer uniform, her straight white teeth, and the pink retainer she carefully wrapped in a napkin before eating. "Don't see it," Victoria had said, and gone back to sweeping. The usher shone his flashlight on the couple and the man held his hands up like the kid was a cop or something. The boy laughed quietly and kept walking.

Wyatt handed me the popcorn box and stood, whispering, "Need something to wash this down with. You?" I shook my head, and as I watched him move toward the exit the older man and I made eye contact in the dim flashes of colored lights. The girl was a senior, probably eighteen, but Jesus. The man seemed to rack his mind for how he knew me, resigned to giving me a friendly nod and turning away, his hairy arm curling around her shoulder. Explosions and beams of light blasted the walls of the theater and I felt uncomfortable, wishing we'd chosen seats higher up. When Wyatt came back, he touched my knee and

I leaned my head on his shoulder. Tried to relax into the space between old and new, the movie of us.

We held hands walking to the parking lot. Disorienting to me was the darkness. Like lying down for a quick afternoon nap to wake past supper, it was an unsettling feeling, tinged with a slight sense of loss. A group of boys rode skateboards down the street, the scrape of wheels on the asphalt the only noise; the second theater hadn't let out yet and by the time we exited ours the lot was empty. Flickering streetlamps illuminated glittery sprays of broken beer bottles and crushed popcorn boxes.

Wyatt squeezed my hand. "Maybe we should grab a drink."

The sudden growl of a diesel engine broke the quiet calm. Then, headlights. The boys hopped onto the sidewalk as a water truck rolled right through the intersection outside the theater. It shifted into gear, spewing exhaust and clanking down the two-lane road with the grace of an invading army tank.

I dropped Wyatt's hand. "Those damn trucks."

"Honestly, traffic's the least of my concerns."

"What, exactly, was it you found out about the pipeline? You know, what you were going to tell Victoria the other night?"

"That my department chair, the one from the cleanup group, was saying that chemicals can leach into the groundwater," he said, and started rubbing his palms together. "That pipeline will stretch from West Texas to Houston when completed. It's ridiculous to think there aren't ever going to be breaks. I'd found some information for her about well water contamination. I wanted her to get in touch with this environmental group out of Austin— they're doing some community organizing in affected areas."

"Was she interested in getting involved that way?"

His eyes lit up. "Hell, she could have joined a suit. Any involvement would've been a huge commitment on her part, but—and I think you'd agree—people need to speak up."

"The legal fees alone, though."

"I know, I know," he sighed. "There's so much money tied up in the pipeline. A billion, if not more."

"Damn." I swallowed hard—another bitter dose of resignation. "So, you're thinking about working for an environmental agency after this? Or what, teaching?"

"Teaching's not as easy as I hoped and I'm just a TA. Don't get any respect," Wyatt said, laughing a little. "I like it, though. I'm giving my first lecture next week—I mention that to say I hope we can spend some more time together before things get busy midterm."

"Promise me more fancy dates like this," I said, and relaxed my shoulders. "Sorry I spoiled the mood. It's hard to think about anything else. We probably should go for that drink."

He responded only by kissing me. He seemed nervous, a slight shake in his arms, and so was I, but I closed my eyes and kissed him back. We stumbled backward until I was pressed against the hood of my car. "Hold on," I said, and pulled away to unlock the door, then dropped my purse in the seat and turned to face him again. My heart beat faster, meeting his gaze.

But instead of leaning in, he frowned. "What's that?" he asked, looking to the side and over my shoulder.

There was a paper, a folded flyer of some kind, tucked under the wiper blade. "Palace Buffet's takeout menu? Or maybe an invitation to meet Jesus," I said, reaching for it.

"No, this." He turned my shoulders and pointed to the back window. The words UR NEXT were written in pink paint.

My face felt tingly, the blood drained from it.

Wyatt shook his head. "Some kind of inside joke? You hate

text abbreviations. Remember when I sent you 'thx' instead of 'thanks'?"

"You think this is funny? It's a threat." I crumpled the paper and threw it on the seat. "I ought to leave."

"What do you mean?" He reached for me, but I swatted his hand away. "Should I take you home then?"

"I'm not leaving my car."

"At least let me follow behind you," he said.

After I turned into the driveway, Wyatt pulled up behind me and got out. I rolled down the window to stop him, to tell him I was fine and good night. I squeezed my eyes shut and waited for the engine to turn, for him to drive away. I opened my eyes and took a deep breath. But he hadn't left—if he wanted to wait until I was inside the door, fine then. The Bluebird was under the carport. Nikki was home and I felt okay. Whoever painted my window was a chickenshit and wouldn't be so bold to come to my house, unless—no, Wyatt wouldn't have. He had left the theater when the show started, but still. I shook my head, grabbed the stupid flyer off the seat, and was about to shove it in my purse when I realized it wasn't a flyer or a takeout menu. It was a folded piece of computer paper. Smoothing it on my leg, I turned the dome light on and saw a grainy reprint of a photo, pixelated like it had been resized or maybe was a screenshot captured from a website. It was a photo of a naked woman with the word "STOP" handwritten in block letters underneath. Hands shaking, I stuffed it in the console. I felt outside myself. Like I was watching someone else lock the car, walk down the driveway and through the front door.

That night I took the past to bed with me, ghosts pressed and curled against my back.

Chapter 31

Cross-country practice started fifteen minutes after the last bell, and I was late.

The team captain, Tricia, tapped her wristwatch at me. "Nice of you to join us."

"I'm sorry; I was—"

"No excuses. No 'I'm sorry.' Do you want a win at regional as bad as the rest of us?" When I didn't answer, she poked me in the sternum. "Do you?"

"It's only ten after."

"You need to start showing up and pulling some weight. I don't know what's gotten into you lately." She had a habit of looking over you when she talked, maybe because she was five-eleven, but still, her gaze was distant, like there was a point of fixation just beyond the horizon. *I do want it,* I thought, *just not bad enough to be your boot camp bitch.* I nodded and silently joined the others in a wall sit.

Tricia was a star. In the spring, she ran track and field, a scholar-athlete who'd likely get a full ride to a D-I school, one of those athletes who really showed out during meets, her legs shiny and taut as she eased into the blocks, grinning as she gracefully crossed the finish line, barely sweating, waving to the stands. It was hard work looking flawless as an athlete. Only her coach and her teammates knew the strain behind her smile, the grinding in her back molars, her blistered feet. I was no athlete. I'd heard you needed extracurricular activities to stand out in your college applications. But I wasn't bad either—I worked at it like I worked at everything. And there was the endorphin high, the purely physical task of going as hard as you can for as long as you can. We had a solid, championship-likely team, and I was proud even if no one in Garnett cared because we weren't football.

The grass was damp from a brief storm, staining our shirts and shorts. Tricia had us hold a plank position on the field. "First to collapse has to organize the equipment room," she threatened, biceps flexing as she held position. My arms burned. My abdomen burned. My teammates entered into a no-blinking contest to distract themselves while I stared at the ground. I needed to shower, to print out my paper for lit review, highlight my chemistry notes. The muscle between my shoulder blades made a sharp spasm. I told Nikki I'd call her. She wanted to tell me about something crazy her new roommate had done. Or should I make flash cards for Spanish first? My arms quivered—

"Annie! Equipment room! I had a feeling you'd be the one to break."

I lay on my stomach for a moment. Felt my breath push my chest into the ground and the tired chug of my heart. Every day that fall my pace had been off. Floundering with the stress of college applications, my classes, a boy I loved and a boy I ached for, my loneliness wide and blue as water, I felt like I was drowning.

I'd been spending a lot of time with a girl new to our school named Elise. We had calculus, and looking back, I think she studied with me because she knew I'd end up writing most of the proofs. Her mother was an adjunct professor at State forced to downsize after a divorce in more ways than one—renting in Garnett, transferring Elise and her sister from Catholic school— and the few times I'd met her, she made it clear this stay was temporary. One night, Elise and I had been doing our homework, had stopped for microwaved egg rolls, then ice cream that I ate sitting on the foot of her bed. Tricia would give me five laps if she knew I was eating sweets, I thought, licking the spoon. Elise rolled over onto her elbows and peeked at me from under her down comforter and picked at a spot of chipped paint where an *Austin City Limits* poster had fallen off the wall. I could hear her sister Cecily's music coming from her room. Elise rolled her eyes, said, "Ever since we got back, she's played that song over and over. Do you know them?"

I nodded and she frowned. She often seemed to dislike me liking bands that she wanted to have discovered. She and Cecily went to Bonnaroo that summer and talked about it at least twenty times a day.

"We should go out," I said, wincing at the eagerness in my voice. I'd only hung out with Elise once or twice outside of school, still a bit uncertain of our relationship. Her father had taken her to France for her sixteenth birthday, she wore vintage dresses, had big eyes, delicate features, and very short bangs that instead of looking weird made her vaguely gamine, and so she seemed sophisticated to me—I think now she was a precursor to the kinds of girls I'd befriend in college, that back then I thought your friends defined you more than anything—and I wanted to impress her.

"Tell me more."

"There's this guy I'm talking to, Justin—"

"Oh, Schneider! He's so cute."

"Yeah." I nodded, blushing. "He said they were having some party at his brother's frat house."

"It's Wednesday night, girl!"

"I'm going. I'm too curious not to." *And I've fallen for Justin*, I didn't say, or that if I didn't go to that party, if I didn't show up for him, I was sure whatever connection we had was over. Acid rose in my throat— God, why was he so stubborn? Why didn't he listen when I told him the truth about Wyatt? That was over, dead. Wyatt was no doubt having the time of his life away from home, like I would, next year. But he'd said, *I miss you.* If he meant it—a mix of pain and pleasure, the thought stung, then cooled, as though someone had touched an ice cube to the back of my neck.

Elise giggled. "Whatever, I'm in."

"I finished the history presentation last night. Might actually lose it if I have to sit and study one more second," I added. Mine was on Julia Morgan and Hearst Castle. I'd never been to California, much less the central coast, but I fantasized about the curve of the drive leading to the castle overlooking the sharp cliffs. Could imagine Morgan walking through the vaulted hallways, the click of her heels echoing, her gazing down at an azure pool—something so lovely—her vision made real. How I wanted to go somewhere like that. Get the hell out of here.

"You would be already finished. I'll drive. Won't drink much since I can't afford to lose any more brain cells," she said, swinging her skinny legs over the bed. "We can use my mom's parking permit so we won't have to walk far. I have some friends from St. Paul's there too. I'll text them."

Her mother was away at a weeklong conference, another foreign aspect of their lives: the freedom Elise and her sister enjoyed without having to sneak around or work at it.

"I can't be out late—I have to present my part of the paper in class," I said, and took out my phone to let Justin know we were coming. It would be more fun with Elise. My skin felt itchy in anticipation, like if I didn't go out, and fast, I would miss everything worthwhile.

We dressed in baby doll tops and skintight jeans. All their clothes—Elise wore heels and I her sister's strappy gold sandals despite the first chill in the air. Techno chimed and pinged against her car's windows, and when we arrived she was able to squeeze between two big silver Land Rovers right in front of the redbrick and white-columned house. Right in the middle of fraternity row, a few blocks off campus where the street started to narrow and the sidewalks widened, each house's metallic Greek letters shining under the cool beam of the streetlamps. Two guys sat in rocking chairs on the porch and didn't even notice as we pushed open the massive double oak doors.

"Ladies." A guy in a stiff white button-up shirt and navy Dockers shorts nodded, coming up on our right. Music, indecipherable except for bass notes, came from downstairs. I nodded hello and Elise ignored the guy, looking at the group photos of men hanging from the wall. Another shorter, heavier-set guy joined him. They wore matching outfits down to the boating shoes and sunglasses hanging from their necks. We headed toward the basement stairwell and the source of the music. Elise fidgeted with her massive handbag, digging for her phone. She bored quickly, I'd noticed. For some reason I took that personally, like it was my fault she wasn't at least intrigued by the situation like I was.

"Who do you know here, girls?" The tall one cut us off at the stairs. Elise shrugged and deferred to me. She gave the best *I'm judging you* face—rolled her eyes, beamed them with her stare.

"Justin invited me," I said, unsure of the vibe. He hadn't texted me back yet—were they trying to keep us out? Did I make a mistake? They were leading us toward the basement, though, toward the main party.

"Bro, do you know a Justin? We don't have a Justin. Maybe a pledge?"

"True Gentleman," the short one said.

"Ah, yes, we don't have pledges anymore, ladies. All of our new brothers are part of the 'True Gentleman' program. New thing with campus hazing rules."

"So, Justin's not here?"

"What does he look like?" the tall one asked, leaning his elbows against the railing on the stairs in mock seriousness.

"Guess he's about six foot, blond hair and blue eyes," I said. "Troy Schneider's brother?"

"Schneider! You know Schneider? He's out back."

"Well . . ." I hesitated, thinking how silly I'd feel coming up to Troy as if we were friends. He was four years older than me and probably didn't know I existed. "I know Justin," I said.

Elise got her phone out of her bag again. Her ballet slipper pink nails made a faint clicking sound as she tapped out a text.

The short guy smiled. "Haven't seen him. But anyway, ladies, let's get you a drink. It's Wine Wednesday and we're having a party down here . . . ," he trailed off as we came down into the basement, the other one behind us on the stairs. "I'll tell Troy y'all are here." There was a bar set up in the corner with several giant punch bowls and two guys doling out drinks. The floor was sticky and even in the dim light I could see it was filthy. The speakers played old southern rock and the beer-pong table had a CCR sticker.

"Hey, girl, that friend from St. Paul's just texted me back. He lives two houses down and I promised if I ever made it to the row I'd stop by and see the house. He doesn't really want to crash here. I'll go over there and be back in a short bit. Unless you want to come?" she asked as the guys disappeared behind the bar. My phone vibrated in my pocket—probably Justin, I thought, finally.

"You go ahead. I'll stay and wait for Justin. They're already making us drinks," I said, spying a familiar face in the corner. It was Megan Miller. She was a year ahead of me in high school, but we'd had Spanish together last semester and I knew she'd just started at State. Megan dated Troy, and everyone at home always talked about how sweet it was they were still going together. I felt more at ease, seeing someone I knew, which lessened the blow of Elise ditching me. God, I hated Elise just then, how she only did whatever she wanted first. She scurried back up the stairs just as one of the guys returned.

"Where'd the other one go?" He smirked.

"Her friend lives a couple houses down—she'll be back."

"Ah, okay." He poured the contents of the second cup into mine. "Well, here's some of our pink sangria. House special. Let me introduce you to some of the brothers. Maybe sign you up for the next round of beer pong. I actually feel like I've seen you before? Have you come to the house?"

"No, but I've been to the row," I lied.

"Okay, party girl." He grinned.

The drink was not like the grain alcohol–laced hunch punches I'd had before. It tasted good. Fruity and like the rosé wine coolers my mom kept in a box in the refrigerator. After I'd met a few of the guys, I waved to Megan and started walking toward her. She and her friends were all wearing low heels and pretty, picnic-patterned shift dresses, conservative and tailored. I couldn't tell if I was extremely underdressed in my jeans and top or extremely overdressed, like I was trying too hard. My whole body blushed when she explained that this was "a little mixer" thrown by the sorority she was rushing. The girls shuffled around each other close, like they were hens and I was the fox. I felt like an idiot. Vowed to throttle Justin when he showed. No wonder the vibe was borderline unfriendly.

My phone vibrated again. I went to the corner of the room to check it, my back to the party, and saw the text was from my mother, not Justin.

—HI, SWEET GIRL! Hope you're having fun! Love, Momma

I always laughed when she signed off on her texts, like I didn't know who'd sent them. I felt a pang in my chest then, thinking about her and Daddy drinking iced tea in the folding chairs under the chinaberry tree in the backyard, enjoying the cool night breeze, knowing how disappointed they would be if they knew I'd lied about doing homework all night at Elise's. I'd been quiet and moody since both Nikki and Wyatt had left, so they were probably just happy I was being social again. Always, they had trusted me. Already I felt woozy from the sips of the pink sangria. Tasted something metallic and salty in my mouth—a bit of blood from my tongue, maybe. I slid the phone back in my pocket and sidled up next to one of the brothers who wasn't playing beer pong. It felt good to touch and be touched. I put down my cup and leaned into the guy as he put his arm around me and told a story about something I can't remember now. I felt burning hot, and moments later so cold my teeth chattered.

My head buzzed with loud laughs and blinking lights, no solid shapes, no sense of time. My cheek pressed against something hard and cool.

I would learn from Elise that I was mumbling gibberish, then out cold. She'd come back to pick me up, ready to go home, and couldn't find me. She'd asked around, and finally someone led her to me. She found me on the floor. One of the guys carried me to her car, and when we got to her house she and her sister, Cecily, dragged me inside. Elise skipped school the next day and checked on me every hour but didn't call for help because we had been drinking underage. She'd said if I had been passed out any longer, she would have called a doctor.

"Do you remember anything?" Cecily tucked a piece of my hair behind my ear. Her blue eyes were pink and watery like she was going to cry.

"No, what happened?" I licked my dry lips and saw I was still in my clothes from the day before. "Oh my god, oh my god," I chanted under my breath. I looked around the room and at my body under the blanket. I still had my sandals on. I smelled.

"We were worried," Elise said sternly, and I wondered if I should apologize. I looked between the two of them, their mouths set, eyebrows raised. I felt somehow both small and like a giant lump of trash at the same time.

Cecily cleared her throat. "How much did you have to drink?"

"God, shut up, Cecily." Elise pushed her to the side.

"Whatever," she hissed. "You said it first."

I tasted vomit in my mouth. "Just one, no, half a SOLO cup of sangria. I think."

Elise frowned and said, "Girl, this is not good. I don't want to put you on the spot, but do you, um—"

"What?"

"You know, down there. You okay?"

Oh. God. I nodded gravely and nearly fell getting out of the bed, stumbled down the hall and into the bathroom. I'd only had sex once. I would have felt sore, I assured myself, maybe bled. I looked at my underwear. I would know. Wouldn't I?

Dizzy as I stood again, the walls of her house seemed to tunnel and cave. Blinking back tears, I found my way back to the bedroom and sat on the bed. "It's fine. I'm fine."

Elise sat next to me. "If you want, we can go to the clinic by the university."

"No." I looked out the window. The light through the trees was wrong—thin and coppery. "What time is it?"

"Almost five. Do you want us to take you home now?"

I groaned and held my stomach.

"Or if you need to puke, there's the trash can."

Dizzy again, I tipped forward.

"Right by the bed, girl. Please not the carpet."

Dusky shadows cast across the floor. I took a deep breath. Looked at my backpack in the corner of the room and sat up straight. "I missed class. I'm going to fail that paper and our entire presentation. God, what even happened to me?"

"This is really embarrassing," Elise sighed, and turned to Cecily. "Should we?"

They showed me after I'd had Gatorade and a few crackers— all I could keep down. A picture of a woman naked from the waist up in front of a glass trophy case, her eyes closed. Mouth partly open. It was an anonymous body that was mine. Every mole, line, fold of skin, the brown birthmark just under the left breast by my heart, was a mirror image. But how could this object of flesh—slack necked like a crash course dummy— actually be mine? The photo had been posted anonymously on a web page. The site was called Juicy Campus—regularly trawled for bits of gossip by State students and Garnett kids alike—and whoever ran it deleted the post by the next day. The comments called the girl in the picture a slut, a drunken bitch. But the worst was the one that said: *Party Girl Looks Dead. She Must Be Dead.*

You're alive, alive, alive, I thought whenever the image came to mind, whenever my hands would start to tingle and numb, alarm coursing through my veins, my mind starting to hover outside the body. I closed my eyes and there it was, grainy and flat. There was me, dissolving into pixels.

For a solid week, girls at school wouldn't look me in the eye. For a solid month, boys at school winked when they saw me. My partner on the history presentation, my friend Hazel, didn't forgive me for ruining our grade. *This is so unlike you. Who are you?* I can still hear her saying. Elise and I didn't talk much after that night. Justin never called. The shame, it lingered. But I put my head down. Tried to ignore it and move on. I think a lot of people live in such states of in-between with their ghosts.

A few days after the party was our big cross-country meet. I was on the ground stretching next to the water cooler when Tricia crouched beside me.

"Annie, we need you to step up today since Mariah's out. Pull some weight. Make a personal record," she said.

"I'm not feeling too hot," I said, picking at the grass. I always felt nauseated on meet days, though usually it was performance anxiety.

"We have full faith in you. Mean it," Tricia said, rocking on her haunches. I nodded and tightened the laces in my running shoes. She patted my back and went off to stretch on her own.

At the starting line I took the stance, felt my calves lengthen as I raised my body, bolted at the gun, and then I did something I never did: counted my steps. It was weird. When I thought about counting, I lost count, hesitated, took an extra step, and nearly tripped over my own feet. I kept going, the course seemingly endless. I lost my balance and skidded down a hillside about a quarter of a mile to the finish, spun out, and fell. Back up again—no penalty, just had to finish—but I was slowed, hobbling into last place. After, I wondered why I distrusted my body to get me through the course, why I imagined falling before it actually happened, and when I did—gravel and dirt stippling my skin—I had felt so good. I had landed hard on my right ankle, now swollen, and when the coach brought ice and held it to my skin I felt calmer than I had in days.

The rest of the meet was somber; we'd come in fourth place, had originally projected to come in first. Tail between my legs, I limped toward Tricia. Her eyes squeezed closed, she folded into a yoga pose and reached her arms over her head.

"I'm sorry," I said.

"Hmmm." She stayed bent forward, speaking to the grass. "No, you're not."

"I just apologized. I don't know what more you want."

"You came over here to show me your damn ankle, well, I don't have much sympathy."

"You're a great team captain."

She sat up quickly. The veins in her forehead throbbed and her braids tight to her skull seemed to pull her eyebrows back. "I know you more than you think I do, party girl. Maybe this little injury will keep you in the library. The orthotic boot the doc will give you won't look cute with a SOLO cup."

My mouth went dry. There was a chance she didn't see the picture, had meant "party girl" in a general way, but still, I hated that she thought me so shallow.

"You have to work hard, show up for us. Just because you have a boo-boo doesn't mean the world stopped turning."

"I hate that I let everyone down," I said. "Maybe there's still a chance at finals."

She shook her head. "Whatever, it's not your problem anymore. You'll probably be out for a couple weeks."

I looked at her and knew that all she had accomplished at this school and as an athlete was because she worked twice as hard as anybody. It wasn't fair—God, what was? I was red and ashamed, but fully aware of the pulsing pain in my ankle and the livid pain in my heart as I turned toward the locker room.

The photo was gone. What remained was the feeling of someone watching me. It hovered at the periphery of my vision, a waning shadow. I didn't report anything because I wasn't sure. It could have been that I was tired, I don't hold my liquor well, and I had little to eat before the party. It could have been that after blacking out I drank more than the single glass I remember. But here is what I do remember from that night:

Falling onto the floor of the women's restroom, my cheek hitting cold porcelain. My legs and arms are paralyzed. My tongue cannot form words. Being lifted over a shoulder, and later, Elise pinching my arm, and a man's voice saying, "She's so light. She weighs practically nothing, nothing at all." Waking up in Elise's bed hours later still in my clothes and shoes. A sticky pink stain, fruity and ripe, down the front of my shirt. A blackish bruise forming on the meat of my thigh. And this surge of grief—for time lost, perhaps. For everything loosed from my tight grip.

Chapter 32

Victoria said to me, maybe a week before she died, "The difference between you and I is that—"

"You and me."

"What?"

"It's you and me."

"That's one difference." She laughed. "You're a snot. What I
was going to say—"

A customer walked in, interrupting our break. I'm not sure
what else she would have said. I don't know what Victoria
thought. It could have been a million things that separated us
in her mind, and sometimes I think it was hardly anything at
all. Washing the bullet at dawn, I was thinking about this, and
I choked up at not knowing, at never knowing, not for certain.
The paint on my window smeared and ran in pink rivulets into
the wheel well and down the drive.

The screen door slammed behind Nikki. "What the hell," she
said, voice still hoarse with sleep.

"Didn't mean to wake you."

She inspected the soapy water, the pink blot.

"Some 'Go Steers' thing. Guess whoever did it thought it was a senior's car. I was parked by the field," I said, and when I did the words sounded funny in my mouth, heavy and unnatural. Scared, unsure who could have threatened me, I hadn't slept. *Wyatt,* I thought again—who else knew where I was parked just then? But the bullet was recognizable, especially if this person had been following me. The bigger question was who would have had a picture from *that* night, nearly five years ago now. It could have been anyone from the party at State, or someone who'd been at Garnett High at the same time as me. But who would have held on to that file for all this time?

Nikki touched the paint with her finger. "When did this happen?"

"Last night. Just a harmless prank." I cringed at the thought of explaining the picture to Nikki, my grandfather, or, God forbid, my parents. I knew they hadn't heard, back then, because there's no way they wouldn't have said anything to me. I took a wad of paper towel and rubbed the last smudge from the window.

There, all clean.

"I needed to get up anyway. Busy day today. Bethany's out and we've got a consultation for the Miller girl and her bridal party. Will probably be awkward for that poor sister of hers," she said, and pulled her arms inside the sleeves of her T-shirt. "Dang, it's a little chilly out here. Might come fall soon after all."

My heart thumped in my neck. "Miller girl, as in Layla? Megan's sister?"

Nikki nodded. "Bet Megan feels like they should be planning her wedding, not her little sister's."

"Want help?" I asked, thinking if I could get Megan alone,

I'd question her about that night. Just the thought made my stomach flip. "I can cover the desk, if you'd like."

Nikki narrowed her eyes. "That's awfully nice. You sure?"

"Of course," I said. My phone vibrated in my back pocket. I almost silenced it before looking—I'd ignored one call from Wyatt already—but it was Mary-Pat. "I'll be just a minute, Nik. Make the coffee?"

She yawned and walked toward the house. "Fine."

I waited until the screen door closed before answering.

"Morning," Mary-Pat said, and cleared her throat. "I called because you need to lay low for a while. On mine and your grandfather's orders."

"Why?" I braced myself—how could they already know about the car paint and the picture?

"No big deal. We'd only rather you be watchful. Someone's, well, bothered Leroy."

God, how self-centered I'd been. If someone had the nerve to threaten me, they most certainly would go after Leroy. I should have called him last night. "What happened? Is he okay?"

"Petty vandalism. Nothing he's not used to. Keep an eye out, and mind yourself now."

"Wait—" I said, but she'd already hung up.

When I got to Leroy's the street was quiet. I don't know what I expected—a flurry of activity? A mess of graffiti on the walls of the house and a group of vandals?—but the air was still and the sun slanted through the pecan tree over the driveway like any ordinary morning. Cats slept on the porch and a neighbor walked to the edge of the drive to check the mail. The only thing out of place was Mary-Pat's Silverado parked crookedly, a spray of gravel on the sidewalk and her front left tire in the dewy grass. I went around back, but it looked as it always did: dirt paths worn in the yard like a racetrack, from the dogs, an old mattress on the ground for them to sleep on with its creamy white filling spewed out, a slow-turning windmill, chipped pots, and a raised flower bed overgrown with Texas sage and lemon balm.

Then I saw the side window: a baseball-sized hole with a web of cracks spread across the pane, and through it Mary-Pat and Leroy arguing. I couldn't hear what they were saying, so I came closer, touched my index finger to the sharp point of glass where the impact had been.

"Granddad, you aren't hurt, are you?" I called, and stepped back so I wouldn't cut myself—the glass hadn't been swept up.

Leroy looked a hundred years old. I came around and walked up onto the porch just as Mary-Pat came out the front door.

"You two idiots got a bunch of no-good people riled up. You know that Randy Huber has a record, don't you? He might not have killed the girl, but he sure as shit might have something else to hide."

My cheeks flamed. "What was it? A baseball?"

"A rock, no note," she said.

I pushed past her and went inside the house. "Well, what are we going to do?"

"We?" She was on my heels. "We aren't going to do anything. I thought you both were going to take my lead."

Leroy stood shakily in the center of the room. I noted the handgun in his tooled leather holster belt. He'd taken his arm out of the sling and he held it strangely against his side. I went to hug him. "I'm sorry," I said into his worn-soft shirt, the pearl snaps pressing against my cheek. Squeezed him tightly and breathed in deep. He smelled like he always did—alcohol and the mustiness of his clothes closet, trace of Old Spice—but slightly acrid, like sweat, like fear. His heart raced.

He didn't move to hug me back, so I let go and he sat in a recliner—his old favorite, the one with duct-taped arms and a sunken cushion—with such a sigh of relief I wondered if he would curl up into a ball and fall asleep. "It's not your fault. We caught one, I like to say," he said, finally.

"I should have told you last night, but," I stammered, "I—"

"What?" Mary-Pat crossed her arms over her chest.

"Someone painted 'ur next' on my window."

Mary-Pat shook her head and walked outside.

"Jesus H.," Leroy said, loudly. I'd never heard him raise his voice in anger. One of the dogs was startled awake and butted his head against the coffee table, knocking Leroy's rum and Coke onto the floor.

I looked around me for something to wipe it up with.

"Over there's a cup towel," Leroy said, and pointed to the dining room table, too tired to get up. "You can toss it."

I held it, pausing—this was a gift I'd given to Leroy. One Christmas, years ago, Mamaw had shown me how to embroider and the cup towel had been my project. I still remembered: a single, straight stitch all along the pattern line, my misshapen drawing of a moon clustered with stars, come up a space ahead on the pattern and bring your needle back down into the same hole at the end of the last stitch. A step forward and a step back. Focused on getting it right, on balancing the wooden hoop on my knee, I didn't realize I'd been sewing through both the towel fabric and my loose pant leg. I'd stood and Mamaw laughed long and hard at the towel stuck on me, at the needle dangling around my kneecap. I ripped out all my work and started over, and still it turned out ugly. But it had been a gift. One I'd made special for him. I wiped up the Coke and rum with it. "You can wash these, you know."

"Pat's right," Leroy said. "This is it, little darlin'."

"What? What is it? You saw someone?"

"No," Mary-Pat said, back inside. I tried to ignore her staring daggers at me from the corner of my eye.

"Get out of here. Go home," Leroy said.

"No," I said. "We're in too deep. We're obviously getting closer, else they wouldn't have done something so desperate."

Leroy turned sideways so he wouldn't meet my eyes. "Tell the girl to go home," he said to Mary-Pat.

"Annie, come on," she sighed.

Leroy didn't smile and he didn't wink. He turned away. So, this was the cold shoulder, I thought. Literally. I went to the door, intent on them not seeing me cry.

"I'll call you tomorrow," he said to my back.

"Whatever." I walked to the bullet with the wet towel still balled in my fist.

Chapter 33

I never liked Bethany. Even still, she and Nikki remained close. "She on vacay?" I asked from her chair at the reception desk, willing the phone to ring—anything to distract from the dark thoughts roiling in my head like thunderclouds.

"Don't laugh," Nikki said, hands sudsy from shampooing Mrs. Buford. "She's at a youth ministry conference. Her fiancé's got her going to the church where his dad's the preacher. Thinks John David and Bethany have a way with the children."

"Have to admit that's rich," I said, thinking of the aesthetician-in-training's penchant for trouble. She and Nikki made a splash their freshman year by getting kicked off the varsity cheerleading squad—an enviable position for two freshmen—after only half a semester. Nikki for never bringing her players baked goods on game days and "being mouthy," Bethany for putting vodka in the girls' water bottles. Rebellion wasn't the quality I disliked about Bethany, more so that she was a hypocrite. Kind of girl says she hates drama, then starts it. And we'd always divided Nikki's attention. Last time we spent any significant amount of time together was cheer camp in fourth and fifth grades. We practiced our routine at Nikki's because she had a trampoline—just shimmying and high kicks set to Shania Twain—and at the time, Nikki was going through a phase where she acted like I was a baby to put up with, ordering me to fetch them Capri Suns, rolling her eyes when I attempted a joke. I didn't like cheer camp either—afraid of climbing to the top of the pyramid, too shy to enjoy myself—and spent the next summer camped at the public library. Bethany reminded me of times I felt like I didn't belong. Yet hadn't I always felt that way? My loneliness receded but always returned, that blue feeling lapping at my heels as soon as I turned my back.

"Annie." Nikki looked at me in the mirror. "Don't be mean."

I bit my tongue. Sherrilyn came from the back and handed me a stack of bills to process. Nikki sat Mrs. Buford under the dryer, and not long after my mother walked in the door with lunch. She normally ate at the bank, a salad with tasteless low-fat dressing most days, but when she'd heard I was filling in for Bethany she'd swung by Richie's BBQ.

"Line was out the door. My stomach was starting to think my throat had been cut." She looked around and laughed a little, her eyes widening when she handed me a plate. "Sweet pea, you look ragged."

Sherrilyn nodded. "You ought to sit in my chair, let me try something with more layers. At least let Nikki do your nails for once."

"Maybe then she'd stop biting them," Nikki said, and motioned at the shelf behind her, the pastel and jewel-toned bottles like rows of Easter eggs. "Go on, pick one."

"Gee, thanks," I said, hiding my hands in my lap.

"What's wrong, Annie?"

"Nothing, Momma," I said, and looked down at my food—

sliced brisket on white bread, a scoop of potato salad, and pickle chips—and forced a bite. Mouth dry, the food stuck in my throat. I'd never gotten used to the Beauty Shoppe's distinct smell: floral yet chemical with a hint of singed hair.

Momma put her hand to my forehead. "Baby."

Nikki swirled the ice in her Diet Dr Pepper. "She's not sleeping."

"I'm fine," I said, inching backward in the rolling chair.

"You think I don't notice." Nikki looked to me. "But I do."

Sherrilyn shivered. "I know I'm all worked up, everything that's happened."

Momma looked at me. "Two people you know—one's been killed; the other's a killer—it's a terrible thing. Being tragedy adjacent is still trauma."

Sounds like something she heard in a therapist's office, I thought, though I was certain no one in my family had ever been to a therapist, and then, praise be, the phone rang. I wiped my hands with the flimsy paper napkin and scrambled to answer. As much as I wanted—needed—to vent, I knew I couldn't. Not with them. If they knew what I knew they would be in danger. There was someone out there watching me. Someone bold, desperate. I took down the appointment in Bethany's datebook, busying myself and keeping my eyes down, but listening. Momma talked about the unsolved Chavez case; Hector's wife, Delia, was a former classmate of hers. Sherrilyn, too, had known the man.

It all started with the hit-and-run, hadn't it? That first cruel act set a curse on this town. Like tipping over a row of dominoes. Spooky Sheila waving her arms in the crowded café flashed across my mind. Leroy and Mary-Pat's gray, worry-worn faces. A naked body, eyes closed, mouth parted, bright red tongue. Pink paint—God, the fluorescent light on these bubblegum pink walls hurt my eyes. I put down the phone and put my head in my hands, tried to slow my breathing.

Sherrilyn sighed. "Some folks are saying the Garza boy's innocent."

I wondered if by "folks" she meant Nikki and knew this was why I couldn't tell them a damn thing.

"Annie, what do you think?" Momma asked. "Your daddy told me you've been sneaking around with the old man. He's worried."

"That's over," I said, but felt a jolt in my chest. It wasn't true. The investigation was not over. How alone I felt, just then—Leroy and Mary-Pat didn't want me, fine. I didn't need them either.

"Y'all about done stuffing your gullets?" Mrs. Buford called from the chair in the corner. "How long have I been sittin' here?"

"Hold your horses, Nan," Sherrilyn said, and snapped her fingers in Nikki's direction. Nikki's face soured as she closed the container of coleslaw and gathered up the trash.

"Well, then. I better get," Momma said. I could tell she was hurt by my avoidance. She looked in the mirror and checked her teeth, straightened her First Bank of Garnett name tag and applied her lipstick, a shade of mauve she kept in her purse called rum raisin.

"She's only squealing 'cause her head got hot. Thanks for lunch, Aunt Tina," Nikki loud-whispered.

Sherrilyn hummed along to the soft rock station piped in on the speakers and leaned over the reception desk to check the next appointment—the bridal consultation for the youngest Miller girl—and as she did, Momma met my eyes in the mirror. "Sweet pea," she said. "You sure you're okay?"

All I could say was yes, and nod, knowing that if I said more I'd risk a gush of tears. Admit to her my panic, my fear, or that

I was losing control. On her way out the door she blew me a kiss, and like a child, I held out my hand to catch it.

Uncombed hair now reddish from a henna rinse, clad in yoga pants and Birkenstocks, a silver stud in her nose, Megan Miller looked different from the sorority girl I remembered.

"Congrats, doll!" Sherrilyn ushered Megan, her two sisters, and their mother inside and into the salon chairs. The bride, Layla, talked a mile a minute about waterfall ringlets versus chignons, and how she wanted to incorporate her colors—red and gold—into the makeup. I watched Megan shift in her chair uncomfortably. When asked if she'd consider extensions, she shrugged.

"Please stop acting like you're so much better than this," Layla said to her sister through gritted teeth.

"She's just got her heart broke is all. This is hard," their mother said, making meaningful eye contact with Sherrilyn and Nikki in the mirror. "She and Troy Schneider broke it off."

Megan rolled her eyes. "Jesus, it's not about that. I'm happy with whatever you decide, princess, so excuse me."

"Bitch, you're my maid of honor. Start acting like it."

"Let her go," the mother said, and the bell rang on the front door as Megan exited. The mother, perhaps to save face, started in on how great Megan was doing, something about a juice cleanse—I wasn't really listening. I followed Megan outside.

The day had grown warm. The asphalt glittered in the sun and black crickets bounced in the weeds and off a cracked stucco wall, its color a sad, sun-faded ochre. Megan was down the sidewalk under the shade of the old LAUNDROMAT sign, digging in her canvas bag for her earbuds.

"Hey, wait!" I called after her, and shut the salon door. "Remember me?"

She stopped and looked at me for a moment. "Didn't we have Spanish together? God, that old bag of bones hated me. Remember how she'd wag her finger in your face if you called her 'Mrs. Stewart' instead of 'señora'? Please," she said, and dropped the earbuds back in the bag. She was thinner now, too thin, but she still looked like Megan Miller: clear skinned with a dash of freckles, blue-eyed. Her roots were beginning to show the color of summer wheat. She looked me up and down expectantly.

"Actually, Megan, I was thinking about a party at State."

Her face stiffened.

"When I, um—"

"Yeah. About that, about what happened," she said slowly, her voice cold. "No one knew you."

"What—what does that even mean?"

"They slipped you something."

"Who did?"

She shrugged and her eyes darted over my shoulder. "I had to pull your pants up."

"Oh." I took a quick breath. "I had no idea you did that."

"I'm not trying to embarrass you now; I'm just sorry. See, I nearly tripped over you. You had fallen down. I pulled you back together best I could and led you onto the landing because it was gross in there on the floor. Left you to go find that girl you came with—I didn't mean for the guys to all see you and make fun of you like that."

A bead of sweat rolled between my shoulder blades and I didn't know what to say. I felt like I was on fire. "Makes me sick just thinking about it," I said after a few moments, my voice shaking, my chin trembling. *God, stop,* I thought. *Don't cry. Why are you crying?*

"I don't hang out with any of them now, just so you know. Troy—hell, all of them—they'll keep acting like that, like such assholes. Keep going back to the house for game day tailgates, alumni luncheons, keep patting each other on the back and acting the same, only with more money and more beer bloat."

I took a deep breath, plucked my shirt for air. "I shouldn't have even been there that night. I was supposed to meet up with Justin. That's why I told Elise she could leave. And then Justin didn't show. Thanks for looking out, best you could anyway."

"You were talking to him," she said, and squinted—the sun was in her eyes and she held her hand like a visor while seeming to consider me, to consider what I'd said for a moment. "You don't remember that part?"

"No." I thought Justin hadn't come and he'd heard the next day at school how big a fool I made of myself. Saw the photo and then decided what kind of girl I was. Realizing he witnessed me in that state—God only knowing what I said or what I did—made my head feel light. "I thought he didn't show."

"Justin was there. When your friend finally came back, he carried you to her car. That's how I realized he was the one who invited you two girls. I told Troy, afterward, not to let his little brother invite people to our parties anymore," she said, and kicked a pebble down the sidewalk. "As if I wasn't doing the same thing a few months earlier. Finishing my homework early, or not doing it at all, so I could spend the night at the fraternity over the weekend because he missed me. As if I was so special. Troy is the kind of guy who should only date girls younger than him. It is a type, you know."

"Is that why y'all split up? Another girl—younger?"

She rolled her shoulders and sighed. "Take a wild guess."

I jumped when the bell above the salon door chimed.

"Annie." Sherrilyn stuck her head out. "Get your butt back in here. Phone's ringing."

Megan looked relieved. "Think I'll wait for bridezilla in the car," she said, and took a step back from where she'd been leaning her shoulder against the building.

"Good luck in Houston," I said.

"You take care of yourself." She dipped her head and walked around the corner to the parking lot. I watched her get in her family's white Lincoln, feeling both drawn to her and repulsed, her words stinging like she'd given me a slap across the mouth.

I sat behind the reception desk, picked up a magazine, and pretended to read, unable to focus on anything but knowing how she remembered me. On knowing Justin saw me in such a state and I didn't have a clue as to be doubly embarrassed until now. The Millers left soon after I came inside, and though I was sure they didn't know a thing about it, I felt lighter after they were gone. After listening to the whirr of dryers, Nikki and Sherrilyn's debating whose duty it was to drive Aunt Jewel to her eye exam next Tuesday, biting back the urge to scream or maybe cry, I stood and gathered my things. "See y'all later."

"No, ma'am!" Sherrilyn called after me. "We don't close for another half hour."

"You're not even paying me," I said without turning around.

The long shadows of telephone poles stretched over the empty street. Troy had been messing around on Megan again. Maybe with Victoria. Maybe he was the one who saved, then threatened me with that image. Maybe everyone's favorite quarterback had been so bold as to hurl a rock through Leroy's window. He was the one who drugged me those years ago. Likely, the desire to overpower a woman, to make her limp and pliable as a doll, had never really left Troy Schneider.

Chapter 34

"Have you seen this man in here before? Remember seeing him with Victoria Merritt the last time she was here?"

I held out a profile picture of Troy's I had printed out at the library. The bartender moved toward the lighted beer sign to examine it and the neon made him rosy. Nikki spun in her stool and gave the old honky-tonk the once-over—when I left the Beauty Shoppe, she had followed me outside, had stood in front of the bullet until I told her my plans—and frowned as if I'd made her come along. Yesterday Once More seemed quieter compared to when I'd come with Leroy: a handful of dancers out on the floor waltzed to a slow, sad song, mostly "olds" as Nikki had said when taking stock of the crowd.

"One of the Schneider boys, ain't he?"

"Yes." I leaned forward. "Troy."

"Thought so. Can't say for sure I seen him with Vic. That night was slammed." The bartender handed me back the photo. "Sorry, babe."

"Thanks anyway," I said, and looked to see if Jimmy Ryland

was back from his break—if anyone had seen Troy come in here with Victoria or had overheard something, it would have been Jimmy at his perch by the door. I shouldn't have assumed the blond man in an Artemis polo shirt Sonny remembered arguing with Victoria was Randy or Steve. Troy knew the group of roughnecks in here that night. He also might have been there himself, to meet Victoria. He fit the bill perfectly. I craned my neck to look around the room and decide if there was anyone I could talk to. I had to be careful, Troy being well-connected and likely to hear any gossip. I wasn't ready to confront him, not yet. Nikki scooted her stool closer to mine.

"Troy? You really think Troy Schneider's got something to do with this?"

"Best lead I've got."

"Have you talked to Justin?"

"God, no!" I grabbed her wrist. "And don't you tell anybody a thing. I'm going to see what I can dig up and take it to Mary-Pat and Leroy, and if they don't care I'm going to Fernando's lawyer directly. Hell, maybe I'll talk to Sheriff Garcia."

She nodded solemnly and, after a moment, spun around on her stool and looked across the dance floor. "I can see Leroy here. He always did like a party."

The disco ball was on and turning slowly. The bartender cracked one can of beer after another, a puncture in the slow song, the pedal steel notes climbing higher, higher, a keening sound.

"What's the matter?" Nikki asked.

"Sorry." I wiped the corner of my eye with my T-shirt. "It's just that I think now Victoria must have been drugged."

"Oh." Nikki looked down. "But, why does that matter?"

"What do you mean, why? It's basically assault! Or intent!"

"Well, yeah. Course. I guess I meant even if she was rip-roaring drunk on her own volition no one should have messed with her."

"Well," I said, my face hot, "I'm not trying to absolve her of anything. You know I didn't say that."

"So defensive." Nikki looked at my face, then down to my white-knuckled grip on the bar top. "Is there something you're not telling me? Did something ever happen . . ." She paused, sliding her hand over to touch mine. "Like, to you?"

"No." I drew my hand back. "There's nothing to tell."

"Good," she said softly. She set her beer on the bar and stood. "I'll be right back. I'm gonna put a song on the jukebox."

The lie was reflexive, so quick. My eyes watered again and I blinked hard. Relieved, I knew she wouldn't ask me again—but why did part of me wish she would? I heard my name being called across the bar. Sonny came through the door and a smatter of moths floated in with him. He folded me into a hug. I bought him a beer and he sat on the stool next to mine.

"Who's that?" His eyes widened as he motioned toward Nikki.

She turned from the jukebox and I waved her over. "My cousin, Nikki Avery."

He shook her hand. "Hey, gorgeous."

I rolled my eyes a bit, but she only smiled. I realized, with some astonishment, that Nikki seemed shy—blushing, even. She tilted her head just so. She leaned. "You played football, I think."

"For Parr City. And you cheered for Garnett."

"Just my freshman year. Guess you were memorable."

"Likewise." He inched closer, grinning now.

"Sonny—" As much as I hated to break the spell, I pulled out Troy's picture. "Remember how you told me some guy met up with Victoria once the last time she came in here? Does he look familiar?"

Sonny turned his attention back to me. Nikki stepped on the toe of my shoe, but I handed him the picture and he studied it. "Yeah. I think that's the guy."

"You're sure?"

"There aren't that many younger guys come in here that aren't vets. He played ball, too, for Garnett. I remember him. But haven't seen him since then. What's the deal? Is he in trouble? I thought they arrested that other guy. Is your granddad looking into it?"

"I'm helping the family tie up some loose ends with the property and was curious. Troy's a landman for Artemis these days."

Nikki looked back and forth between us. "You didn't tell me how you two know each other."

"Old dancing partners," he said. "Want to?"

"Isn't this one of Jewel's favorites?" She looked back at me as the two of them walked onto the floor.

Charlie Rich's "The Most Beautiful Girl" had come on. I smiled for the first time all day. Let myself forget for a moment what had brought me to this place, the shadow of fear and doubt in the back of my mind, the knowledge that I had very little time to make headway on this. Sonny at least could confirm that Troy and Victoria were more personally involved than he let on. That they had fought not long before she was killed. This could be big. I needed to call the others. But Nikki looked happy out on the floor. I let my shoulders relax, decided we could stay for another song because I knew that together with Leroy and Mary-Pat I'd figure out the best course of action. Narrowing in on Troy would redeem me in their eyes. I waved at Nikki and Sonny, was about to order another round when my phone vibrated in my purse.

"Hey, Daddy," I said, my shoulders tightening again.

"I'm sorry, honey." His voice caught in his throat. He was crying. "I'm afraid I have bad news."

"What happened?"

"It's your grandfather."

The music stopped.

Part III

Chapter 35

Blood stained the front of his faded denim shirt, and in his hand was a crumpled Stetson. It took me a moment to realize neither blood nor hat belonged to Bill Schneider.

"I got here as fast as I could," I said. The emergency room at the county hospital smelled like antiseptic and sweat. The receptionist argued with a shoeless, shirtless man bent over her desk, and through the walls I could hear someone moaning, someone crying.

"Your folks got to meet with the doc just a minute ago," Bill said. "Asked me to wait for you and let you know what happened. They only allow so many people back there."

"My dad said there was a wreck. Are he and Mary-Pat—"

"He was alone in the vehicle. Don't think anyone's been able to get ahold of her. The EMTs weren't sure if he had a heart attack before or after he went off the road. Might've been why he lost control, or might've been a result of the trauma. All I know is he drove right through our fence. Totaled his truck. Luckily, we were down that way and heard the crash. I pulled him out while one of my boys found cell service and called the ambulance."

"No, no way—"

Bill hung his head. "Sorry, honey."

This can't be happening. I had a hard time focusing between the whoosh of blood in my ears, the intercom static, and the man at reception—either very drunk or very high—now pacing the room talking to himself, but I finally noticed the two of them in the corner. Troy seated and scrolling through his phone, and Justin, pushing back his chair and coming toward me.

"Oh, Annie."

I opened my mouth, but no words came out. He pulled me in for a hug and I felt his Adam's apple bob against my cheek, thinking I could hide my face in his neck forever. To even look him in the eye felt impossible, not now—and not with what I knew. I felt a firm hand press against my back and turned to face Bill, Troy now at his side.

Troy looked me up and down. "You drove yourself?"

"My cousin's parking the car," I said, my head throbbing. "She drove me."

"Your granddad and your people have been my neighbors for all my life. Leroy is a good man," Bill said, and sighed. He placed Leroy's hat on the chair next to my purse and stared at it. He, Troy, and Justin were tired looking and sunburned, their boots and jeans streaked with dirt. And radiated heat—I could feel Justin's body like an open flame beside mine though we'd separated.

"Thank you all for being there for him," I said.

Troy straightened his shoulders and nodded, but at someone behind me. I turned around expecting to see Nikki, but it was Sheriff Garcia charging through the automatic double doors toward us. A deputy went to subdue the man from reception, who'd since stumbled into a cardboard display and sent hundreds of diabetes awareness pamphlets flying. Garcia hooked his thumbs through his holster belt and shook his head. "That fellow and another were fishing—fishing, my ass—down by the river. Says his buddy fell on a broken bottle, but the one back there getting sewn up claims assault. I have to help him handle this and then I need to hear what happened with McIntyre," he said, and as he looked at me his face softened. "Your grandfather."

"Sure thing, Ray," Bill said, and also excused himself, pulling his phone from his pocket. I looked around the waiting room, the harsh light and palpable urgency contributing to its surrealness. My head felt cottony, my thoughts blurred. The same words played over again—*car wreck, heart attack, critical condition*—as if by repetition they'd make more sense. What was Leroy doing alone out there? Was he headed to the crime scene? Legs shaking, I moved to sit, and as I did, an old woman in a wheelchair rolled past us, a full dialysis bag in her lap and an even older man pushing her.

As soon as they were out of earshot, Troy crinkled his nose. "This place is gross and fucking depressing."

Justin's face turned pink as Troy gave a commiserating wink and smile to a pretty young woman bouncing a fussy baby in her lap. I wanted to throw up. There was a monster in the waiting room. How was he keeping up appearances like this? How could he be so two-faced as to stand here at a time like this, with me—not to mention law enforcement—and smile?

"Sorry, had to take a call," Bill said, taking his place back between Troy and Justin. "You know, Annie, I've been thinking—remind me to follow up with your dad after all this. Your grandfather and I had a conversation not too long ago that could make this, uh, easier."

The hair on the back of my neck stood up. "Conversation about what?"

"We talked about the land." He crossed his arms over his wide middle and looked down at me. "About, well, if something were to happen to him. How there'd be no one left who cared about that little spit of dirt. More a burden than anything. And now with it being the scene—"

"That land has been in my family for three generations," I said, and stood up quickly, chair screeching on the tile. A hundred acres was nothing to a man who owned an operational ranch more than ten times the size. A desert island in the middle of a vast ocean, the place was surrounded on three sides by the Schneider ranch and the even bigger Shaver family ranch, and the highway on the other.

But it was ours.

Bill put his palms out. "First refusal on the sale was what Leroy said. Like I was going to tell your dad, he and I had a handshake deal I intend to honor. No need to worry; we'd get it taken care of quickly with an honest offer. Even if he pulls through, it's something for you and the family to consider."

"His blood is all over your shirt!" I shouted, my face and neck searing hot. "Oh, but I see. That must have given you pause. Made you think this was an opportune time for a land deal."

Bill sighed, nodding slowly. "Honey, let's calm down. I should've known this wasn't the time or the place—"

"Listen up, all of you," I said even louder, pointing to Garcia and the deputy in the far corner of the room, still talking down their suspect. "Y'all know my family. You know me. You know there have been ups and downs and things change, but seeking out the truth? That runs in our veins. It's as much a part of us as this place is. . . ." I paused and locked eyes with Bill. "As much as that little spit of dirt. Maybe my grandfather let some of you down occasionally, or quite often, but thing is, when he thought something was wrong, he interrogated that. He got hurt on the job today, so I intend to finish the job for him. To hear the call of the living and the dead."

"Excuse me, ma'am?"

"I'm fine, I'll shut up, just—" I said to the nurse coming around the desk toward me. I felt a rush of adrenaline so strong my teeth chattered. "What I mean to say is, I won't stop."

Garcia frowned and his deputy looked confused. Half of the people waiting weren't listening, though a handful hesitatingly tipped their chins in salute. The suspect laughed and clapped. Troy leaned against a wall, his face a sheet of ice.

"Annie!" a familiar voice called from behind me. Nikki had come back from the parking lot. "Your mom texted. She said they'll let us back there now."

Chapter 36

I couldn't look at Leroy. A wave of nausea hit me as soon as I saw his bruises, his swollen face, and the plaster encasing his limbs. So bedside, I watched my father. Twenty-four hours since Leroy's surgery, he maintained the stunned look of someone unprepared for all of this. His skin was sallow, face pale, his eyes wide and darkened with fear. A nurse came in and asked us to move, tapping him on the shoulder, and he didn't speak or help move the stiff-backed chairs that ringed the bed, only stood in the corner with his hands in his pockets until she left.

The monitors beeped, the IV dripped, and the room was still again.

I have always worried about my father. I'd known from a young age that irrevocable damage beyond the physical had been done to the two most important men in my life the night of *that* accident, nearly twenty years ago. Twenty years—was forgiveness possible when the other person was gone? What would Dad do with all his anger, all his frustration, if he couldn't direct it at Leroy?

Needing some air, I followed Momma out of the room. She

always said she didn't smoke—only pilfered the occasional one from Uncle Curtis—but outside pulled a new pack from her purse. She paused on the edge of the grass outside the lobby, looking adrift. Her life had also been shaped by the choices her father-in-law had made. Leroy loomed so large—his legacy was one Dad had rejected, but even that choice was something they danced around instead of through to the other side of. Dad would always be known as the son of the sheriff. He would always be a former cop. Momma had been the breadwinner most of my childhood, and yet she was still known around town as the wife of a cop. "He's a lawman, through and through. A fighter," Garcia had said at Leroy's bedside, and the words echoed in my mind as we stood in the building's long shadow. A security guard cleared his throat and pointed to the NO SMOKING sign, so I steered Momma toward the parking lot. I always forgot she was shorter than me until we were this close, shoulder to shoulder. She dropped my hand and started to cry.

"He'll get better—" I said, though my chest felt tight, my breath hard to catch. "And after this is over, maybe everyone will finally stop being so mad at him."

She stopped pacing and turned to face me. "Everyone meaning me?"

"I meant Daddy, mostly."

"I know you think I resent your grandfather. Or that I believed what happened to your daddy was his fault. Truthfully, I was relieved he was there that night. Worst night of my life," she said, dabbing at the mascara under her eyes with her sleeve. "I never once thought he would do anything to hurt William. Or anyone, for that matter. I thought Leroy was probably the only person could protect him."

"Protect him?" I placed my hand on her arm. "Protect him from what?"

An old, beige-colored Buick sped into the lot and screeched to a halt a few spaces ahead of us. Nikki was in the passenger seat, and Aunt Jewel rolled down the driver's side window. "Brought y'all supper!" she called, and took off her sunglasses—massive prescription lenses that looked like the Terminator's—and glared. "You put that cigarette out, Tina. It'll stain your teeth."

"Oh, Lord," Momma sighed, and stubbed her cigarette on the asphalt. She pulled me close to her, whispering, "From himself, sweet pea. Protect him from himself."

Even with Jewel gone, Leroy's room felt overcrowded. Nikki had decided to stay along with my parents, and until he was asked to leave so had Marty Santos. He'd brought a portable cassette player and a George Jones tape that he thought playing would aid in Leroy's recovery. It was nearly nine at night when there was another rap on the doorframe. I looked up expecting to see the nurse—I'd since learned her name was Brenda and that we'd gotten on her last nerve with that music—but it was Mary-Pat, standing stiffly at the threshold.

"Came to see him," she said. Her eyes were watery, and her visitor pass was stuck on upside down. "Is he awake?"

"He drifts in and out of consciousness, but no, not really," Momma said.

Mary-Pat's chin quivered. "I didn't know he'd get behind the wheel. I'm sorry."

Momma went to her and gently patted her back. "It's not your fault."

"I was telling him he ought to come stay with either me or with William until things settled down with the investigation. Told him I'd be back later and for him to gather his things. I don't know why he couldn't have just waited."

"Investigation." Dad lifted his head from the cradle of his hands and stared at Mary-Pat. His face was expressionless as stone, which frightened me even more than if he were swearing or yelling. "That's why he was out across the river. That's why he was so worked up."

"He was worked up because, well . . ." Mary-Pat paused and looked at me. "There were credible threats being made and—"

"Just go," Dad said, and put his hands over his eyes. "All of you. I'm going to stay the night again. I'll call you if anything changes."

"Fine, I'll leave." Mary-Pat wiped her nose with a tissue and took a deep breath, pausing in the doorway. "It's not my fault he had a heart attack, or that he was stubborn, or that he worked the case. But I do take blame, of course I do, because I knew he wasn't supposed to be under stress. I should've handled things better. I'm really sorry, William."

If Mary-Pat took blame, so should I—the thought shuddered through me like stone through glass and I felt cut, stung. On the other side of anger, I realized, was everything else: sadness, cold and black. I clenched my jaw, tried to focus on my anger, to razor it into some kind of purpose. But I was so tired. Momma motioned for the rest of us to get going. My leg tingly and numb from sitting in the same position for hours, I hobbled down the ICU corridor toward the red EXIT sign. Nikki trailed me, the automatic doors making a shushing sound as they closed behind us. After the cold, sterile-smelling hospital room, the rush of warm night air gave me goose bumps. I dropped my keys and, when I squatted to grab them, could barely stand again.

"Don't say I should feel bad, Nik. I already do. I'm afraid he'll, he'll—"

"Annie, stop it," she said, and crouched down beside me. She hooked her arm through mine to pull me up. "This sounds

275

harsh, and there's all kinds of accusations being thrown around back in there, but at the end of the day, know that if it's his time, it's his time. It's not so unnatural. And he was on a case, doing what mattered most to him."

"He was scared. If this is it, I can't stand thinking he died feeling scared," I said.

"I bet you more people than not go away feeling scared. Even people who say they know about heaven or anything are just guessing."

"'Don't fear the mystery.'"

"What?"

"Nothing. Just something he said."

When we got back to the house, I broke. I hadn't cried until then. Nikki curled up beside me on the couch and we stayed that way for some time, until she nodded off to sleep and my eyes grew tired watching the sky streak with light near dawn. When Mamaw died, she had been sick for a long time. Hospice had been called in. We all had a chance to visit with her, hold her hand, and tell her we loved her. I remember about a day or two before she passed, sitting on the edge of her bed, the sheets freshly changed and the window open to let in sweet-smelling air, feeling drowsy and content watching her sleep. I felt like a kid again, pretending to take a nap in her bedroom while wide-awake listening to birdsong and wind chimes, memorizing the faces in the pictures on the walls. A cardinal landed on the bird feeder, there were pale buds on the trees, and her breathing was soft and low as a kitten's. Warmed by sun streaming through lace curtains and surrounded by family photos, I willed time to stop. I felt outside of time for that hour or so, being with her. It didn't make me any less sad, but it made me less alone. That feeling of passing through time, savoring the sweetness of a moment, would not happen for me if Leroy died, no—instead I felt time's mad ticking. The last time we spoke he told me to leave. He turned his back. And I could not feel anything but regret having listened.

Chapter 37

"Dot would have covered for you, sweetheart." Marlene came up behind me and placed her hands on my shoulders, the bite of her peppermint soap strong so close to my face.

Business was slow, as it normally was midafternoon now that the morbid curiosity of strangers had worn off. The "café with death on the menu," as one reporter had phrased it, was back to being simply the café, our café, but to say that it felt the same inside would be inaccurate. It was blue all over. As though a film coated the windows and the walls, as though my eyes had misted over with a cold-hued gloss.

"No, ma'am, I want to work, take my mind off it for a few hours."

"I'll keep praying for him. Lord have mercy. With everything's happened between Victoria and Fernando, I feel numb and I bet you do too."

I nodded, unable to speak, and tucked into the bowl of black-eyed peas and snaps I was having for a before-shift meal. The peas were fresh picked and shelled, had come with Marlene's cousin down from Haskell, and after so much fast food and vending machine snacks tasted heavenly. I closed my eyes. My head felt swimmy and strange. I'd had a vivid dream the night before: slightly rocking, I realized I was on horseback, chasing the source of cartoonish sounds, the clop-clop of hoofbeats and a high-pitched whistle. On a dirt path down a narrow canyon green with spring growth, I came upon a strawberry roan. It drank at a creek, its mane coppery in a sudden shaft of sun. No rider, it was alone, and suddenly gone again. I turned a corner but couldn't quite see around it, and I'd woken drenched in cold sweat.

Melvin Baker and a patrol cop came in and sat in their booth. They looked at me quickly and then away, probably hoping I wouldn't be their waitress so they didn't have to bring up Leroy. I couldn't blame them; the fact of it was a balloon ready to pop with the slightest poke. It was like that with Victoria, Fernando too—but I wouldn't cry in front a group of people again, so I bit my tongue and went to rinse my bowl out in the kitchen. "I'll be right with y'all!" I yelled in their direction, and they nodded back somberly.

I returned with a notepad and their waters.

"I was telling my girl we arrested that kid out to Cedar Springs and she just looks at me unbelievable that we already cracked it," the younger cop said to Melvin, his chin and his chest out. "I told her yeah, not to say it's easy. It's basically like going into combat. Got to have a certain edge."

I wondered if most of his afternoons were spent congratulating himself for doing his job or if today was special. Melvin nodded. "I hear you. People always think criminals are so slick. They aren't. Most are dumbasses. They always leave something or make a mistake. It's not *CSI*."

Samantha Jayne Allen

"Oh, God," I said, breath catching.

"Hon?" Melvin looked up at me and I flushed. I'd been standing there, wheels turning, probably looking half-crazy. "We've been thinking about your family, all of us. Say, me and this knucklehead better run to court, so how about just the usual? Maybe bring it to go with the check."

"Sure thing." I scrambled to the counter with the ticket and nearly tripped over my own feet. He said every scene has at least one stupid mistake. That was it. The police said Victoria got picked up from the highway, but I—and maybe only two others—knew that she'd come back to the bonfire a second time. What if the crime scene was wrong? They hadn't searched the back path from the Schneiders' property to the place, I was sure of it, only the path up from the road, since they assumed she was killed in someone's car and dragged to the creek post-mortem. If I was right about Troy, when would he have picked her up in his truck? More likely was that he would have taken her, maybe walked her, away from the others. He would have walked her where no one would see the two of them, over the fence line and out to the place. I took a deep breath, and with the pen, I wrote *SCENE* at the back of my pad. As I did, it occurred to me that this very reason could be why Leroy had gotten behind the wheel.

Marlene, who'd been at the window and watching my tip get smaller and smaller, came over to me. "Why don't you get some air and let me take those tables? I was gonna run errands today, but figure I can trust you to come back." She smiled and walked toward the men. "Take cash from the drawer and go on out to Greene's. Get me some tomatoes if he still has any."

"Yes, ma'am," I mumbled, heart hammering in my chest. I hurried to the back, took off my apron, and grabbed my keys.

"I'll be on my way," I said, hand on the door, but Marlene

280

didn't look up, too busy chatting with the table. Greene's farm was to the west of town, out across the river and near the place. Marlene wouldn't miss me for an hour, maybe longer. I stepped outside and pulled out my phone.

"Artemis Oil and Gas."

"Is Troy Schneider in the office today?"

"Sure, let me put you through. I don't think their meeting's started yet."

I hung up, knowing what I needed to do. A rap on the café window made me turn around. It was Sheila, seated inside. She pressed her palm to the window and stared out.

Chapter 38

Cloudless, the sky's blue seemed muted. Something about the way the light seemed canned, slanted, it felt for the first time like fall. I sat for a few moments in the bullet, worrying over what I might find, worrying I didn't even know what I was looking for, hoping that I would know when I found it, thinking it might be foolish to imagine the cops had not searched the back of the property. I opened the door and stepped out. A light breeze floated over the top of the tall grass off the dirt road. Victoria had been found not far from where I stood, and there were still torn strips of yellow crime scene tape at the sides of a fresh path that led down a small hill toward the dry creek bed, toward her makeshift grave in a thicket of cacti and honey mesquite.

Since I knew Troy was at a safe distance, my plan was to take some time and track backward toward where the party was, hoping to search the periphery of the Schneider land. Troy would have walked her directly from the party to somewhere private, somewhere he was comfortable—maybe one of the clearings, or even the old hunting shack.

Grasshoppers pinged against my jeans as I waded into deep grass and down the hill toward the property line, marked by a few posts and single strand of barbwire, enough to stop a cow but certainly not a human. I crossed the properties and almost immediately noticed the difference in how the land was kept: ours was overgrown with brush, wild, while theirs was easier to traverse, the presence of livestock noted in the broken branches, hoofprints, and dried droppings. A short distance ahead and over the creek it was rockier and wooded. I walked up another hill. Turned to the side, through the clearing I could see the escarpment on the far side of the place, slightly purple in the distance, a long, shallow depression between the high point where the house had stood and my current location. I turned forward and climbed, nose to the ground, until the hunting shack was before me. The wooden boards were gray and splintered from age and years of weather. Farther back and up in a big red oak was a blind. Shadows cast across the earth and the air was cooler.

On the ground, underneath some prickly pear, I saw something that didn't belong: a yellow gas station lighter and a red plastic SOLO cup. I knew I shouldn't touch them—they could be evidence, I had the foresight to consider—and took a photo of the items and my location with my phone. As I stood quickly, my head spun. Hardly getting any air, my breaths came fast and shallow when I noted a faint path worn in the grass. The path seemed to cut from the shack down toward the property line and the creek.

Something terrible had happened here. Bone-deep, I knew. Fear was a taste on my tongue—bitter, coppery spit of blood—and yet I couldn't turn around. Silent, lethal, a Mexican eagle dove for a mouse in the grass up ahead. I stopped to double-check the time on my phone, calculate how long I'd been away from the café, when I thought I heard something behind me, something like the scud of boots on dirt.

"Annie." Justin jogged up from behind me.

I relaxed some—what would I do, confronted with his brother?

His face was sweaty and red. I remembered his embrace at the hospital, his touch tattooed on my skin, his obvious emotion, his feeling for me, so why, then, did the hair on the back of my neck stand up? *He is not okay,* I thought so clearly I could've said it aloud. *You were wrong.*

"Justin," I stuttered. Looked over his shoulder and back around. "Where's your truck?"

"Parked far enough behind that you wouldn't see or hear me. I knew where you were going."

"Why—what are you doing? Me, I'm just getting some air, playing hooky," I said, and tried to smile, a sinking feeling in the pit of my stomach. Before he spoke again, I knew. Like getting burned touching a stove you didn't realize was on—slow build to shock, to stinging pain.

"Annie, don't play dumb. I don't want to do this, but you won't stop. I tried to scare you off, but you kept on. If you hadn't already figured it out you might have, or gotten too close."

With shaking hands, he pulled a pearl-handled bowie knife from a sheath on his belt. The only people who might be around were Marty Santos or Justin's dad, Bill. I screamed as loud as I could, but the only reaction was the caw of a vulture scared off something dead down in the grass.

"In the small chance that my dad heard you from up at the house, he probably thought it was an animal."

Justin blocked the fastest path between the car and me. Even if I had time to pull my phone out and make a call, there was no cell service, not until you were closer to the road.

The blade glinted in the sun and I knew I was going to die.

For the first time in my life I was so certain. My face felt tingly like I was about to vomit, and I felt like crying, I wanted my mother, I wanted God, and I wanted to open my eyes and wake from this bad, bad dream. The sun shone through the cedar brake behind him, but I knew beyond it was only more ranchland, hundreds of acres of nothing. I swallowed hard.

"You strangled her," I said, and stuck my chest out, thinking I needed to buck him a bit, as if that might work.

His face and neck looked nearly purple with rage. "She was going to tell everyone. She wanted to ruin my entire life."

They slipped you something, Megan said. *Justin was there. You don't remember that part?*

"Justin." I shook my head in disbelief. "Did you drug her, like you did me?"

"You? *I* didn't, but yeah, it was just what they did. Dumb girls always came sniffing around the house. Begging. They didn't know you or care." He looked me up and down and pointed with the knife. "Troy didn't care one way or another about Victoria. He was acting all drunk and weepy. Ignoring her because he'd gotten twisted over Megan again. So, I figured I'd make a move. All I wanted was a good time. She was just some trash my brother hooked up with at that country bar—oh, please, wipe that self-righteous look off your face. She was, like, into it. I gave her a Xanax 'cause she wanted to chill."

"Oh, of course. And after that, you figured you'd take her out to a dirty shack to fuck, but damndest thing, she woke up?"

"She didn't have to start screaming about it being—"

"Rape? That would be rape, Justin."

"No." He came closer. "No."

"How could I not see what scum you really are? You don't even care about the fact that her life is over, do you? You only care about yourself, and it's clear you never cared about me either."

He laughed—an ugly, guttural sound.

You can do everything wrong or everything right and somehow it doesn't matter. The realization is both stunning in its freedom and stifling in its unfairness. It is a primal scream and it is a wheezing death rattle. The person to blame was no one but the man standing in front of me, the man incapable of seeing me as a human person with memories, dreams, a future like a long bright ribbon of chance and infinite possibility spooled out. I was not real to him, not in the way I knew myself to be.

"I only took that picture to put you in your place. Posted it to show you a lesson. You were jerking me around." Eyes wild, he laughed so hard he snorted. "Why do women do that shit?"

Get control or he's going to kill you.

"Justin, let's both just calm down."

"Damn it." He smacked his forehead with his free hand. "Shut up! Shut up!"

I didn't want a chase. Justin was half a foot taller than me and in good shape. But he was a wreck—his laughter had turned to crying, his breath was ragged, and snot dripped from his nose. His unwashed hair stuck to his forehead and he wore the same soiled shirt he'd had on at the hospital.

"Someone's going to miss me at work," I said, and looked around me. "We can figure this out. You don't want this on your conscience too. Let's go over our options."

My pulse thrummed so hard I could feel it in my neck. *You only have to get far enough away that you can use the phone.*

Justin took a step closer. "You made me do this."

Go.

I pumped my legs as hard as I could. My feet slid as I cut sideways across the hill thinking I could create a wide enough radius to loop back to the road. Lungs searing, my feet wouldn't go as fast as the top half of me and I tripped, tumbled down.

I was halfway up, still on my knees, when he kicked me in the stomach. Again, to the ribs. I looked up at the sky because I couldn't stand to look at his face. I didn't want it to be the last thing I saw.

And yet—

I don't know where it came from, this strength inside me. Maybe it was anger, red sparks of rage like kindling in my chest, maybe it was the half-formed prayer that I didn't want to die and no, please God, let this not be it. Oddly calm, I made eye contact and said, "No." As he was about to swing the blade down across my sternum I stood and reached for his knife. First, pressure, next, a white-hot sting like a thousand needles. Throbbing pain shot through my hand and up my arm and neck to the base of my skull.

I held the knife by the blade.

Justin startled so he weakened his grip, dropped the knife, and drew back long enough for me to aim a swift, hard kick to the shin.

And then I ran. As hard as I've ever run before. Blood seeped through my clenched fist and pooled in the cup of my palm like water.

If I ran along the bottom of the hill going north and cut right at the creek I could wind around and lose him in the thick knot of scrub oak, then switch direction to the road. My vision tunneled and I felt my stomach spasm where he had kicked me, but I sucked air in my lungs and ran. I could hear him behind me. Unsure for how long I could keep going, going, if I could hide so I could wrap my shirt around my hand, why my knees were buckling—"Run; you're running for your life," I said aloud—I smelled his sweat; I heard him breathe.

Gunshot sounded like a crack in the stratosphere.

Dull *thwop* as the bullet hit flesh.

Justin made a terrible, faint "oh" sound before his footfall ceased and, finally, his body collapsed into the tall grass. Blood leaked down my arm. The wound pulsed in my fist as if it held my own beating heart. *You're alive, alive, alive,* I thought, my vision clotted with green spots. I could see the sun on the horizon, and then total darkness swept the plain.

Chapter 39

I woke. Tried to turn over, but my hand was wrapped tight, an IV drip fastened in the crook of my arm. The drive to the hospital had been a blur and I'd passed out not long after the doctor stitched my hand, sealing the gash where I'd held the blade.

"I'm going to need a formal statement, but for now, just tell us again what happened," Sheriff Garcia said. My eyelids felt heavy and weird, but I focused my gaze on him.

"She's lucky," Mary-Pat said to him while pacing around my bed. She tapped her foot and jingled her keys. "It's lucky I went for a bite at the café and asked after Annie. Marlene said she sent her out to Greene's and for some reason, maybe it was that old kook Sheila flapping her arms with her premonitions, I had a terrible feel about it," she said. "Truth be told I've been keeping an eye on the girl. Given the threats, I thought it would be best to keep her in my sights."

"You knew she'd gone up to the place?" My father's voice sounded so tired.

"No, but I was driving past on the way to Greene's farm after her, and I noticed the gate. It was open, unlatched. Chain dangling. You or Leroy couldn't have done it; Annie wouldn't have, not after what happened—it just bothered me, so I came down a short ways and saw the Schneider boy's truck. Kept going a little further and saw her Pontiac and two people running toward the creek, one chasing the other. Grabbed my gun and aimed for the leg." Mary-Pat's voice sounded heavy. "Have you an update, Ray?"

"He lost a lot of blood, but he made it through surgery."

"When that little bastard wakes up, he'll be in restraints." Momma's voice trembled. She always cried when she was angry and then got mad at herself for crying.

"Yes, ma'am, I have two of my deputies there with him."

Nikki touched my toe through the blanket. "She's awake."

"The doctor gave you painkillers, so you might be groggy for a while," Dad said, hand to my forehead. "Try and rest for a bit. They want you under observation for a few hours."

I nodded but fought hard to stay awake. Fought against the darkness of my unlit room, my inability to sit up, to open my eyes wide, to meet face-to-face the monsters that crept unseen under a starless sky. How could I have not known—how, how, how?

When I opened my eyes again, everyone had gone. Its evening rhythms known to me now, the hospital seemed unusually quiet. The IV drip was no longer attached to my arm, so I stood with quivering legs and went to the door. A dull pain throbbed in my stomach and my ribs. The adrenaline having worn off, and the painkiller starting to, I realized just how hard he'd kicked me. Winced every time I breathed. The nurses' station was empty, so I walked down the hall toward Leroy's room, the path familiar as a recurring nightmare.

Dad was sleeping sitting up in his chair. Leroy was not awake, not that I could tell, but the swelling had gone down in his face so he looked almost normal. Almost. My bandaged hand, numb from the stitches but beginning to tingle and burn, hung heavily at my side. I took Leroy's hand in my other and laced my fingers through his. He didn't squeeze back—but I felt a charge when I touched his skin, a jolt of static maybe, and warmth.

I heard footsteps behind me and turned to see nurse Brenda.

"This family, I swear. Some kind of trouble you are," she said, and came to stand beside me. "Heard he was awake earlier. Tried to speak."

"Is he doing better?"

She patted my back. "You all can talk to the doctor, but in my opinion that is a good sign. Go on to your own room now. I'll see if they're ready to discharge you."

But I stayed through the night. Entertained visitors both real and imagined. I dozed, dreaming Leroy sauntered across the threshold to my room. I dreamed Victoria leaned against the doorframe, a brass cowgirl in her outstretched hand. Whispered voices rose and fell, clumsy with anger, one stubbed a toe on my bed and cursed his name, someone brushed my hair, and someone brought me clean clothes. Maybe the reason I came back to Garnett was not some sense of purpose to be found at the root, but rather because here I was loved and loved well. On the other side of the darkness were the ones keeping watch. On the other side of it was everyone I'd ever known.

Chapter 40

The Steers had a winning season that fall. School buses led the caravan down the road to the playoff game in Odessa. Kids hung out the windows, cheers and bright streamers trailing in the wind. Streamers were everywhere—all around town the telephone poles and street signs were wound with purple and gold—while plastic pom-poms and discarded confetti poppers littered the sidewalk. Marlene painted a sign in her window and had held a supper party for the team, the boosters, even the alumni and their families. Fernando didn't come. Couldn't come. Since he'd been released from jail, he'd gone to live with his older brother down in Corpus. Justin pled guilty and was awaiting sentencing. I feared the day I'd have to walk inside that courtroom and face him.

But that day, the day of the big away game, I stood at the window of our office on the square and watched the cop cars drive in the opposite direction of traffic.

They were going to arrest Glory Barnes for the hit-and-run. Charge her with manslaughter in the death of Hector Chavez.

"What tipped you off?" Sheriff Garcia had asked me. I

explained to him how I'd been kept awake by what Glory had said that day I'd confronted her and Brandon in front of the courthouse. How she'd accused her daughter-in-law of hooking on the highway on the night she was killed. There was no way to know Victoria had stood out by the road unless you had seen her there with your own eyes. The police hadn't leaked that information to the press or her family, I'd confirmed. No one had told Glory about Victoria's phone dropped in the tall, trash-studded grass on the side of the highway.

Glory saw Victoria on the night she died. She had been driving back from her sister's house, back before her weekend away had even started. Called back to babysit her granddaughter once again, she must have felt so angry, and there was the irresponsible party herself—drunk, weaving, thumbing for a ride—oh, Glory was furious when she saw Victoria. Shaking, blinded by her anger, she hadn't seen the truck drift over the center line in time, did not see Hector Chavez walking on the other side of the highway, and she swerved. Heard him on impact. Panicked and sped off. The new truck wasn't bought with a payout from the oil company, no—they'd been banking on an insurance check after she lied and claimed to have hit a deer.

Blue and red patrol lights pierced the sky.

Heartsick, I turned from the window. Mary-Pat had left paperwork on my desk to file, a list of court records to pull, but I would find the time later. I decided to lock up for the day. With Leroy stuck in a long-term rehab facility at the VA, she'd been training me herself, granting me the hours needed to apply for a license. There was still so much uncertainty. Yet I knew a chapter had closed in my own life the day Justin nearly ended it, that another had begun. Mary-Pat and I had started down a long road together. Our rapport was unsteady at times. My gratitude for all she'd done was overwhelming, and I think it made her uneasy, my affection—my first day on the job, she had been no-nonsense. Endless lists, assignments. Had barely made eye contact with me until the end of the day, nearly dusk, when she'd come up the stairs to find me sitting at Leroy's desk. Her face looked stricken, but when I said hello she smiled. I laid my hand up on the desk and unclenched my fist. She stood beside me and looked down at the raw scar.

"Hurts," I said, eyes welling.

"If I were a palm reader, I'd say looks like you have an extra-long life line." She laughed and squeezed my shoulder—that was all she'd say about it.

Checking the lock, I gave the door to the building a quick tug. Got in the silver bullet and drove down the highway, picking up speed. I wanted out of my head. Foolish as it may seem, a part of me felt unable to relax, to not imagine the dead unquiet in their graves, to awaken from slumber and see an object moved by no hand, to feel a cold gust of air at my back on a windless day.

To be doubled over by sadness.

But it was getting better. I could see around it, most days. Feel lucky in the present moment. We even had gone dancing at Yesterday Once More to celebrate my gainful employment at the firm—Wyatt and me, Nikki and Sonny. Loud inside, nearly midnight, the air was thick with smoke and laughs, sweet with perfume and spilled whiskey. The band played "San Antonio Rose," and Nikki began to sing.

I groaned. "Nik, please."

"Why did God give me a voice this loud if he wasn't going to give me one that could carry a tune? I mean, I can belt out a song. It'll scare you how loud I can be," she said.

Sonny touched her knee under the table. "Here's to the singers of songs."

Wyatt raised his beer. "And here's to the wild waters of the Geronimo River. That salamander might save us yet."

Nikki looked confused. Sonny shrugged. "Cheers," they said at once, and tipped their beers back.

"Wait." I touched his arm. "What do you mean?"

"My professor said today one of the big landowners whose property would be in the path of the pipeline near the river filed a lawsuit. The salamander's an endangered species, so it's protected. The pipeline might disrupt its environment if anything leaks into the water table. Not certain Artemis won't eventually get its way, but construction has to be halted for the time being."

"Wow," I whispered, looked down at the scuffed wooden boards, and bit back the urge to whoop and raise my fist, to cry out.

"We'll see what happens," Wyatt said. "One can hope."

The room was a blur of candy-colored lights and swishing skirts. That old honky-tonk was like a distinctive sound in my mind—mournful yet bright, like pedal steel, heavy and sure like a bass fiddle—but really it was no sound at all. Yesterday Once More was a memory of a time and a place I'm not sure ever really existed. I drank my beer and listened to the band. Felt the drumbeat. The fraying guitar sound and tremolo voices swirled in the air around my head, and I tapped Wyatt on the shoulder, asking him to dance.

Pumpjacks nodded on the horizon. I drove over the fault line and the plains were before me. I stopped the bullet at the old railroad tracks and parked. Yellowed grass and blazing blue sky, sun shimmer over twisted metal, the ghosts didn't hold as much allure now, and yet out here I felt the presence of the dead around me as strongly as I felt the sun on my skin. God, if there was one, seemed closer when I thought about the ones I missed. I hadn't made it across the river. I hadn't gone back to the place. Not yet—though eventually I would return to walk out of the green mesquite and up the ridge, step over the stone foundation, touch the soft dirt to my lips and taste it, bitter, but not yet. It hadn't been so long since she died. The sun was high in the sky and it would be a cool, clear day.

Acknowledgments

I'd like to thank Anne Hillerman, the Western Writers of America, and Minotaur Books for sponsoring the Tony Hillerman prize. It's truly an honor to win this award.

My wise editor, Joe Brosnan, brought out the very best in this book and in me as a writer. Many thanks to him and to the fantastic, hardworking team at Minotaur Books.

Thank you to my brilliant agent, Sharon Pelletier. It's a privilege to have her in my corner.

I'm fortunate to have had many wonderful teachers, first in the English Department at Agnes Scott College and, later, while attending the MFA program at Texas State University. I'd especially like to thank Ben Fountain and Debra Monroe, for their insight and advice, and Tom Grimes, who told me to keep going. Thank you as well to the Eckerd College Writers' Conference, for having me, and to Laura Lippman, for her feedback and enthusiasm for the early chapters of this book.

Thank you to my workshop cohort and my writer friends, and especially Lauren Hughes, who swapped pages with me and gave great notes.

ACKNOWLEDGMENTS

Thank you to Frank Reiss and my former coworkers at A Cappella Books, for cultivating the arts in our community, and for your kindness and encouragement when I told you I was writing a novel.

I'm infinitely grateful for the love of my family: the Tanners, Allens, and Lindseys. My sister, Olivia Tanner, for being my best friend and most trusted opinion. My dad, Joe Tanner, for his unwavering support, optimism, and sense of humor. My mom, Donna Tanner, for instilling a love of stories and for being the biggest influence on my writing and in my life. And my husband, Dane Allen, for believing in me as I believe in him.